EARTH MAGIC
Hot Water

CASUAL
MAGIC
BOOK TWO

RE NNO

EARTH MAGIC & HOT WATER

LAUREN CONNOLLY

CITY OWL
PRESS

EARTH MAGIC & HOT WATER
Casual Magic, Book 2

CITY OWL PRESS
www.cityowlpress.com

Cover Design by MiblArt. All stock photos licensed appropriately.

Edited by Yelena Casale.

For information on subsidiary rights, please contact the publisher at info@cityowlpress.com.

Print Edition ISBN: 978-1-64898-367-2

Digital Edition ISBN: 978-1-64898-368-9

Printed in the United States of America

Also by Lauren Connolly

Casual Magic:

Fire Magic & Ice Cream

Earth Magic & Hot Water

Healing Magic & Playboys

***

Forget the Past:

Rescue Me

Read Me

Resist Me

Praise for Lauren Connolly

"Cleverly crafted, sweet and spicy, *Fire Magic & Ice Cream* is wittily written and explores all the emotions! With very imaginative world building, the elementals' that live alongside humans all have certain 'gifts'. Ms. Connolly has crafted a plethora of characters that are unusual, endearing, and full of loyalty." — *InD'tale Magazine*

"If you are looking for a fun, delightful, and super steamy romance that's a quick read, look no further! *Fire Magic & Ice Cream* brings it all in one charming package." — *Kat Turner, author of the Coven Daughters series*

"The relationship between Dash and Paige, in *Rescue Me*, will bring the warm-fuzzies, as both step out of their comfort zones to give it a chance, and boy is their chemistry sizzling. A page turner from start to finish, the reader will be reluctant to put it down!" — *InD'tale Magazine*

"If you're looking for a fun, low stakes, lighthearted, magical, and steamy read for the summer you HAVE to read *Fire Magic & Ice Cream*! This book was so much fun and I breezed right through it. I loved Quinn and how she had to learn to control her magic and the cinnamon roll ice Viking man August who balanced her out. Their chemistry was on point, and the way they navigated their relationship was so adorable." — *E.E. Hornburg, author of the Cursed Queens series*

"*Read Me* is a perfect sunshine-and-grump tale that is an absolutely delightful addition to the Forget the Past series! Readers will feel the gamut of emotions throughout this tale, from laughing out loud to reaching for tissues, and it will be worth every second. If one loves a second-chance-at-doing-life-right tale, this book is definitely one to add to the must-read pile! Unputdownable from start to finish!" — *InD'tale Magazine*

"All of Lauren Connolly's books that I've read this year put a smile on my face. This book was what I needed after a long and hard day. Her books are my mental cinnamon rolls. Thank you for being a 'Dash' of joy in my life." — *Meg Fitz, author of Best Laid Plans*

"Once again, Ms. Connolly has written a tale full of heart, fun, and adorable animals with *Resist Me*. Pig, the adorable rescue pit bull will bring smiles to reader's faces, and the ending will leave one wanting even more! Utterly delightful from start to finish!" — *InD'tale Magazine*

To the pissed off women of the world.

Chapter One

CAT

My wig itches, and once again I silently curse the man who made me wear it. The jellyfish exhibit at the local aquarium is supposed to be my happy place, but today the need to scratch thwarts the marine animals' relaxing powers. I sneak a finger under the false hairline, searching for the irritating spot.

I never used to wear a wig to the aquarium. This building was always my haven. Now, I'm forced to don a disguise if I want any chance of finding peace in the dim rooms lit only by the blue glow of fish tanks.

After my finger finds and scratches the itch, I sigh in relief, resettling into my casual stance in front of a round window that peers into the jellyfish enclosure. A mushroom-shaped head leisurely pulses, dragging spindly string legs in an arc through the water. I try to match my breathing to each of the movements, easing my anger to a simmer, hoping to extinguish the harsh emotion fully.

"Are they really made from jelly?"

The high-pitched voice at my elbow has me flinching back a step. I thought I was alone in this room in the early afternoon of a Tuesday, or at least alone in front of this display. But a little girl stares up at me, beads clacking together on the ends of her tight braids, as she watches my retreat.

She's a cute kid: gap where she's missing a front tooth, rounded cheeks, and curious brown eyes a few shades darker than her skin, except for where someone painted a mermaid on her face.

People always assume I'm good with children. I think it's the combination of being a short, soft-spoken—for the most part—woman in prime birthing years, but I know *zero* about what to do with them. Or how to talk to them. I was the youngest of my siblings, and neither of my sisters have any offspring that would force me to improve my skills.

If I had candy, I'd consider throwing some treats to distract her as I hustle away. But my pockets are empty.

At least this child isn't screaming, or crying, or trying to grab me with sticky fingers. She stands still, her eyes going back to the glass to watch the beautiful aquatic dance.

I could answer her question. There's no harm in that.

"Well, not exactly. Jellyfish have three layers. The epidermis, the mesoglea, and the gastrodermis. The mesoglea is jelly-like, but not the kind of jelly you eat," I say, using the same tone I'd tell a drunk customer at my job they're getting cut off. The tone says, *Look how nice I am! Please don't yell at me.*

"Wow." The girl steps closer, peering at the jellyfish from a different angle. "What do they eat?"

Again, it's a simple enough question to answer, so I list off a few items on a jellyfish's menu.

"Mommy says they sting, but it's all wet and squishy."

Not really a question. Still, I start to explain about venom, until a yelp cuts me off.

"Shay! There you are. Oh my god, I've been looking everywhere." A woman jogs across the room, going straight to the girl and scooping her up as if perching the kid on her hip is the most natural action in the world. Not sure I could manage that move, so it's a good thing I had no plans on trying.

"Aunty Mo, did you know jellyfish are made of jelly you can't eat?" The girl points to the creature.

"That's nice, baby, but you can't go running off on me like that. I didn't know where you were." While she scolds her niece, the breathless woman offers me a grateful smile, as if I helped her when, really, I just answered a few of the kid's questions. The fact that my first thought was to throw candy and run, rather than asking her about adult supervision, is one more indication babysitting is not the job for me.

"I didn't run. I walked. And I was here," the girl, Shay, says in a completely rational tone that has me fighting a snort of amusement. Even the woman, Aunty Mo, presses her lips together as if to suppress a laugh. I can see small traces of relation between the two in the shape of their noses and color of their eyes.

"Still, we need to stick together in here." The adult meets my eyes. "Thanks for looking after her." She doesn't give me time to point out that I didn't, really, before she's shifting to the side and talking to someone else. "And thank you for helping me look. Sorry I got so frazzled."

My instinct is to turn and find out who the fourth is in this sudden grouping, but my muscles weld into an immovable mass at the sound of a smooth, flirty voice.

"No problem at all. I'm happy to help."

Oh no.

He's here. Right here. A few inches behind me, here.

The reason for my wig.

Time to discover if my itchy disguise does the job I suffer constant scratching for.

Aunty Mo says something else to the man, but my mind is so focused on unlocking rigid joints and taking careful, casual steps to the side that I don't register a single word. His responding chuckle, though—that rolls through my body, touching each one of my nerve endings.

Don't shiver. Don't even breathe. Don't let a drop of blood fall in the water if you want to escape this shark.

Luckily, the room we're in is circular, with multiple halls branching off. I only need to shuffle a few more feet, and I can retreat like the coward I am.

No, I silently chastise myself. *I am not a coward. Anywhere else, I would be the shark, and tear his handsome head off. But I* cannot *get angry here.*

I'm only a couple steps from freedom when a shout fills the dimly lit space. "Lady! Your phone! You dropped it. Aunty Mo, she dropped it."

What hell dimension am I in!? I silently wail to myself.

Time to prioritize. Who even needs a phone anyway? We're all glued to a screen for most of our lives, the constantly glowing glass killing our eyes and our souls.

Let's everyone drop our phones and never, ever pick them up again.

But just as I've come to terms with my off-the-grid lifestyle and brace to sprint from the room, a body blocks my way.

Eyes on the tile floor, I take in his shoes first: brown, polished, laced and tied neatly. Not at all dangerous. The treachery comes when I drag my gaze upward. Muscular calves, wonderfully formed thighs, all shamelessly on display in a set of khakis that look painted on. Equally form-fitting is his white polo, with the stitched logo of Saltwater Oasis.

Is it even legal to wear such tight clothing? Is this how immaculate conception happens?

Everyone with functioning ovaries must merely look at him, and they're fertilized through the divine power of his sculpted body.

If I walk out of this aquarium pregnant, I will be *so* pissed.

I take juvenile pleasure in the fact that this sculpted specimen of a man fails to claim the coveted six-foot-and-over category most guys seem to desire. Unfortunately, because he stands at a respectable five-eight or so, my eyes reach his face faster.

Loose curls the color of cola brush skin tanned by genetics and the heat of the sun. Gray eyes—a hypnotizing shade I've never been capable of erasing from my memory, no matter how hard I try—burn through all my protective layers, despite having walls fashioned from firmer material than jelly.

Rafael Aguado gapes at me, recognition unhindered by my itchy faux hair.

Note to self: wear a masquerade mask next time.

A grin crashes across his face, so joyous I gasp in my next breath.

"Cat." He sighs my name, as if enjoying the taste of the letters on his lips.

My body has the opposite reaction. I'm wrenched back to fourteen, to another time he stared into my eyes and spoke my name—only then, my now ex-best friend wielded words against me like a weapon. Years have passed since that night, but still I feel the phantom of past tears running down my cheeks and shame flushing through me, heating the watery tracks until they dried in salty riverbeds across my skin.

The fire magic living in my veins rises in a dangerous pulse.

"No," I hiss, as I snatch my forgotten phone out of his loose fingers and shove him aside.

I need to get out of here.

Chapter Two

RAFAEL

Cat Byrne is in the place where I work.

Is she here to see me?

Her fleeing toward the exit points to not likely.

"*No,*" she had said. Was that a no to me saying her name—or maybe, *No, don't talk to me.*

Could be, *No, I'm not your former best friend, and you've just conjured a ghost of her to torture yourself, because all you want is to find her and make up for the wrongs you did.*

I chase after Cat, navigating the many rooms that make up Saltwater Oasis. The idea of letting her go leaks out of a convenient hole in my brain, left as a forgotten puddle on the floor behind me.

Two months in town, and I've only run into her once. A few weeks ago, my friend, Damien, held a barbecue at his house. The guy hosts them regularly for our kind, elementals—people able to manipulate water, fire, earth, metal, or air with natural-born magic. We even have affectionate—if slightly insulting—nicknames for each group: Squids, Pyros, Petal Pushers, Stoners, and Airheads. And among the collection of magic wielders, there she was, standing beside the pool, so familiar yet so different from the girl I knew in high school. I wanted to hug her and find out if her body fit against mine the same. If there was still a subtle scent of hot roses in her hair.

Cat—on the other end of the greeting spectrum—wanted to shove me into the pool. She promptly followed through on that urge, then ran. Just like she's doing now.

The sun shines painfully bright when I push through the front doors. Phoenix midday is no joke. I shade my eyes and spot her powerwalking across the parking lot, then pick up my pace, worried that if she leaves now, I'll never see her again.

I have no way to get in touch with her. No one, not even my best friend, Sammy, will give me Cat's phone number. To be fair, he said he's pretty sure she gave him a fake one, but still. Seems I'm on my own when it comes to fixing this decade-long mistake.

"Cat, wait!" The heat of the day has me sweating by time I reach her. "Please."

"Leave me alone." She pulls the driver's side door of a Prius open and chucks her purse across the console. The angry movement sends her short black bob swinging around her cheeks, one of the many changes my hungry eyes catalogue.

My old friend looks the same in some respects, with her white, lightly freckled skin, short, sharp nose, and expressive mocha eyes. But there are new, if subtle, curves to her figure, a plushness to her lips, and a generally mature sculpt to her face.

When I grip the open door, she pauses long enough to glare at my tense knuckles as if she wants to break each one. Or burn them to cinders, more like.

"I want to apologize," I press. The words are long overdue.

"No need. I'm over it," she says, the fury gone from her voice, replaced by an eerie calm. Cat's breathing is weird, her chest expanding and staying that way for longer than normal before slowly deflating. Like a dragon taking deep, threatening inhales, all in preparation to release a fiery breath that will incinerate the presumptuous knight who waltzed into her lair.

I should back away, hands raised in surrender.

But I've only ever wanted to get closer to Cat.

"You don't sound like you're over it," I say.

Her head turns toward me slowly, and I flinch when she offers me a creepy doll smile. Too wide, emotionless eyes, obviously plotting my death.

"It's been twelve years. Of course I'm over it."

I'm tempted to point out that knowing the exact amount of time since our falling out might be proof that she's *not* over it, but I'm smart enough to keep from correcting her.

"Okay. You're over it." I offer my own smile, but not a scary one. "And since you're over it, we can be friends."

Irrefutable logic. I mentally pat myself on the back.

Far too soon.

Cat's haunted happy face wipes away, leaving a scowl. "We tried friends. It didn't work out for me."

"See!" Triumph has me grinning wide. "You're *not* over it. So, let's hash this out." Taking a chance, I step back from the car, spreading my arms wide in case she wants to throw a few fists. I'm ready to act the punching bag, if that's what Cat needs to move on from how big of an asshole teenage me was. "You can yell at me as much as you want."

Cat shoves away from her car, getting into my face.

"I don't want to yell at you!" Her shout sends a few parking lot pigeons into flight. At the sight of their flapping wings her face only gets redder, and she starts up with the heavy dragon breathing again.

"That felt good...right?" I usually find shouting cathartic. But the woman looks like I struck a match and lit her fuse. As sweat trickles down my sides, dampening my shirt, I realize that the Arizona sun might not be entirely to blame.

Maybe I've been living around humans for too long. I've forgotten how hot fighting with a fire elemental can get.

Literally.

Her magic rolls off her body, boiling the air between us.

Another tactic. Try something else before you lose her again. Or she sets your pants on fire.

Of course, whatever inferno she starts, I can immediately put out with my own abilities to manipulate water. But I like these pants. And I need them, so I don't get fired from my job for indecent exposure.

In another life, Cat used to love compliments. If she wore a new pair of shoes or painted her nails a fun color, I would make a huge deal, waxing poetic about the alteration. My words would get so flowery that, eventually, she'd end up rolling on the floor, clutching her stomach, giggling hard from my ridiculous adulation.

Gods, what I wouldn't give to hear the sounds of her amusement again.

My attention catches on the dark strands surrounding her furious face.

"I love your hair. Did you just get it done? So gorgeous. Like a raven's wing. Or a bat's!" Cat always thought bats were adorable with their little squeaks. At least, she used to. "Such a dark, lustrous—"

"Oh, shut up!" Cat digs her fingers into the hair I was applauding and rips the entire mass off her head.

Well, there goes that plan.

Her familiar, fiery locks sit in a short muss I want to run my fingers through and fix for her. Then, I want her to let my hands linger against her skin, teasing and touching. More than a decade might have passed, but I want her just as badly as I did when I was sixteen.

"What can I do?" The question spills in a desperate groan from my lips, all urge to tease and charm her replaced by raw need. But she's already turning away.

"You can leave me alone." Cat tosses the faux hair into the car next to her bag. "I'm *over* it. You wanted me out of your life? Fine." She hits me with molten eyes, the brown shifting to golden with the heat of her anger. Hot magic continues to roast the air. "I grew up without you. I'm not looking to get you back."

Pain crashes into my heart, a massive wave battering the organ against sharp rocks. The hurt keeps me immobile, watching as Cat climbs into her car and pulls away. Leaving me behind.

Paying me back for the way I drove her off in the first place.

When Cat's bumper disappears around the corner, I find a way to breathe again and remind myself that it's the middle of the workday. An aching heart doesn't mean I can pause the rest of my life. I'm supposed to be meeting with my boss in—I check my watch—five minutes ago.

Shit.

Problem is, when I try to dejectedly trudge back to the aquarium, my feet stay still. And not because misery drained all the strength from my body.

I'm stuck in place because, at some point during my argument with the beautiful Pyro, she melted the soles of my shoes, leaving them adhered to the pavement.

Despite the inconvenience and the persisting heartache, I can't help a small, sad smile.

"Gods, I've missed you, Cat."

Chapter Three

ASPEN

Not for the first time, I wonder if going to the strip club is a bad idea.

"ID," a beefy Black guy instructs when I make it to the front of the line. On a Thursday night, I wasn't expecting a wait, but maybe the weekends start early in the Phoenix nightlife. Or maybe, The Jewelry Box is just the place to be.

I hand over my California driver's license and wait the extra couple of seconds it takes him to discern if the clean-shaven man in the photo is the same as the bearded one in front of him. The facial hair is new. I scratch my chin self-consciously, still not sure if I make the look work.

After my breakup, I wanted a change.

"Twenty-dollar cover," the doorman instructs me, handing my license back. I pass him the required amount. "Only touch if invited to. We have a one-strike policy, and you're done. Ejected and blacklisted." He nods me toward a thick metal door. "Tip your waitress."

I dip my chin in return, then head inside where I come to a desk with a curvy, tan-skinned woman with dark eye makeup that intensifies her stare.

"Coat check?" she asks, voice husky and smile inviting.

"No. Thank you." The service is nice, but I wonder how often people take advantage. Phoenix isn't exactly chilly. I point to a curtained doorway in silent question, and she waves a hand to encourage me on.

The lights register first, and not because they're the techno spinning spotlights I expect at a strip club. Instead, this place has more mood lighting. Reminds me of a speakeasy.

There's still plenty of sparkle, mainly from chandeliers dangling from the ceiling. The crystals refract warm light, which then glows in large, gilded mirrors, each strategically placed to offer views of the main stage no matter where you sit in the club.

That's not all that's suspended. Scarves dangle from the ceiling with a woman twined in their lengths. She tangles and untangles herself in sensuous moves, wearing only enough to keep the most intimate parts of her body hidden.

Not your typical strip club.

A massive wooden bar stretches along the right side of the room, and I aim for it as a good starting point. The place smells like leather and a vaguely floral scent. I wonder if the latter is from one woman, or all of them. The scent is natural, with true elements of rose. With the tease of the rich fragrance, I can almost feel the soft petals against my fingertips.

The same velvety texture of her skin.

I shake my head to clear the thought. My reason for showing up here isn't to seduce my ex-girlfriend. I just...needed something familiar.

So I came home.

And sought her out before even saying hi to my family.

Trying to listen to the music instead of the pesky voice in the back of my head, I realize that while the song plays loud, the sound isn't overwhelming. If I were here with someone, I could hold a conversation. The Jewelry Box may be a strip club, but I get the sense it's more.

Reaching the bar, I settle on a stool with the supple softness of true leather, rather than the stiff, creaky quality of the fake stuff. Only a second passes before a bartender appears in front of me.

"What can I get you, handsome?" She flicks a curtain of black hair off her shoulder before leaning on the bar, bracing her elbows on the surface, and giving me a clear view of the ample breasts straining at her crimson corset. The color sets off the golden highlights in her skin and matches her lipstick perfectly.

"Could I get tequila on the rocks, with lime and mint?"

She nods, flashing me a flirty smile then swaying her hips in their skin-tight black pants as she goes to pour my drink, working for a good tip. While she's gone, I scan the club, searching for a head of fiery hair. But the place is crowded, and the bartender soon recalls my attention.

"Here you go, big guy." She swipes my card, then lets the plastic slide slowly from her fingers as she hands it back. "Let me know if there's anything else you need help with." She practically purrs out the words, and I silently applaud her technique.

"There's something," I say, while pushing her tip across the bar, and she leans forward as if serving me is all she wants to do. "Is Cat Byrne working tonight?"

Even though her smile doesn't fall, something about her demeanor cools and hardens. "Sorry, big guy. Waitresses don't offer dances, and we don't give out their schedules." With a hand that I now see has sharp, red acrylics, she waves toward the closest stage. "If you like one of the performers, someone on the stage, or silks, or pole, you can usually follow their social media to find out when *they're* working."

That was icier than the initial greeting, and I want to kick myself for the major flaw in my plan to surprise Cat. This is her place of work, and any guy showing up asking about her is going to sound like a creep.

"We're old friends," I offer halfheartedly, then immediately want to bury my head in a giant pile of dirt.

The bartender's eyes go diamond-hard. "Mm-hmm. And that's why you don't know when she works?"

Focusing on my drink, I do the smart thing and keep my mouth shut. There's no reason to answer and dig myself deeper. Not unless I plan on laying out every detail of my and Cat's past for this woman.

Obviously, my abilities as a lawyer—the ones that let me easily charm every member of a jury—don't translate to day-to-day life. Of course, when I'm in the courtroom, I always pretend that I'm *him*, the other person in Phoenix I considered seeking out tonight.

But I don't expect a warm greeting from Raphael Aguado.

As I consider a new plan, one where I set up an intentional meeting time, a familiar heat teases the surface of my skin.

"Hey, Mia. Could I get a bottle of top-shelf whiskey and three glasses? Have some big spenders at table eleven."

The voice, sweet yet firm, sinks into my muscles like stepping under a warm shower after a rough workout. Turning carefully, I catch sight of the bartender grimacing as she comes to the same realization I do. Continuing to shift my stool, I find her.

Cat.

Words lodge in my throat, so deep, I'm not sure what I would say if I could speak. All I can do is meticulously catalogue every detail of the first person I ever fell in love with.

Ruby red hair, still cut in the short style she wore while we dated, and skin the same whipped cream shade that always had me worrying about her in the desert sun, while simultaneously wanting to devour her like a dessert. Cat's nose possesses the same sharp slope, her ears the same familiar curve, only now with three piercings along the rim instead of one.

Her body—praise and damn the gods. She's a few inches taller, a few pounds fuller, but still pixie-like. Every bit of her shouts the word *gorgeous* in my skull. The outfit she wears enhances her subtle curves. Tight, evilly short shorts with ruffles clutch the orbs of her ass. The top, some tantalizing silver bra with delicate metal chains dangling from it, hypnotizes me.

For a girl who once asked me if her cardigan was too sexy, I'm struggling to believe what I'm seeing.

Happiness at the sight of her uncurls a power in my palms, the magic twining like vines longing to reach toward the sun. I clench my fists to keep it at bay. The fire elemental tilts her head my way, following the bartender's attention, and her eyes, looking like pools of melted chocolate, take me in. A gaze I can't believe I allowed myself to go years without singes me.

"Hello," Cat says. Then, she smiles—and turns back to her coworker.

As if I'm like every other customer in this club. No one remarkable. Not worth another second of attention.

She doesn't remember me.

The realization hits hard, shorting out the magical urge, and I struggle to pull in a breath. Doubts bombard me, a storm threatening to rip my roots from the ground.

Did I make out our emails to be more than they were?

Cat never made me any promises during our sporadic correspondence over the years, but I thought the messages at least meant a tenuous connection remained. That she hadn't weeded me from her mind completely.

This was a mistake.

Self-consciously, I clutch my drink and scratch my beard. When the rough fibers brush against my palm, I pause. And I hope.

We haven't seen each other in years. I'm not on social media, and the few photos I've sent were all before my post-breakup facial hair. The bartender, Mia, subtly attempts to draw her coworker farther down the bar, away from me, when I stand.

"Cat." Her name is need on my lips. The redhead pauses, glancing at me in surprise. When wariness shadows her gaze, I press on. "It's me. Aspen." Vulnerability twines through me, and I cross my arms, then immediately uncross them because I've been told my muscles bulge in that position and can be kind of intimidating. "Aspen Baumann."

Her lips, which have a glittery gloss on them, round in shock.

"Red, why don't you head to the back?" Mia isn't smiling anymore. In fact, she looks ready to vault the bar to defend Cat. Instead of annoying me, I find myself grateful for her instinct. It's good to know there are people here who have the Pyro's back.

"Aspen?" My name in her honey voice is like a straight shot of sunshine, warm and coaxing my earth magic to the surface. When the mint in my drink starts sprouting extra leaves, I clench my fists again to stifle my erratic power.

Cat's in front of me, suddenly, hands on my chest, heat from her skin seeping through my T-shirt.

Gods, I want to melt into her.

"You're *here*?"

Chapter Four

CAT

I had to touch him to believe it.

He's here. Aspen Baumann is standing in front of me in all his mountain man glory. Gods, that beard is new and somehow makes him more handsome. Or maybe it's the years of maturity. Because I haven't been in the same space as Aspen since...

No, I don't want to think about that now. Not when he's here, giving me that familiar sheepish grin.

"I'm here." His deep voice sinks into me like roots in soil. "Surprise."

"Can I hug you?" *Please let me wrap myself around you, even though I was a silly little girl who broke your heart.*

"I—" When Aspen hesitates, I try not to show my devastation. But he clears his throat and throws a glance toward the entrance. "Customers aren't supposed to touch."

Relief has me giggling. Of course Aspen would make sure to follow the rules. He was always the responsible, steady presence I could count on.

"You can touch with permission. And I give you *enthusiastic* consent." I try not to blush when I realize how that sounds. "Please hug me right now, you big oak!"

Something I said earns me a beard-crinkling grin, and next thing I know, Aspen scoops me up in an embrace, my feet fully off the ground as he clutches me tight—but not too tight—against his chest.

This is right.

I use all my willpower not to let out an embarrassing groan of pleasure. Years later and his body engulfs me in warm support, just like it did when we were fumbling kids in high school, trying to figure out lust and love. With my arms around his torso, face buried in his chest, I breathe his scent in deep. Mint and warm soil. The fragrance unlocks memories, images flicking through my mind like a slide show.

Aspen scooting his chair closer to mine in math class, asking for help with his homework.

Aspen inviting me to come watch his football games on Friday nights.

Aspen offering me a fruit ice pop at lunch, his eyes on my mouth as I sucked on the treat.

Aspen smiling wide when I gave him a bunny-ear cactus for Valentine's Day.

Aspen hoisting me on his shoulders after my volleyball team won the championship.

Aspen murmuring my name against my neck as he kissed me in his bed, his cactus sprouting new segments and flowers on the bedside table as the Petal Pusher's magic overflowed.

Suddenly, I'm worried I might start crying in the middle of the strip club.

Pull yourself together. All that was a decade ago.

But until this moment, I never accepted how much I missed Aspen Baumann.

"I can't believe you're here!" I loosen my hold enough to stare into his hazel eyes, loving how they scrunch in the corners just like they used to. Over his shoulder, I spy a basil plant Mia uses for specialty cocktails. Extra leaves slowly—but faster than is natural—unfurl.

Whatever Aspen thinks of me now, at least I know he's happy to see me. Unlike my fire, which is fueled by anger, the Petal Pusher's power has always connected to his joy.

Lucky man.

I meet Aspen's gaze again, unable to smooth away my gleeful smirk. "You're making things grow," I whisper.

His brows pop up, and I feel his fingers fist against my back, trying to stifle the earth magic. Then he lets me down, my body sliding against his as I come to stand on my own. I can't help but shiver as I soak in the shape of him.

"When did you get to town?" I ask to distract my libido, even as I hold onto his biceps and stare up at him. Our eyes are closer than I remember thanks to the set of high heeled boots I'm wearing.

"Just a few hours ago. Dropped my stuff off and headed over here."

"Couldn't wait another second to check out the club?"

Aspen has known almost from the start that I'm a waitress at The Jewelry Box. In the emails we exchanged over the years, I never lied about the odd jobs I took to pay my bills. That's what this waitress gig is about for me, and I won't pretend otherwise. Even if the metal elemental who fashioned this metallic bra successfully made the thing fit like wearing a cloud, I'd still rather have a different uniform that didn't focus so much on my boobs and ass. Maybe if I had more of either to show off...

But I'm not ashamed of this job either. It pays well, and I chose it, and I'm good with that. Still, I may have painted a more upbeat version of my work life to Aspen than is accurate. Trying to portray a woman living in a bohemian manner, who doesn't care that she has no plan.

I *do* care, but I just don't want anyone to know how much.

Especially not Aspen Baumann, my first boyfriend and the guy I thought I was over until he wrapped his arms around me and shattered that rosy eyeglass lie. I half-hate him for still being so lovable.

Why can't I fall out of love with you? I wail inside my head as my eyes trace down the slightly crooked slope of his nose. I was at the football game where his helmet popped off and a stray elbow broke it. Later that night, he lay his head in my lap, and I held an ice pack on the bruise.

Why can't you fall out of love with anyone? The insidious voice brings another nose to mind. This one perfectly straight beneath two gray eyes pleading for forgiveness.

I don't still love Rafael, I remind myself, *and this moment is about Aspen.*

"Couldn't wait to see *you*." Aspen corrects my lighthearted joke, starting up a non-magical fire in my belly with the way he focuses entirely on me.

"Sorry to break up this reunion." At the sound of Mia's dry voice, I glance her way. "But your table just gave me the 'hurry up' wave. Better get your ass in gear, Red."

"Sorry. I just wanted to say hi." Aspen steps back when my hands drop from his arms. "I can head out."

"No!" I shout the word, desperate not to lose sight of him now that he's returned to my life. I hook an arm around his waist and half-guide, half-shove Aspen onto a stool. "Stay. Drink. If it slows down, we can catch up."

Don't disappear on me.

Before he can protest, I scoop up my tray of drinks and stroll off. It's not fair, this overwhelming urge to keep him close by. I'm the one who separated us in the first place. Besides, I'm not trying to recapture a relationship I had in high school. But I can't handle the idea of Aspen walking out of this club without me getting to hear more words from his lips and taking a leisurely moment to catalogue all the changes in him.

Maybe then, after a little gawking and silent pining, I'll be able to let him get on with his hotshot lawyer life back in California.

Tonight though, he's mine.

Chapter Five

ASPEN

Happiness fuels my magic, and being around Cat means this strip club risks turning into a jungle if I don't restrain myself.

In high school, I was great at containing my powers, because I had to do it all the time. Cat was constantly at my side, and every funny thing she said, or cute smile she gave, or innocent, sexy move she made threatened to make my heart bust out of my chest. After the night everything ended, I didn't battle with my power for months as a weight of melancholy hung over my life.

My mind shies away from the painful prick of that memory. Instead, I focus on the present moment. The rosy scent of her hair. The way her body softened against mine even as her arms tightened around my torso in an almost threatening embrace. The airy gasp of her breath, just beside my ear.

If only I could taste her, too. Find out if her lips hold the same intoxicating effect that they used to.

Don't push your luck.

"I guess you do know her. My bad." Mia leans on the bar in a less-provocative manner than before and has lost the flirty edge to her voice. I get the sense I'm chatting with the woman behind the customer service smile now. "We get plenty of creeps in here. Can never be too careful."

"No problem." I palm my tequila. "Should've thought through my unannounced visit." Even though I'm talking to Mia, I can't take my attention off Cat. The fire elemental strolls around the room with utter confidence, chatting with customers, smiling at whatever they say to her, appearing to have a grand time.

When she told me a year ago in one of her emails that she got a job waitressing at a strip club, I didn't know what to think. After learning that her sister, Harley, set her up with the gig, I decided not to worry about the legitimacy of the place. Harley may not be what most people would call a role model, but I know that she protects her baby sister like a fire-breathing dragon and would never let her work at a dangerous club.

Instead, my mind focused on the other aspects of working here. What it would be like to come across Cat in a room thick with lust. Now, I have a front row seat, and I'm considering if I should've brought a coat just to cover the stirring in my lap. Even the entertainment on stage can't distract me from the redhead as she bends over to collect empty glasses off a table.

"So, you're her..." Mia taps her knuckles on the bar to grab my attention. I meet her amused, curious stare.

"Friend." I scratch my beard and sip from my glass, savoring the fresh flavor mixed with alcohol. "Ex-boyfriend, too. Amicable. We kept in touch."

Mia smirks as she reads an order another waitress hands her. The bartender starts pouring drinks, but her attention wanders back to me. "Amicable, huh?"

"Yeah." I lose sight of the Pyro in the shifting crowd. "Hard not to be with Cat."

Mia's lips twitch down, and her eyes slide to the side then back to me. "She goes by Red here. For privacy."

My face heats, and I silently curse myself. "Red. Got it."

Before stepping into this club, I would have considered myself a confident guy. Self-contained and self-assured. But bring Cat into the equation, and I'm a stumbling, crush-stricken teenager again.

"What brings you to town, big man?"

A desperate hope.

"Time to come home," I say out loud. "Wasn't happy living in California anymore."

Mia aggressively mixes a shaker, and I wonder if the movement is supposed to seem as threatening as it's coming off.

"And what do you do for a living, amicable ex-boyfriend?" she asks while pouring out the foamy alcohol into a martini glass.

"Worked at a law firm. I—"

A yelp cuts me off, and I swing around on my stool. I'm not sure how I heard the distressed sound over the thrum of the music. Maybe I didn't catch it in my ears, but instead through the invisible vine I've always imagined sprouting from Cat's body and twining around my heart.

Either way, my eyes immediately find her across the room, arm in the meaty palm of some Neanderthal.

No conscious decision goes through my mind. One second, I'm sitting at the bar tracing the condensation on the side of my drink, and the next I'm sprinting across the room, rage twisting through my veins.

"How much to get you, me, and a bottle of bourbon in a room alone together?" The sleazy, overconfident asshole leans over Cat, as if he can use his superior height to earn her submission.

No way in any hell dimension.

The next second, I've crushed his wrist in my grasp, tight enough that his hold on Cat loosens.

"Hey! What the fuck?" the piece of shit shouts, then lets out a pathetic whimper when I wrench his arm high behind his back, an inch or so away from dislocating his shoulder. After having my own popped out of its socket—twice during my football days—I know the sensation hurts like a motherfucker.

"You okay?" Half my attention stays on the assaulter, but I let my eyes run over Cat, searching for signs of injury.

"Yeah. I'm fine." She wipes her palm over the skin the guy grabbed, as if she can erase the memory of his greasy grasp. "You saved me the trouble of kneeing his precious jewels, so thanks for that."

I nod and try not to let on how furious I am. Calm on the surface, tangling vines of poison ivy underneath.

"What do you want me to do with him?" I ask.

"You'll fucking let me go is what you'll fucking do you—ah! Fuck!"

Cat's red brows raise as she glances between me and the customer, finally realizing I'm at her whim. This is her house, and I'm just a visitor. Something this primordial ooze of a person I have in submission obviously forgot.

Turning, she waves a special hand gesture at Mia, and the bartender nods.

"We're going to wait for my boss, Yasmin. The club owner," Cat tells me.

I nod and stand as still as the big oak she affectionately referred to me as. Gods, I missed that nickname.

The other men in this guy's party have finally taken notice of what's happening to their friend. Some start to rise with anger on their faces. Keeping mine devoid of emotion, I meet their glares, conveying that I will take every single one of them down if they step out of line. This is Cat's place of work, and I refuse to let her feel unsafe.

All the while, the man in my hold mutters unintelligible curses and threats my way.

"Here she is." Cat nods toward a woman headed our way.

The owner of The Jewelry Box strolls across the floor toward us, power and sensuality in every swing of her hips. There's a sharp edge to her movements that acts as a warning: this beautiful woman will cut you before you even have a chance to cross her. Black hair braided in a tight style leaves her angular face and hawk-like eyes on full display. The silver pantsuit she wears is tailored perfectly to her body, and I wonder if the fabric is silky soft, or finely woven metal. Fashion and armor.

"What," Yasmin purrs once she's close enough to fully take in the scene, "happened here?"

"This guy went fucking nuts!" the customer barks out, his face mottled from anger or pain. Maybe both. "I was just ordering a drink, and he fucking attacked me!"

I don't refute the lie, but I also don't loosen my hold, keeping the man in the same position as I watch Cat for direction.

"I wasn't talking to you." Yasmine turns toward the Pyro, ignoring the spluttering man. "Red? From the beginning."

Cat lays out the series of events from the moment she approached the table. Yasmine's only reaction is a slight narrowing of her eyes, gaze dropping to Cat's wrist when she tells her about the grab. I stifle the urge to break this man's wrist to teach him a lesson.

"You touched her without an invitation." Yasmine speaks the words at the customer, rather than posing them as a question.

"We're at a strip club, for fucks sake!" He tries to shake out of my hold but gets nowhere. The club owner steps closer, looking down at the man because her heels give her already tall form a few inches over him.

"My jewels," she says, gesturing toward the stage where a woman in blue is currently hanging upside down from a poll, the dusky shadows of her nipples visible through the sheer fabric of her top, "offer a range of services. Services that they have the power to choose to provide or not. This is not a toy shop, with toddlers grabbing whatever colorful object catches their eye. You must be invited to touch, and we have a one-strike policy—two rules you were told upon entering. You are banned from this establishment." The guy gasps in outrage, but the woman is already turning to face the other men at the table. "You all are done for the night as well. You may return another. In better company."

There's a hum of resentful muttering as they stand from their seats, and I overhear one guy in a suit say something about not coming back if this is what service is like. Yasmine homes in on the whiner, a gracious smile curving her silver-painted lips. "If that is the case, we could always make it official. I can permanently ban you as easily as I did your friend."

The group shuts up collectively, and I wonder over the threat. Getting banned from The Jewelry Box seems to mean more than finding a new strip club to go to.

At Yasmine's wave and Cat's nod, I walk with the owner to help escort the men out of the club. Once they're out the front door, I dive back through the curtain and find Cat clearing the table.

"You sure you're okay?" My urge is to gather her into my arms, but she's steady on her feet and hasn't asked me to hold her.

"I'm good. Not the first time it's happened." She grimaces as if regretting the admission. "But not a lot, I swear. This isn't some sleazy place. The Jewelry Box is great."

As I mull over her defense, Yasmine approaches us with a speculative look in her eye.

"Do you need a break, Red?" she asks, and Cat shakes her head. The owner keeps her attention on Cat as she tilts her chin my way. "What's this one's deal?"

"Aspen Baumann. He's an old friend. We went to high school together. Petal Pusher." Cat waves from me to Yasmin. "She's an Airhead." When the sentence leaves her mouth, the adorable Pyro's mouth drops open in horror at what she just called her boss. The silly names made up for each of the elemental groups have only been around for a few years. Someone from a different generation, or not in the know, might take offense to being called a Pyro, Squid, Petal Pusher, Stoner, or...Airhead. "I mean—you know—she can—"

Yasmin's lips soften into a smile. "Calm down. I'm not offended." Her focus roams over me as I stare back. "One of my bouncers is on paternity leave, and another just broke her leg in a motorcycle accident—which means I'm temporarily short-staffed," she says. "Would you consider applying for a position?"

Work at a strip club?

When I went off to college on a football scholarship, I knew what career I wanted. Law has always fascinated me, even though I'm not the most charismatic in the courtroom. The past few years, I've risen through the ranks at a prestigious San Francisco law firm. Even though I loved the work, I lost my connection to the city. Which is one of the reasons I left it all behind.

But the thing about crossing state lines is, I can't just jump into the first law firm that hires me. I need to pass some important check points to practice in Arizona.

Which means I've got some time on my hands.

My gaze tracks over to Cat, where she's paused with her tray full of half-empty drinks, waiting for what she no doubt expects will be a polite refusal.

Working with Cat.

"I'm interested."

Chapter Six

CAT

My eyes threaten to close on me as I sort lights and darks in front of the washing machine. I didn't get home from work until three a.m., and then thoughts of Aspen kept me from falling asleep.

Aspen living in Phoenix.

Working in the same club that *I* work in.

Maybe that didn't happen. Maybe him filling out a job application at The Jewelry Box was a vivid dream. I need a cup of coffee—or three—to lubricate my brain enough that I can distinguish between fact and fiction.

My phone dings in the pocket of my sleep shorts. I let my dirty clothes slip from my fingers into the basket, before reaching to see who's texting me. My big sister's name flashes on the screen, and I swipe open to see what she has to say.

> Harley: Just sent this to everyone. Hope you don't mind.

Beneath the text is a picture of a colorful invitation with the words "Pool Party Today" blaring at the top of the image. My eyes trace over the invite three times before I recognize the address.

My address.

"By the Goddess," I mutter. A heated pulse starts up under my skin as I type out a response.

Cat: Did Quinn sign off on this?

If my other sister and roommate agreed to a party without talking to me then...I don't know what. That's just not Quinn's style. It's Harley's style for sure.

Cat: And who is everyone?

Harley texts back a minute later, completely ignoring my first question and listing a long stream of names. I recognize most. They're all magic-wielding elementals like my sisters and me. People I like hanging out with most days. But not ones I want showing up at my house unannounced when I'm still exhausted from being on my feet all night.

Then, my eyes snag on two names in the list, and the fiery pulse thrumming heavy through my body increases tenfold.

Sammy

Rafael

My phone slips from my hand to land among my laundry, but I'm glad it's not in my palm anymore because I'm at risk of melting the device. Instead, I grip the two handles of my laundry basket and grit my teeth against the fury I feel toward my older sister.

How could she? Not only is Harley setting up a gathering that involves the two people I never want to be around again, but she invited them over to *my* house. A house she does *not* live in.

I suck in deep breath after deep breath, but the unfurling of my power is unstoppable, leaking out of my pores and filling this small space as if I set the dryer on max and let it run for hours with the door open.

"Gods damn it!" I shout. When I turn to start some angry pacing, releasing my grip on the basket, something comes away in my hands. I glance down to find my palms coated in a sticky blue substance.

Plastic. I melted the handles off my laundry basket.

Just as I'm muttering a wider range of curses, I hear a footstep, then—

"Ah ha! I knew it!" Harley leaps around a corner, scaring the magical fury out of me. I thought I was alone in this house.

"What in the Goddess's name!" I pant, clutching my chest and getting plastic goo all over my boobs.

"Not a goddess. Just your lovable big sister who brought you donuts and is ready to solve all your problems." Harley's hand snaps out to grasp my wrist before I can think to hide my palms. "Caught you blue-handed. I knew you hadn't figured it out. You've been fooling us these past few years with that meditation bullshit, but you're just as bad as Quinn was, am I right?" She wiggles her set of perfectly shaped crimson brows. "Powers going wonky whenever you're pissed?"

"Harley." I try to keep my voice light, normally proud of how I'm the calm, rational sister. "What is this party? I didn't agree to it, and I doubt Quinn did either. We don't host parties here."

My sister rolls a set of brown eyes a shade lighter than mine and blows a loose red curl out of her face. Quinn and I have straighter hair for the most part, but our wild older sister has a mass of gorgeous curls that always bounce with her dramatic movements.

"There's no party. I was trying to piss you off to prove my point. And I did." She raises our hands higher so I can't ignore the still-liquid plastic. "Your control is on the fritz."

"There's no party?" Relief infuses my chest, and the molten pulse under my skin slows as my anger fully dissipates. Annoyance remains, but that doesn't call my heat as much.

"We're past that." Harley lets my hand fall, and I return to the laundry room to grab some paper towels to wipe my palms clean. "You're ignoring the obvious issue here."

"There's no issue."

"Your laundry basket would claim otherwise. How did this happen?" Harley strolls past me and boosts herself on top of the dryer, looming over me more than she usually does. "We knew about Quinn all this time, but I thought you had it handled."

Like all elementals, our sister Quinn's powers are tied to a certain emotion. Mine is anger, but hers is lust. Caused a lot of relationship issues, until she fell for an ice elemental and was able to practice enough to control the heat.

"I *do* have it handled," I insist, trying my best not to sound petulant.

Harley's eyes flick from the mangled basket back to me.

I sigh. "That was a fluke. You know me. Unless it's a big deal, I don't get mad. So it's handled."

Harley chokes on air, coughing to clear her throat before she responds. "Excuse me, what? *That's* how you've dealt with your fire all this time? You just...tried not to get mad?"

With a shrug, I avoid her gaze. "I'm not an angry person."

"Gods, Cat! That's not real control. Don't you know how dangerous you are?"

My face heats, but this time from embarrassment rather than magic. I feel like a kid getting lectured by a teacher for not being prepared for a test.

"Nothing has happened." The excuse is meager even to my ears.

You're always scared something will, though, the nasty voice taunts from the back of my brain.

"Yet," Harley presses. "You're in the same boat as Quinn."

"I'm not," I insist. "Lust, that's a good thing. Especially when you want to be in a relationship. But anger...it's just better that I don't get angry. I shouldn't have to."

Harley laughs as she tangles her fingers in her riotous hair. "No, no, no! That is exactly the wrong way to think about it." My big sister hops down from her perch to grab my shoulders, forcing me to meet her eyes. "You have every right in the world to be mad. If you're pissed at me, I want you to feel that anger with every bone in your body. Too many people tell women we need to smile and be happy all the time. That's bullshit. Get furious! Scream, shout, tear me a new one for inviting a load of Squids to your house."

"And then melt the skin from your bones?" I mock back.

"You're allowed to feel your emotions." Harley drops her forehead to mine. "It's just that our kind have a dangerous edge to some, so we need to learn control. But that's the thing, Cat— you control the *magic*, not the emotion."

Her words make sense, but I can't help wanting to argue against them, if only to work around the possibility that I'm behind in yet another category of my life.

"Besides," Harley continues when I don't respond. She steps back and gives me a smirk. "You're going to have a bitch of a time suppressing your anger now that a certain Squid-who-will-not-be-named is back in town."

And just like that, the heat builds in me again as the image of Rafael's face flares across my mind.

But on the surface, I keep my expression passive. "You can say his name. What he did is in the past. It would be childish for me to hang onto a grudge for so long. It's ancient history. "

And yet look at me, digging it up every time I think of him, like an immature archeologist.

Harley scrutinizes me for longer than I'd like. To prove I'm fine, I go back to throwing dirty clothes in the washing machine.

"You know, I've always wondered..." Harley leans against the wall, her arms crossed, gaze probing. "Does the nameless Squid have some connection to why you always choose boyfriends from the bottom of the barrel?"

I pause with a pair of panties balled in my fist. "What's that supposed to mean?"

She scoffs. "Come on, Cat. You love to date a loser. There was the guy who asked to move in with you after the first date because he didn't want to pay rent. Then the one who lived with six roommates and danced a very bad robot on the street for tips as his full-time job. The pet psychic who told you your rabbit was very happy in heaven—when you never owned a rabbit and don't believe in heaven. And now...are you still seeing that DJ? 'Face Smasher,' or whatever he called himself?"

"Ear Basher," I correct, knowing that I'm not helping my case. "And there's nothing wrong with being a DJ. It is a particular kind of art form."

"There's nothing wrong with being a *good* DJ. But Head Crasher just fades one popular song into another and wears a lot of glow sticks. He's a man baby, just like every guy you've dated since high school. I don't get it."

I bite the inside of my lip to keep from agreeing with her. Because she's not wrong. It's just...there's something nice about dating a guy who has zero of his shit together. When I tell him I have health insurance and a Roth IRA, his eyes go all wide, and he asks me how taxes work. For a moment, I can pretend I'm a properly functioning adult, because compared to him, I am.

Harley does not need to know my insecurity, though.

"Maybe I just want to hook up with someone who's fun. Nothing serious. And who I date has nothing to do with...*that* Squid." Gods, I can't even say his name. "He and I were never together, anyway. We were friends when we were kids, and then he dropped me." And I *definitely* didn't choke on those last few words because I am *definitely* over it.

Harley tilts her head to meet my eyes, her expression no longer teasing. "I remember."

On a rare occasion, my eldest sister can be entirely, deadly serious. The experience is disconcerting, having the weight of her focus undiluted by humor. Right now, she holds me still with her sincerity, and I'm sent back to that night when Rafael ended my favorite thing in the world—our friendship. Harley found me sobbing in my bedroom and held me through the night. The next day, she took me to the salon, claiming that break ups—even though I insisted it wasn't a breakup because we weren't dating—needed haircuts. She insisted I take control of a part of my life that I could.

Rafael used to tug on my long red hair in a gentle, playful gesture. I never wanted to think about it again. Now, I reach up to finger my pixie style. The one I chose then, and still love to this day. Short hair is a certain kind of freedom.

Aspen was the first one to compliment my hair when I showed up at school rocking the new look.

"You said since high school," I point out. "So you don't think Aspen was a man baby?"

Harley bobbles her head. "Not a baby. He was a boy. But that's because you were in high school. And he was further on his way to becoming a man than any of the duds you've dated since." She opens her palm and a little flame rests in the center. The fireball starts to dance around her fingers, moving in intricate patterns I could never imagine attempting.

Harley is a master of control.

"Besides, as great as Aspen was, you ended things. I figured there was something wrong with him I didn't know about." She collapses her fingers, and the fire extinguishes. "I'm going to make coffee and then have my own little pool party. Join me when you're not such a grumpy pants. We can brainstorm how to deal with your power problem."

Harley struts away, heading for the kitchen like she lives here. Quinn and I need to start charging her rent if she's going to keep using the pool more than we do.

Staring into the cave of the washing machine, I think over her words. *"I figured something was wrong with him..."*

There was nothing wrong. Aspen was perfect. Well, not perfect. He did bite his nails when he studied and always guessed the ending of a movie before it happened, then blurted it out like he couldn't help himself. And if he falls asleep on his back, the guy snores like his throat is fashioned from a chainsaw. That last one made it impossible for him to sneak into my bedroom for secret sleepovers, because no one in my house would believe I could make such a horrendous noise.

But those were all just quirks. As a man, or boy as Harley said, he was wonderful.

I was the reason I ended things.

As I pour the fragrant blue detergent over the clothes, I decide not to mention Aspen's return to my sister. I don't want to risk her hearing the truth in my voice: that I never really moved on from the Petal Pusher. That I never found a way to fall fully out of love with him.

If Harley finds out, she'll use the unstoppable force of her will to get me to ask him out again. That would be bad either way. One, he says no, and I'm crushed. Two, he says yes, realizes how unimpressive of a person I am, eventually breaks it off with me, and I am once again crushed.

But what I wouldn't give for a chance to explore the man he's become. Those emails were just a tease. I want to know it all. His return to town has my veins buzzing with excited energy—much different than the heated anger that pulses whenever I think of another unmentionable elemental moving back to Phoenix.

Another man with a distracting body I *so* don't want to explore.

Chapter Seven

RAFAEL

Water cradles me from all sides as I float in the saltwater pool. After a week of work, there's nothing better than a swim. The element surrounds me in an embrace, like an old friend coming home.

At least, that's how some friends greet one another.

Others melt your shoes to the asphalt, so you have to lie to your coworkers and tell them you dropped chum on your feet and then you drive home barefoot to grab a replacement pair of shoes and bring a crowbar back to work to pry the evidence off the parking lot.

So yeah, the water feels nice.

"Beer?" Sammy's voice comes from just near my shoulder, and I pop my head up to see my best friend and fellow Squid reclined on a flamingo floaty, extending a sweating can to me.

This is a good greeting too.

"Thanks." I let my feet sink to the bottom of the pool and accept the libation. Without my ears mostly submerged, the noise of the party rises again. Since moving back to town, I've learned Saturday afternoon get-togethers are a common thing among a group of young professional elementals, all of them gathering at Damien Cortez's house. Damien used to throw a different kind of party when we were younger. The Squid was the one who provided beer to us in high school, as he was a couple years our senior.

I seek the dark-haired man out where he stands in front of a massive grill. He's no longer the lanky fuck-up smoking weed behind the school gym. At some point, he filled out, started standing taller, and became one of the most successful real estate agents in the Phoenix area. His house is a testament to his success. But the girl in the lounge chair next to the grill is the true indication he's changed.

Drifting over to the side of the pool where she is, I settle in close enough to chat with the pair. "Hey, Marisol. What'cha reading?"

The teenager pops her head up, sending her wavy hair bouncing with the movement. "Calculus." Her grimace shows how exciting the subject matter is. With a heave, she lifts the textbook off her lap to show me the cover.

"Seriously, Damien? You're making her study at a party?" Sammy has floated his way over to join us.

The older Squid snorts. "She chose to torture herself. They've only been back a few weeks, and she's already worried about her grade."

"It's not my fault that Mom and Dad gave you all the brains and me all the beauty," Marisol snipes at her brother.

Damien grabs his stomach as if in pain. "Low blow. You know I'm sensitive about my grotesque face."

She snorts and disappears back into her book, missing the almost paternal smile her brother sends her way. According to Sammy, the Cortez parents got tired of living in one place and decided to travel the world—without their daughter. That left Marisol in the care of her older brother since she was thirteen. He's done a good job, but I know from firsthand experience how having a below-par parent can fuck with you, even if there are still people in life showing you love.

"Studying on a weekend," Sammy groans, still stuck on her studious choice. "When we were your age, we were going wild. Breaking rules. Barely avoiding bodily injury."

Damien waves his spatula in a threatening manner. "Shut up. Don't put those ideas in her head. Studying is good. So is sticking to curfew and not getting fired from your job for holding a midnight rave."

"I sold more pizza in one night than the shop did in a month," Sammy defends himself, thrusting his beer into the air in a victory toast, and almost topples off his flamingo in the process.

As the two go back and forth, my mind travels the road to my teenage memories. There's a mixture of good, bad, and cringeworthy. Sammy and I hung with a group that loved taking risks. It was fun, I guess. But when I examine how I felt back then, the reckless drive was more of a need to prove something. To who? The world, maybe. As if I could reach a danger level that would convince the universe I didn't give a shit.

And then maybe *I* would have stopped caring. Especially about the things that hurt so much back then.

As if the gods want to punish me for the irresponsible acts of my youth, Sammy calls out the name of the last person I'd ever hoped to see again.

"Aspen!"

It's all I can do not to let out a groan as I watch the earth elemental weave his way through the crowd toward our spot in the pool.

When did he get back to town?

The Petal Pusher has changed since I last saw him. Aspen was always big, which served the guy well as linebacker on our high school football team. He never had trouble filling out those tight pants, the stretchy fabric showing off a muscular ass that should've been against school rules but wasn't for some reason. Now, he's even more solid, the biceps of his arms at war with the gray sleeves of his T-shirt. My eyes trace over his tall, muscular build, hating how good he looks in clothes he obviously put less than five minutes of thought into. Effortlessly handsome.

My entire body heats, a rush of different emotions crashing through me with every step of his approach. I try to straighten them all out, but suddenly he's standing next to Marisol's chair, and I'm out of time.

"Damien." The Petal Pusher's voice rumbles low as he greets the host. "Thanks for having me."

"Of course." The two men clasp hands and go in for a half-hug back slap. I, meanwhile, try to ignore how the sound of Aspen's voice drags down my spine in a firm caress, the way I used to wish his hands would.

Hell no. Do not go back to that.

"Marisol." Aspen holds out a fist, and she taps her knuckles against his without leaving off her reading. "Sammy." Aspen nods the guy's way and gets a beer raised in a toast of a greeting. Then heavy hazel eyes land on me, thick lashes giving an almost imperceptible flutter. "Hey, Rafael."

"Aspen." I clear my throat when the Petal Pusher's name comes out higher pitched than intended. "You're here."

The guy nods.

"Since when?" Hard as I try to suppress it, accusation still leaks into my voice. Him being here fucks with my plan.

It's simple really: Get Cat to forgive me. Convince her to fall in love with me. Live happily ever after with the Pyro of my dreams.

Problem is, last I checked, she's the Pyro of *his* dreams too.

"Just a few days," Aspen says.

"You're visiting?"

Silently, he shakes his head.

Fuck. Fuuuuck.

"Cool," I mutter, then chug my beer. "Gonna grab another." I use the empty can as an excuse to get away from the group, pretending not to notice Damien's raised brows or Sammy's smirk. Water swirls around me more than my movements should elicit, a current created by the rising tide of my jealousy. The magic rocks in me, a stormy ocean in the bottle of my chest.

If Aspen's back in town for more than a visit, it's only a matter of time before he reconnects with Cat.

Are we in high school all over again?

With careful, controlled breaths, I subdue my power enough that half the pool doesn't cling to me as I use the steps to climb out. The backyard party is a chorus of conversation around me, but I'm so stuck in my thoughts I don't hear any of it.

Has he already gone to see her? Are they already back together?

If that's what the guy wants, no doubt he'll get it. The two were devoted to each other in high school, always holding hands in the hallway and laughing together about jokes only they knew, sneaking off to a back stairwell to make out during study halls.

Because how could a guy go a full school day without kissing Cat Byrne?

How could anyone say no to a heavy petting session from Aspen Baumann?

The memory of the day I happened upon them in that stairwell rises so fast I don't have time to suppress it.

The two of them were so wrapped up in each other they never saw me. Aspen had one arm braced on the concrete wall and the other supported Cat's ass while she wrapped her arms around his neck and legs around his waist. The Petal Pusher's hips had rocked in slow waves, miming erotic thrusts even with their clothes on. The sounds of their gasps and the smack of lips plays like a torturous pop song I can't get out of my head, even now.

I find my way into Damien's house and stumble into the bathroom, locking the door behind me, breathing heavy.

Gods, I know exactly what it felt like.

What it felt like to be Cat in that moment. Because that's exactly how Aspen had kissed me that one night at a party.

And I knew *nothing* of what it felt like to be Aspen.

Because I'd never gotten the chance to kiss Cat before I imploded our friendship.

That day in the stairwell, I experienced one of the strongest surges of jealousy I'd ever known—so forceful the school's sprinkler system went off, the water pulled forth by my magic. Luckily, the couple was too caught up in their kissing to realize what happened at first, giving me time to disappear. But I've never been able to escape that memory, and the playback won't let me go now.

Instead, as I gasp in ragged breaths, the scene morphs, replacing the young versions with the ones I've seen recently. Cat with her new curves, and Aspen with that tempting beard and bear-like figure.

"Gods," I curse as my erection presses against my wet bathing suit. Gripping the edges of the vanity, I try to push past the lust that threatens to drown me. But my brain is a ship lost in a storm of erotic fantasies, pairing Cat and Aspen in new positions with less clothes. As I envision him bending her over, sliding into her from behind, I can't help my hand seeking the ties of my suit and freeing my dick, which juts forward, aching with need.

"This is so fucked up," I mutter as I finally let myself sink into the fantasy. Gripping my shaft, I imagine walking up to the two instead of running away. Imagining the soft grin Aspen would give me as his cock slipped out of Cat's glistening pussy. He'd guide me forward, let me take his place as she gazes over her shoulder at me. Smiling, finally, after all these years. Smiling at me again.

"Cat," I whisper as I stroke myself, my hand a sad replacement. Closing my eyes, I can imagine pumping into her, burying myself deep as I slip my hand around to find her clit. And just as I coax her to clench around me, a pressure against my ass. "Aspen," I mutter.

Then I'm the one filled with the hard length I've only ever felt a hint of through two sets of jeans.

"Fuck." My balls tighten at the idea of being inside Cat while Aspen fucks me from behind. With a quick lunge, I'm able to grab a handful of tissues before I come hard, clenching my teeth, and leaning against the sink when my knees threaten to buckle.

After the last pulse of pleasure fades, I'm left feeling cold, unsatisfied, and pissed off. I meet my eyes in the mirror, hating the needy flush of my skin.

"When am I going to stop being such a greedy asshole?" I ask in a hushed voice, as if the reflection will answer. But it only scowls, and I look away.

My mind is a mess, and apparently my dick is too. Wanting them both like that, it's wrong. I know it is. And I'm betting that's what gets me going—breaking the rules.

Guess it runs in the family. The thought sends a spear of guilt through me.

Cat is better off choosing Aspen like she did back then. At least he can commit fully to her, like she deserves.

As the idea returns, of them together, I feel like I'm back in the stairwell, watching again. Seeing the two of them happy without me.

I need to get over this. I turn on the faucet and splash water on my face, finding small comfort in the normally soothing element. Cupping my hands, I take a drink, then stand tall. "I'm going to get over them," I tell my reflection.

There are a lot of attractive elementals at this party. Someone's got to be looking to hook up. With that thought, and as much enthusiasm as I can muster, I whip open the bathroom door.

Coming face to face with Aspen.

Chapter Eight

ASPEN

Rafael smells like sex. I flick my eyes to the room behind him but don't spy anyone. My chest, where a tight knot had formed, eases. I'm not sure how I would have reacted if I walked in on Rafael immediately post hookup, but I doubt the outcome would have been great.

He's not your man, I remind myself, just like old times.

The only person in high school who turned my head as much as Cat Byrne was Rafael Aguado. In fact, I had a crush on the easygoing Squid before I even met the little Pyro. Freshman and Sophomore year, all I wanted was to sit near him in class, hear his laugh, watch him sprint across a soccer field, and imagine pressing my body against his sweaty one when the game was over. But I was too shy to make a move, especially when I didn't know which way he leaned.

Then, he introduced me to Cat, and my world shifted.

My crush on Rafael didn't go away. I just developed an equally intense attraction to the fiery math whiz with a soft gaze and a fierce glare. So, despite one drunken night at a party, nothing real ever happened between Rafael and me.

But hell, seeing his tan skin flushed, eyes flashing, I wish I'd gotten that chance.

"Hey, Rafe. You gonna tell me what crawled up your ass?"

The Squid sucks in a breath, and his stare drops to my crotch, then flies back to my face.

Interesting.

Rafael collects himself, putting on his couldn't-care-less face that's also familiar, but only from the time after his falling out with Cat.

"I don't know what you're talking about." He crosses his arms, just like I've done with mine, and leans against the doorframe like I've leaned back against the wall. Mirroring me. I wonder if he means to.

"You ran away when I showed up." And it felt like a punch to the gut, but I'll keep that to myself.

He laughs, but the amusement sounds false. "I didn't run away. I needed to take a piss."

I don't bother addressing what is probably a lie. "We fell off the last few years of high school"—because I pulled Cat closer instead of pushing her away, like he did—"but we're grown. I want to be friends." Dropping my arms into a less defensive pose, I tuck my hands in my pockets to keep from reaching out to trace a thumb down the happy trail of brown hair under his belly button. "We used to be close." My voice deepens on its own.

Rafael's nostrils flare even as his jaw hardens, hinting at clenched teeth. Then, he relaxes, and pulls the nonchalant mask back on.

"Were we?" He shrugs. "Didn't you spend most of your time with Cat?" The Squid's voice cracks on her name, revealing his true emotions. He clears his throat, trying too hard to sound unaffected. "You happen to see her in the few days you've been here?"

Seeing no point in lying, I nod. "Yeah. Stopped by her work."

The flush drains from Rafael's face, leaving him looking too pale. Well, one thing is for sure. The guy is still in love with her. But that's not the question that nestles like a seed in my chest, demanding attention.

"But we were talking about us," I redirect the conversation. "Sammy got me thinking about old times."

If I'm not wrong, Rafael's eyes are stuck on my lips, and I like that his attention is there. Has me thinking he might be reminiscing the way I am. Suddenly, I wonder why he came out of the bathroom alone, smelling like sex.

"Well, you two have fun chatting about those. I'm personally more interested in the present." Before I can think of something to keep Rafael in front of me, he strides down the hall, returning to the party. I let my head fall back against the wall, pondering the brief exchange.

Once again, I have zero idea about how Rafael feels about me, other than jealousy that I've been with Cat—more now that I've talked with her again. But what does he expect? Rafael more than anyone understands the draw of that pint-sized Pyro. I'm surprised we've both been able to stay away from her for so many years.

After ducking into the bathroom and using the facilities, I head back out to the party, once again drawn to the grill. This time my stomach directs my legs, and I snag one of the waiting burgers Damien took off the heat.

"Five!" Sammy garbles his words around a grape he just caught in his mouth. Marisol giggles and lines up another shot, arcing the small fruit toward the Squid on the floaty. The grape bounces off his lip and Damien grumbles about food in his clean pool.

"Aspen, your turn!" Marisol is already lobbing one my way. Luckily, I haven't lost all my reflexes from my football days. With a quick step forward, I snap the treat out of the air. The teenager gives a cheer and Sammy scoffs.

"It's the beard!" My friend accuses. "You cheated. That massive amount of facial hair is obviously magic."

I can feel the coarse hairs crinkle as I grin. "Pure power." My fingers scratch my chin, chasing a stray itch while trying not to muss up the comb job I did before coming here. I've had the new addition going on six months now, but I'm not fully used to it.

Still, I like the change.

I'd woken up the morning after my breakup, stared at my razor for a good minute, then stuck it back in the medicine cabinet. Memories of Cat inspired the decision. How she'd gained a new confidence after shearing off her long ginger hair in high school, post her falling out with Rafael.

I needed a change. A firm difference that defined before and after. Something reminding me that, as tempting as it was, I didn't really want to go back. I ended the relationship for a reason. It's hard to step away from someone when you want to be with them, and they want to be with you, but not in the way you need.

"Maybe I should grow one. We could be beard buddies." Sammy rubs his clean-shaven chin.

"Don't." Damien digs in a cooler for a beer and hands it to me. "Your beard is patchy as a poorly mowed lawn. You'll just embarrass yourself."

Sammy scoops up a ball of water like a snowball and chucks it at the man of the house, who ends up catching the liquid orb and tosses it back, quickly morphing the attempted joke into a game of supernatural catch. I watch them get more intricate with their throws as I eat my food and drink my beer. Marisol even gets in on the exchange, though her catches have the clumsy fumble of a young elemental just a year or two into her water powers. We all develop our abilities to manipulate an element when we go through puberty.

Hormones and magic. Every parent's dream.

Due to some clever landscaping, and ease of keeping plants watered when you can do it with a flick of your wrist, Damien's backyard has more greenery than the average Phoenix yard. I shuffle to the side, letting my hand drop and trail through the leaves of a Cape Honeysuckle bush. Normally, they don't flower until further into the fall, but I pull on my power. Early on, I figured out that the emotion tied to my ability is happiness. For example, if Cat was standing in front of me, telling me how glad she was to see me, my power would surge to the surface.

Right now, with only a base level of happiness, I'm the one who has to call it. A pressure forms in my palms, a weight in my fingers, drawing against my muscles. The magic creeps out as if spilling from beneath my nail beds, and suddenly a riot of bright orange honeysuckles bloom within the shiny green leaves.

"Oh, so pretty!" Marisol comes up beside me to examine the flowers. "We just planted this last month. I haven't seen it bloom yet." She fingers the flowers, and I'm pleased to have contributed something to the gathering.

"That's it," Sammy declares, "you're coming to my house next. I bought a fern, and it's this close to the death dimension." The Squid pinches his fingers together. "You gotta save it, man. I don't know what I did wrong, and I don't want to be haunted by a fern ghost."

"Sure." After kicking off my sandals, I lower my butt to the edge of the pool and sink my legs into the cool water. "Don't want you to be a plant murderer."

"Yeah, I..." Sammy trails off, his normally jovial expression melting into a scowl. Then, he turns his attention back to me, and tries for another smile, but it looks more like a grimace. "So yeah, man. Life. How's that been? Tell us everything."

His attempt to distract me is amateurish, and I can't help twisting around to seek out what Sammy doesn't want me to see. In less than a second, I find the culprit.

On the other side of the yard, back in a corner that is only partially hidden from view, Rafael has a guy pressed against the side of the house. The two men seem to be doing their best to tie their tongues in a knot.

Multiple emotions surge in my chest. Jealousy writhes like a thorny vine, threatening to tear up my gut. But among the sharp pain is the strange satisfaction of finally getting an answer to a question I've had for years.

Turning back to Sammy, I decide to ask once and for all. "So, Rafael —he's bi? Gay?" I tack on the last but can't fathom it after seeing the way his eyes go liquid every time Cat's name comes up.

Sammy nods as he sips his beer. "He's dated guys and gals. Think he officially came out in college. But I've known since..." The Squid smiles, and for once there's no teasing smirk lingering in the curve of his mouth. "Well, probably as long as you've suspected."

"You were surer than I was," I mutter, thinking back on the party he's alluding to. The one where Rafael and I shared our one and only kiss.

Sammy shrugs. "I'm usually right." He twirls his finger, which shifts the water and sends his floaty in a leisurely spin. "Sometimes it's a burden, being so much more observant than everyone else." The cocky Squid floats away, and I let him go. Talking to the guy can be exhausting sometimes, and I need a moment to think.

Rafael is bisexual.

What other kinds of relationships would he be open to?

Chapter Nine

RAFAEL

Tequila tastes a hell of a lot worse coming up than it does going down.

I rest my flushed cheek on the cool toilet seat, trying to forget that this is where Sammy sets his ass whenever he needs to take a dump. But with that image in my mind, I'm back to heaving for another few seconds. All that's coming up at this point is stomach acid that scrapes against the back of my throat and burns my nostrils.

That's right. I'm also throwing up through my nose.

"Good morning, beautiful." Sammy strolls into the bathroom and hops up to sit on the counter. "I've heard some lovely bird songs welcoming the sunrise, but none match the glory of you puking your brains out. Seriously, I'm considering recording it to use as an alarm."

"Fuck you," I mutter before spitting the remaining sick out of my mouth. Reaching out with a shaking hand, I flush down the evidence of my night of indulgence. The afternoon cookout turned into an evening binge-fest. At least, for me.

"Oh, fuck me, huh? That can't be right. You seemed hell bent on doing that with Carlos, who I'm ninety-nine percent sure you met for the first time yesterday. So was it fated mates at first sight, or are you desperately trying to end a dry spell?" Sammy's voice sounds playful, but

I can't help thinking there's an edge in his tone—or maybe that's just the sharp pound of my headache.

"I was having fun." Cautiously, I take stock of my stomach, trying to determine if I'm safe to move more than a foot from the toilet.

"Fun." He snorts. "You were trying to drown yourself in a bottle of tequila."

"Water elementals can't drown." Carefully, I ease back, propping myself against the bathroom wall and finally meeting my friend's stare, even though the bright bulbs above his head hurt my eyes. "What's the point of being a magical being if we can't use our powers to get rid of a hangover?" I complain.

The Squid smirks and waves a phone in the air. "Next best thing. We're going to your mom's house for breakfast. Or brunch, more like, seeing as how it's almost noon."

"Is that my phone?" The case looks awfully familiar.

Sammy affects a pout. "How'd she know it wasn't you texting her? Two messages in and she guessed. Your mother is psychic."

"You've been texting my mom? On my phone?" I lurch forward to snatch it from him, then immediately collapse back when my stomach rebels against the sudden movement.

"You weren't using it," he says, as if this is a valid excuse. Sammy tosses the device into my lap before sliding off the counter. Then, he picks up a bottle of water and a container of ibuprofen, setting them at my side. "Sober up, buddy. I'm craving huevos rancheros."

He makes it hard to be annoyed with him for any length of time. A swallow of water helps clear the lingering gross taste off my tongue, and I pray to the gods the pain relievers work fast as I swallow the pills. As I wait to feel a little more like a living being rather than a reanimated corpse, I scroll through my texts.

> Me: Good morning mother dearest. I would be eternally grateful if you could find it in your heart to cook me breakfast this morning.

> Mom: Who is this?

Me: How dare you! I am your son! Your precious
baby boy!

Mom: Hello Sammy. Does my precious baby
boy know you have his phone?

Me: Who is this Sammy you speak of? Never
heard of him but sounds like a handsome devil.
Also, a hungry devil, who would very much
appreciate huevos rancheros.

Mom: I'll make you breakfast if you bring my
son with you alive and well

Me: Would you settle for alive?

A chuckle creeps up my sore throat, and I find my head is clear
enough for me to stand on shaky legs. Somehow, I navigate my way
through the house, which I now realize is *my* house and not Sammy's.
I'm still getting used to the half of the duplex I'm renting. Sammy waits
by the front door, texting on *his* phone this time.

"Did you sleep here?" I slide on my darkest set of shades, grimacing
at the idea of stepping into unfiltered sunshine.

"You have an extremely comfortable couch, and I wanted to make
sure you didn't drown in your own vomit." He slips his phone into his
back pocket and hits me with a wide grin. "I'm sweet like that."

"Um, thanks. I guess."

"You can thank me with breakfast!" He swings the door open,
revealing a morning so bright I wonder if we've somehow relocated to
the surface of the sun.

"Not so loud," I groan, stumbling after him.

We only make it to my mom's house because Sammy drives us.
Apparently, he also drove me home last night, and I wonder if I should
take it as a warning sign that I got more wasted than my wildest friend.
Used to be that I was Sammy's conscience when he started making bad
decisions.

Speaking of bad decisions, my hungover mind brings up the memory of my mouth against a set of lips that tasted like an IPA.

"Did I..." Shit. I don't even know how far I went with...fuck. I can't even remember his name.

"Have a tongue wrestling match with a Stoner named Carlos? Yes. In front of a minor no less. You may have scarred Marisol for life."

"Gods," I groan, letting my aching head drop into my palms.

"Yes, those pesky deities did seem to abandon you yesterday. Or maybe you spurned them. Whatever the case, at least you had me. I made sure to smuggle you away before any more bodily fluids were swapped."

"You...kept me from hooking up with someone?" Not that I'm not grateful now, after the fact, but that's not Sammy's MO—at least, not teenage Sammy's MO. Truth is, we haven't spent more than a week or two at a time hanging out since I left all those years ago for college.

Maybe I'm an ass for thinking the guy couldn't change.

"I know. Seems blasphemous." I glance over to find him turning the wheel, and realize we've made it to my mother's house. "But it's not like you *wanted* to fuck Carlos."

"I...what? What makes you think that?"

Sammy throws the car in park and slides his sunglasses down his nose to stare at me straight on.

"Have you burned out all your braincells with alcohol consumption? How did you even get that fancy marine biology job with a skull so empty? Be honest, all they let you do is throw dead fish into the tank for feeding time, am I right?"

"Shut up," I mutter.

He shrugs, jovial grin back in place. "I'm all for helping you out, but I'm not here to tell you the obvious. You gotta put in some of the work. Now come on. Watching you puke all morning has me hungry."

"Some wires are crossed in your brain." I'm not sure if he hears me, already having jumped from the car. Not that he would care. Sammy is unapologetically himself, and you either accept it, or avoid the guy.

"Hi, Mom," I call out as we enter her small, comfortable home. It's not the same one I grew up in. She downsized after the divorce. I like this place better. The other one was cold even on the hottest desert day, and the walls heard too many shouted arguments for me to ever get comfortable in them again.

"Oh!" She steps out of the kitchen, her hands pressed to her cheeks in the dramatic fashion of the stars on the telenovelas she loves to watch. "My precious baby boy!" Mom smirks, and I shoot a glare over my shoulder at a chuckling Sammy.

"That's all she's ever going to call me now."

But ten minutes later, as I'm making my way through some eggs smothered in pico de gallo that are doing wonders for my hangover, I don't mind so much if I get an overly lovey nickname. As I nurse my aching head and fill my sensitive stomach, Sammy tries, not for the first time, to get my mom to give him special treatment at her job.

"But what if I pay for two first-class seats, and I'm really quiet and well-behaved?"

My mother narrows her eyes, even as the corner of her mouth tries to tick up in a smile. "Not going to happen. Just because I'm the pilot doesn't mean I can let anyone into the cockpit. Only flight crew."

"So you're saying I need to dress up as a flight attendant?"

She throws a piece of bacon at him, and he catches it in his mouth, successful after all that grape training of the previous day. Even as she feigns exasperation, I can see the joy and pride flickering in my mother's eyes whenever her career comes up. For the longest time, she worked at a travel agency, only flying small planes in her free time. But when things finally crumbled between her and my dad, she said fuck it and got her Airline Transport Pilot certificate. For the past six years, she's been piloting flights around the world and loving every minute of it.

I never thought I the kid in our relationship—would be the one feeling proud. But I am. I'm so fucking proud of my mom.

"And how's work going with you?" She turns her attention to me, a soft smile spreading over her mouth. "Sammy hasn't convinced you to let him swim with the sharks, has he?"

"Is that an option?" My friend leans forward, eager eyes on me.

Before I can unequivocally shut him down, the doorbell chimes. Mom's brow wrinkles, then her dark eyes widen along with the grin on her face. If I thought she looked happy to see me, this is nothing. I wonder who could inspire so much excitement. Food twists in an uncomfortable whirl in my stomach when I consider if it might be a guy. Not that I'm opposed to my mom getting back out in the dating world, but I'd rather not be hungover and looking like day-old shit when I meet someone new. Silently, I pray to the gods it's a delivery, although that seems unlikely seeing as how it's Sunday.

"I'll just go get that," she announces, cheeks flushed.

Sammy nudges me with an elbow. "Who do you think it is?" At least I assume that's what he tries to say, through his mouth full of bacon. One of my shoulders is up in a shrug when a brush of warmth traces over my skin, along with a tease of rose scent to my nose.

It can't be.

But when I turn in my seat, I stare into a set of familiar brown eyes that threaten to set me on fire.

Chapter Ten

CAT

This is no one's fault but my own. I should've known that this not only could happen but was likely to. Of course, I run into Rafael at his mother's house.

It's just, I've been swinging by Ms. Aguado's for years and never even had a whiff of Rafael other than the framed pictures on her walls and the occasional mention she throws out of what he's doing. Facts that I definitely do not collect into a secret corner in the back of my brain to bring out later and examine, fit together, and tuck away again.

But those were the years Rafael lived on the other side of the country. Now, he's back in Phoenix, and I should've avoided his mother's if I wanted to avoid him.

Which I *do* want. Of course, I do. Because I hate his squishy Squid guts.

"Cat," Rafael rasps out my name when we meet eyes. Ms. Aguado must have her AC blasting because a shiver trembles through my body in that moment.

"Cat's here!" another voice adds, and I spy a second unwanted water elemental in the room. Sammy Reyes. "Perfect timing. We were just eating breakfast. You want her to join us, don't you, Ms. Aguado?"

I open my mouth to give a retort, then realize it would be too cutting to say in front of Rafael's mom, whom I respect. My fumble gives her time to reply. "Nothing would make me happier!" She grasps my shoulders with a strong set of hands and guides me to a chair. "Let me get you a plate."

While her back is turned, I glare at Sammy and ignore Rafael.

"You don't have to trouble yourself." With effort, I keep my sweet tone despite the annoyed fire unfurling under my skin. "I just came to drop off the shoes my mom borrowed." I set the shoe box on an empty section of the table.

"You brought them back! I was wondering if I'd have to wrestle them from her." As Ms. Aguado chats about the ongoing clothing exchange/war she has with my mother, I do my best to dismiss the tingling sensation of Rafael's attention on the side of my face. Unfortunately, that means I end up looking at Sammy, which has my temper growing hotter. The guy has pissed me off since the first minute I met him.

My first day of high school.

I had been nervous, but had known I could count on my best friend to help me navigate some of the new-to-me world. After all, Rafael was going to be a junior. In fact, with a hint of smugness, I'd silently bragged to my bathroom mirror how most of my fellow freshmen wouldn't have an upperclassman as a best friend. Wearing a new outfit my sister Quinn had helped me pick out, I'd run next door to the Aguado's house to invite Rafael to ride in Quinn's new-used car to school that day, so he wouldn't have to bother with the bus. I was going to be a freshman arriving with *two* juniors, and for a few brief moments, I'd thought I had high school figured out.

Then, Rafael had barely said hi to me before jumping into a convertible with a Squid I'd never met before, and later would learn was Sammy Reyes: new guy in town, and Rafael's coworker at the summer camp they'd both attended months prior. Without me.

Sammy so thoroughly usurped my best friend role that I eventually lost even the designation of *friend*—cast aside for this grinning douchebag.

"You missed a fun party last night." The annoying man in question tells me as he spoons a fried egg onto a tortilla. "Didn't want to come and hang out with all of us Squids?"

Exactly, I silently agree. But that feels too much like running away. "I work Saturday nights," I say out loud, which is the truth. I was at the club until four a.m. My morning nap got me functioning enough to run some errands, but I'm going to have to crash for a few more hours when I get home. Right now, though, I'm wide awake, fueled by simmering anger.

The hot pulse wants out. My eyes drop to the Rolex on Sammy's wrist, and I wonder if it would be petty to melt off the wristband.

Stop it! Control the anger. That's the only way you control the heat.

"Working." Sammy drags out the word with a smirk and an eyebrow waggle, and I forget my goal to suppress my temper and try to determine if I have enough control to singe off his eyebrows. I'm not looking to mutilate the guy, just knock his cockiness down a few thousand pegs.

"Yes," I clip the word off. "Working."

"What do you do for work?" The Squid-I'd-rather-not-think-about asks, and damn my attention for flicking in his direction. Immediately, Rafael catches me in that intriguing slate gray stare of his. Those eyes haven't changed all these years. If we were anywhere other than his mom's kitchen, I'd give Rafael the silent treatment. But I don't want Ms. Aguado to know how petty I am under the surface.

Push the anger away. You're not pissed off. You're the sweetest thing in this room.

"Some part-time jobs." I manage not to drop my eyes, but I can't help the flush of shame that starts to creep up my cheeks. "On Saturdays, it's my waitress gig."

And it pays well, I want to tack on in defense of myself—to mitigate any pitying thoughts about how I'm in the last half of my twenties, have never had a full-time job, and have no idea what career I could even do.

"These burners are all over the place!" Ms. Aguado grumbles, and I glance to the side in time to see her turn one way down.

Is that my heat? Probably. I pull in a deep breath through my nose, then push the air forcefully out my mouth. *Don't think about unhappy things. Don't get angry. I am a pink bubble of happiness, and I refuse to pop.*

"Where—" Rafael starts, but Sammy cuts him off.

"We saw Aspen, yesterday. Said he's been by to see you too."

Sammy almost earns himself a smile from me for mentioning the Petal Pusher's name. Thoughts of Aspen are a soothing balm to my soul. He's a centering presence I love thinking about and being around.

From the way Rafael scowls at his fellow Squid, my guess is we have a different view of the earth elemental. I don't know what happened between my ex-best friend and my ex-boyfriend. Before our falling out, Rafael would regale me with stories of his school shenanigans, and Aspen was a regular feature in the tales. Back then, I was only jealous I wasn't old enough to go to high school with him. A few times, I joined him and his older buddies to play video games. Those were my first few interactions with Aspen, and the teenage Petal Pusher was gruff but kind.

That was back before Sammy moved to town, and Rafael got too cool to hang out with a kid like me.

But that doesn't explain the separation with Aspen. Clearly, Sammy also likes the earth elemental, and Aspen was their age. Plus, he was on the varsity football team, which gave him major cool cred. What never made sense was why Aspen wanted to be friends with *me*, much less wanted to date me.

I was the quiet girl who wasn't cool enough to even hang onto a friend she'd had for years.

But that had never mattered to Aspen.

"I saw him," I offer, unable to suppress the small smile that comes at the memory of him swooping in like a hero at my work.

Rafael rolls his eyes. "Yay," he deadpans. "The Petal Pusher is back."

My tilt toward a possible good mood burns up at his derision. "What's your problem with Aspen?"

The Squid shifts in his seat, focus flicking around the room. "He's just...not very impressive."

"Not impressive?" I snort. "He's built like an oak and stands over six feet."

"Height isn't everything," says the five-foot-eight Squid.

"You won't find me complaining about it," I snap back. "Plus, he tastes like mint."

Rafael's tanned face flushes a deep red. "So you only judge people on looks and taste?" The Squid leans across the table, holding me in his stare.

My breath comes in quick pants that I tell myself will cool my anger. "Not only that. He's more than how tall and handsome" —Rafael scoffs at the second description, which has me pressing on harder— "he is. Aspen is kind and fun to be with. And loyal."

"Loyal?" Rafael growls. "Not in my experience."

"Of course not." I can feel the fire in my eyes, pulsing so the world glows gold. "You use a different definition of loyalty than everyone else!"

"He went behind my back!" At some point both of us rose to our feet, bodies leaning over the kitchen table as if ready to pounce and turn this into an animalistic brawl.

"When?" I mock, sure he won't have an answer because that's *not* Aspen.

"With you!" The shout echoes around the small kitchen, stabbing into me from multiple directions until I'm sure there must be flames spilling out of a collection of puncture wounds in my skin. For a moment, all I can do is gape. But fury creeps around the wall of my shock and fuels my words and magic.

"Is *that* your problem?" Back in high school, I didn't struggle with my fire so much because I was more sad and ashamed than anything. But over the years, rage has taken the place of those emotions. "Aspen's not loyal because he didn't hop on board the 'Cat Sucks' train you were driving? You wanted him to abandon me, like you did? You wanted him to abandon me, like you did?" Hurt makes my head and heart ache. "It wasn't enough that you kicked me out of your life, you told everyone else to shun me too?"

There's a roundness to my words, letting me know that tears are imminent. Because it's not enough that I overheat when I'm mad. I also have to cry.

The angry flush in Rafael's face drains to white when his eyes widen at my words. "No, Cat—"

"Just stop!" I wave my hand to cut him off and, in the motion, I catch sight of a silvery glint. On closer inspection, I realize a spoon drapes over my hand like a piece of warm fabric. In my fury, I've almost melted it completely. Silver drips from the curved tip.

The room comes into focus, and I meet Ms. Aguado's shocked gaze.

I don't even try looking at Sammy, knowing whatever shit-eating-grin he has on will only send me into the inferno.

"I'm sorry," I say to the woman as I carefully place her ruined spoon on the table. "I should go."

"Cat—" Rafael tries again.

"Son." Ms. Aguado cuts him off with a sharp word, and I'm grateful to her.

Careful not to touch anything else in their house lest I set it on fire, I sprint as fast as I can out the door.

Chapter Eleven

ASPEN

I'm struggling under the swarm of wild animals when Cat steps through the front door. The beasts that hang on my every limb and climb up my back shout in glee.

"Uncle Aspen, toss me! Do the airplane!" The demands come from a dark-haired boy with his arms wrapped around my neck.

"One airplane ride each, then I've gotta go say hi to my friend."

There's a cheer, and I try not to throw my back out as, one by one, I toss each of the nieces and nephews onto a nearby couch where they bounce and giggle in glee. If I'm using a walker before I'm thirty, it's going to be their fault.

"Ollie!" One of my sisters calls from the backyard. "We've got water balloons!" The teaser couldn't have come at a better time because despite my declaration of one flight per child, I could see them gearing up for another onslaught. I escape to Cat's side while I can.

"They're...rambunctious." The Pyro stares up at me with bewildered eyes, and I recall her general discomfort around children. She could never figure out exactly how to talk to them, and her stilted conversation with toddlers always made me grin. I wasn't sure she would accept my invite, but I figured a children's birthday party would be a good place to reconnect without her feeling like I'm asking her out on a date. She's the one who broke things off between us all those years ago. As much as I want to date her again, I have to assume she'd rather stay friends.

Still, I want to be around her. Cat just...makes me happy. Hence the earthy tingle in my palms that I try rubbing away on my shorts.

"They're hopped up on sugar, so it's doubly bad today. Let's go find some adults." I curve my arm behind her but don't touch. Not like I would have in the past.

In high school, Cat came to family functions all the time, but back then she was my girlfriend. I would keep her hand in mine or hold her around the waist. If we sat down, I'd pull her into my lap and encourage her perpetually warm body to press into mine, feeling like I'd won the heart of the sun.

Now though, we're friends. Friends means I can talk to her, laugh with her. But the touching isn't a given.

Navigating through my parents' large house is normally easy, with all the wide halls and extra space, but it seems every square inch is filled with kids, and parents, and decorations.

"Oh, I got Ollie something." Cat pauses in the middle of a hallway and reaches into her purse, pulling out a small, neatly wrapped rectangle. "It's just a card game my sisters and I used to play—'Phase 10.' You get different number combinations to move through levels." She shrugs and hands the gift to me. "Is that okay? I don't really know what he likes."

"You didn't have to do that." I accept the present with both hands to keep from reaching for her. Pulling her into a kiss.

She grimaces. "So not a card game kid, huh?"

"That's not what I said." Tilting my head, I catch her gaze with mine. "He's gonna love it. Hazel mentioned he likes math class. Reminded me of someone." When that earns me a smile, I have to fight the urge to cup her face and stroke my thumbs over the creases in her cheeks. "A number card game is perfect."

I lead us on a detour to the gifts table and perch Cat's offering on the top of the pile. Across the room, my sister Geneva has tucked herself behind a large potted plant. Perfect.

"Found someone over the age of eighteen for you to talk to," I announce upon crowding into my sibling's hiding space. Geneva leans around me and joy blooms across her face.

"Cat! Thank the gods. Everyone here either is a child or wants to talk about children." She steps forward and wraps my Pyro in an engulfing hug. I try not to get too jealous. "Please, say something R-rated before my brain explodes."

"Um, okay." Cat's voice comes muffled, as I'm pretty sure her face is fully smashed into my sister's chest. "A customer at the club had to be taken to the hospital because he took too many little blue pills. Last we heard, his erection was going on ten hours."

Geneva's shoulders shake with laughter as she leans back and cups Cat's face. "You are perfection. Do you want a drink? There is booze at this party. It's just up on a high shelf." My sister throws a smirk my way. "I guess Aspen or I will have to reach it for you."

Cat rolls her eyes. "Ha, ha. You're *so* funny."

"Aren't I?"

I end up rummaging through the refrigerator in the garage to find some hard seltzers for the three of us. As I weave my way through the mass of people, my attention homes in on the redhead laughing with my sister. Like a plant, I always turn toward the brightest spot in the room. Which will always be Cat.

"Ugh, you are earth-blessed," Geneva declares, snatching the grapefruit seltzer from my hands. The only reason I don't protest is because I know Cat doesn't like grapefruit. When I offer her a choice between lemon and raspberry, she reaches for the latter. Her warm skin brushes mine as our fingers touch on the exchange, and I hold onto that heat as long as I can.

"How old is Maze turning again?" Geneva cracks open her can in the middle of her question.

"It's Ollie's birthday, and he's turning nine. Maze's birthday is in three weeks."

"Shit." My sister maneuvers around me. "I need to go find the card I wrote. Don't think the birthday boy will appreciate a card written to his sister."

A chuckle creeps from my throat, and I don't bother chiding her. Our mom will do that when she finds out. Besides, Geneva's never been good with dates. When I turn back to Cat, she has her brows raised and a broad smile splitting her lips. The sight teases along my nerves.

"If they wanted us to keep our nieces and nephews straight, they shouldn't have had so many." I keep my voice low in case any of my other brothers and sisters are nearby.

"What's the count now? I think I lost track a while ago."

"Don't blame you. Reed has four now. Poppy has five—two sets of twins. Not sure she's slept in the past six years." Only at my oldest two siblings, and I'm almost out of fingers. "Iris has Ollie and Maze, then Birch has two, which puts us at—"

"Thirteen. Unless you or Geneva have a secret baby to add to the brood?"

"Nope. Thirteen is it." And that number isn't growing because of us younger siblings.

Cat fiddles with the tab on her can. "Is that..." A flush creeps up her face. "Never mind."

I step closer, my body and the parlor palm fully separating her from the rest of the crowd. "You can ask me anything, Cat."

She wavers a moment longer, then stands straight and meets my eyes. "Is that something you want? Kids, I mean. I know in your last relationship you said they were done with that part of their life, but I was just wondering...were you okay with that, or is that why..."

"Why I ended it?" I clarify. Over the years, I had gotten very candid with Cat in our emails. She knows most of the good and bad about my past relationship.

She nods.

"No. That's not why." A memory of family photos filling the walls of a huge townhouse comes to my mind and starts up a muted ache in my gut. But not for the reason Cat is asking. "I like being an uncle, but that's different than being a parent. My older siblings love it. Geneva is a definite no." Which is why I was her ride to a women's health clinic a few years ago, when she discovered her birth control failed. "I'm undecided. Whoever I end up with will have a bearing on the decision."

Cat nods, keeping her thoughts to herself as she sips her drink. I'm considering turning the question her way when a shout goes up. "Cake!"

High pitched screams meet the declaration, and I catch Cat's wince. Leaning in close, I whisper in her ear. "While everyone's distracted singing, you grab some snacks and head up to my old room. I'll grab us some cake. Deal?"

"Deal." She whispers back, and I try not to be obvious about how I'm breathing in her rosy scent.

After a lot of dodging and almost losing a finger to a hungry child's mouth, I extricate myself from the masses with two decent-sized pieces of cake. When I make it upstairs, I find the second floor muffles the crush of voices from downstairs.

My bedroom sits at the end of the hall in the back corner of the house. It was the smallest of the rooms, but I never minded because there was a large window seat. One Cat now sits in, her legs stretched out on the bench, a bag of chips in her lap.

She's staring out the glass, probably not seeing much other than the neighbor's house, but I'm reluctant to disturb her, if only so I can keep looking my fill for a few seconds longer. When she turns her head and catches me staring, the Pyro offers a wide grin and holds out a bag of BBQ chips.

"Snagged your favorite."

She remembered. "I got you a piece of the cake with the berry filling." Cat always loved fruits, especially berries. She'd sit at the cafeteria table with a Tupperware container filled with blackberries, slowly staining her fingers as she popped them in her mouth. Drove my teenage self to distraction. All I had wanted to do was suck on her fingers. Taste her and the juices mixed together.

I trade her the cake for the chips, then sprawl on my bed, keeping distance between us for my own mental health.

"This place looks exactly the same." Her eyes travel around my bedroom, unchanged since the day I left for college.

"Mom and Dad kept all our rooms like this. Shrines to our youth, I guess. Like they thought we would only visit if nothing changed."

"You have visited. At least, a few times, right?" She focuses on forking up a bite of her cake rather than looking at me.

"Yeah. A couple of times." But I didn't seek Cat out on those visits. At first, it was because we weren't talking. The night the silence between us started is still a raw, painful memory I'm not sure will ever fade. We were sitting in my car in front of her house the last week of summer before I left for college. I was mentally filling in the calendar with the best time for me to come home and visit her and wondering if her parents would sign off on her staying with me for a weekend.

Then Cat, my first love, had turned to me and said we should break up.

I'd been too shocked to put up a defense. She had a determined tilt to her brow, no room in her words for pushback. Then, she had climbed out of my car and left me. A few days later I had left Phoenix with dueling urges of never wanting to return but also longing to, so I could talk to her and find out what went wrong.

As I look at her now, carefully eating her cake, attention not on me, I revisit a theory I came up with a few years too late: that maybe I hadn't put up a fight because I'd always been waiting for it to happen. Bracing for the day Rafael got over himself and apologized. In my mind, the Pyro and the Squid were soul mates. Possibly fated by the gods. Anyone who saw the two of them together felt the force between them.

I was just the third party standing outside their aura, with a crush on them both.

But time went by after the breakup, and I never got word of them dating. My parents loved giving me a rundown of the relationships in the elemental community, so I knew if there was something to hear, they'd tell me—gently, I'm sure, because they both knew how much I loved Cat Byrne.

Then, after two years and a few too many beers, I sent her an email. A short one with only two spelling errors, congratulating her on graduating high school.

She'd written back. Then I had. And we'd kept the correspondence going.

But we never saw each other in person again until the other night when I showed up at The Jewelry Box. There was a fear, lingering in the back of my mind, that if Cat saw me, she'd remember why she had ended things, and I'd lose her all over again.

But I'm not an insecure teenager anymore. Just a slightly more secure man who might be scared, but still brave enough to finally learn the truth.

I set my plate of cake in my lap and stare straight at the woman who could easily crush my heart again.

"Why did you break up with me?"

Chapter Twelve

CAT

I should've known this would happen. That things couldn't be easy like they used to be. Just me and Aspen, fitting together without drama or complications.

But I'm the one that made things hard.

It was years ago. We were teenagers. Explaining my reasons shouldn't hurt like telling him would have then.

The thing is, most of the time I still feel as insecure and out of my depth as I did when I was sixteen. And that's the whole problem.

"Full truth?" I sigh out the question, and Aspen firms his lips and gives a curt nod. Bracing himself as if my young rejection still has the power to hurt him.

He feels deeply, I remind myself. No matter how big and strong he looks, Aspen has a soft center.

I suck the last bit of icing off my fork, but the sugar tastes bitter now. Setting the plate aside, I allow my feet to rest on the floor, needing to sit with a straight spine as I dig into that night and the fears that led up to me breaking both of our hearts.

"It was a kind of self-sabotage, but I didn't think of it like that at the time. All I could envision was you on some huge college campus, surrounded by people smarter and more driven than me, and all of them loving you. Because you were—and still are—so great. You had your football scholarship, and you knew you wanted to be pre-law. You just gave off this vibe…" My fingers wiggle around my chest as I try to put into words what had made such fearful sense to me at the time.

"What vibe?" Aspen's deep voice rubs along my nerve endings, and I fight off a shiver. Fire elementals aren't supposed to feel cold.

"An adult vibe, I guess. An *I have my shit together* vibe. An—" I suck in a deep breath "—*I don't need a high school girlfriend holding me back* vibe."

"I never—"

With a staying wave, I cut off his protest. "No, no. It was all me. All in my head. You were the best. You loved me." I rub my hands against the back of my neck, fighting a rising headache from the stress of the memory that still hurts. Because it still feels true. "But I thought I was an anchor—one you would eventually want to get rid of—and the process of untangling us was going to hurt. I didn't want to wait by the phone for that call. I didn't want to hold you back. And I didn't want to watch you slowly realize that I was."

I've made the whole confession to my hands, my eyes fixated on my twisting fingers rather than Aspen's face. But now I chance a look up, discovering he's rested his skull back against the headboard and draped a thick arm over his eyes, as if the dim bedroom light burns his corneas.

"To be clear," he starts after a stretch of silence, "you didn't break up with me because you stopped loving me?"

"No. Gods." My breath gusts out of me. "But…" I cringe in shame. "I knew, at the time, that's what you'd think. And for some reason, I figured that was better." I want to curl into a ball and disappear into myself as I acknowledge the pain I must have put him through. The same pain I had sought to avoid. "Are you mad?"

More time stretches between us, adding to the years apart that I caused. Eventually, his arm slides away, and he meets my gaze, hazel eyes hiding his thoughts behind a stoic shield.

"No. We were kids. Both of us. No matter what you thought." Aspen's thick fingers scratch at the beard I'd really like to touch. "And I don't know what the distance would have done to us. Still, I wanted to try." This comes with a sad smile, and I try not to wince. "I guess we got to grow up, live lives, try things we wouldn't have if we'd stayed together," he muses.

That's a positive for Aspen, I'm sure. In his emails, he talked about studying abroad, living in different states, and dating people who knew what the hell they were doing with their lives. On my end, being without Aspen hasn't been the adventurous existence of an independent woman or even the wild single life a girl could hope for. As much as it stings to admit—even just to myself—Harley was right. Since Aspen, I've only been with screw ups. Guys traveling through life at the same speed I am, allowing me to stay in stasis. Never truly growing up, even though my driver's license claims I'm an adult.

At least the separation meant Aspen never had to witness my steady drive to nowhere.

He was, and still is, better off without me.

Chapter Thirteen

CAT

All week, I've been distracted—playing Aspen's words over again and again in my mind.

"I wanted to try."

We could have, and maybe made it through. Even now, we could have been those sickeningly cute people who talk about how they were high school sweethearts and have been in love since their first kiss.

Could it have worked?

As I climb out of my car into the heat of the day, a scrap of paper falls onto the ground. When I squat to pick it up, I realize it's my receipt from the bank. I'd stopped in to deposit all my cash tips, which make up a good portion of my earnings for the week. The number in my savings account is decent, especially for someone in their mid-twenties, but I can't help focusing on the means I earn my money.

Am I going to be a waitress for the rest of my life? Is that what I want?

I'm scared to voice the answer to the second because it has another obvious question that follows immediately after.

What do *I want?*

The query picks at me as I walk up my front path, then follow a set of slate stones that lead around to the backyard. Quinn and I have gotten in the habit of entering our rental through the back. The front door has a deadbolt that's slightly warped and hard to open and close. It's easier to keep it locked and use the back entrance, which is why I don't even get a chance to kick off my shoes or put my purse away before I come upon Harley sitting on one of the pool-side lounge chairs.

Her being here isn't out of the ordinary. She's a pool mooch. What's odd is that she's in leather pants and a crop top, rather than a bathing suit. As fire elementals, we don't experience the discomfort of heat like everyone else does, but I still have trouble fathoming leather pants when it's over ninety degrees out.

"Hey, short stuff." My big sister reaches out to pat the chair beside hers, inviting me to sit in my own backyard. I settle where she offered because there's an odd note in her voice. Harley's usual bravado sounds off, and she hasn't commented on the bandana I'm using as a cute red headband. I like the look, but it normally inspires Rosy the Riveter or milkmaid jokes.

She's off her game.

"What's up?" I venture.

Harley slaps her palms down on her thighs, her sparkly purple acrylics like sharp, glittering claws in the afternoon sun. "I'm here to help with your problem. You're welcome." She smirks, but the expression is still off. Her lips pinched too tight.

"My problem?" Did my sister suddenly develop psychic skills? How did she know my inability to fully adult was making me feel like an imposter in my own life? And how does she expect to help? Any more than she has, that is. Harley's done enough by finding me my job at The Jewelry Box. At least now I can pay my bills.

"You know, your tendency to melt objects and boil liquids whenever your panties are in a twist. *That* problem."

An image of a melted spoon flickers across my mind. I'm barely able to stop myself from flinching, and I let my fingers fiddle with the strap of my purse as I breathe carefully and pull on my most unbothered expression.

"That won't work." She pokes me in the arm, and I rub away the sting of her nail digging into my flesh.

"What won't?"

Harley gestures in front of her face. "Surface-level stuff. The magic doesn't care how you look. It cares how you *feel*. And we both know you can look like the sweetest cherub in the galaxy, all the while wanting to tear someone limb from limb."

"But I don't *want* to tear anyone apart." Gods, now I'm whining.

"Oh, really?" Disbelief and a tinge of humor color her words. "Want to tell me about the spoon incident?"

Damn all the gods. "How did you hear about that?"

Harley shrugs and fluffs her hair, satisfaction dripping off her. "Ms. Aguado told Mom. Mom told Dad. Dad told me. It's a whole family phone tree. You're now officially on watch. So do you want to work on this with me? Or with Dad?"

"There's nothing to work on." My serene shield grows flimsier by the second, now a scant bit of tissue paper over my features.

In a rare moment, Harley loses all playfulness, staring into my eyes with a seriousness that intimidates me more than her bluster ever has.

"Can you honestly tell me that your powers never scare you? Not once?"

My mouth opens with denial, but a memory shoves to the front of my brain. Not the breakfast at the Aguado's, or even the pool heating incident. Instead, I think of the day Rafael discovered me by the jellyfish.

When the heat rose under my skin that day, there was a single instinct in my mind. *Get out.* And it wasn't entirely driven by getting away from Rafael. That day, the potential ramifications of my powers on the loose terrified me.

"Fine," I relent, "my powers make me uncomfortable sometimes." I smooth my hands over the skirt of my sundress. "But Quinn just proved I simply need to work on it some more."

"Agreed. But Quinn only learned to control her powers when she let herself get horny." That last word comes as a declaration. Harley always likes to say sexual terms with enthusiasm so no one can doubt her utter lack of give-a-shit about the shame ascribed to sex. As a dominatrix, she's dealt with plenty of sex work discrimination. "Avoiding anger is a Band-Aid, not a solution," she presses, bringing my focus back to the discussion point.

"So you plan to annoy me into a practice session?" The clipped edge to my words proves she could.

"Nope." Her finger twirls one of her corkscrew curls in a movement that appears agitated. I can't fathom why she'd be anxious. Harley loves bossing everyone—especially me and Quinn—around. "You've spent your whole life ignoring my poking. I don't think I could get you truly mad. Not like you need to be to master this. I think that was the issue with Dad too."

She has a point about our dad. He was my first teacher and did a fantastic job of showing me how to call up heat and flames, and then do fun and practical tricks with the magic. But I look up to my dad, and I'm the baby of the family, so I never got *extremely* mad during our training sessions. Which—to Harley's credit—means I never got to practice controlling my heat at the height of my power. Not when there was another fire elemental nearby to keep things safe by suppressing any flames I lost hold of.

But then, Harley's words fully register, along with her stiff shoulders and shifty eyes, and trepidation tightens the muscles throughout my body. "Then what, exactly, is your plan?"

"Just remember that I'm on *your* team." Harley's warning only unsettles me more as she rises and strolls over to the back door. Not for the first time, I wonder if it was a mistake to give her a spare key.

Then she opens the door, steps aside, and I know for a fact it was.

Out steps a Squid with a cocky grin and a confident swagger that makes me want to scorch his kneecaps.

"Hey, Red!" Sammy veers toward the pool, kicking off a set of expensive-looking loafers, shucking off his socks, rolling up his pants, then dunking his feet in the water. *My* water. Making himself at home in my backyard. That would be bad enough if the doorway didn't belch out another unwelcome visitor.

"Hey, Cat." Rafael greets me with an apologetic half-smile, his entrance devoid of swagger, but equally as infuriating. Just the sight of his gray eyes trying to lock with mine, as if he has any claim to my time or space, sets up a powerfully heated pulse under the surface of my flesh, incinerating the remnants of my serene shield.

"You," I hiss at my older—definitely not wiser—sister, "invited them to my house? Where I *live?*"

A sharp pop cracks through the air, then a tinkle of glass follows. All four of us look at a mercury thermometer I have hanging on the side of the house to gauge the temperature of the day. Now the thing is a broken mess, shattered by my volcanic fury.

Harley smiles. "Perfect."

Chapter Fourteen

RAFAEL

I consume Cat with my eyes, starved by my fear that this might be the time she finally leaves my life forever. That's the sense I get every time she walks away from me. That this is it, when she disappears, I get no more of her.

When she escaped our last confrontation, where I was immature enough to get defensive over the mention of Aspen, panic consumed me. The toxic swirl in my gut was only increased by the lecture from my mother—the *'I've never been so disappointed in you'* one. Until Cat's raw confession, I don't think my mom had a clear idea of what happened between the girl who was my best friend and me. She thought we'd had a fight. Some disagreement that tore us apart.

She didn't know it was me who ruined something so precious.

That's why, even though I dread the day Cat eradicates me from her life forever, I know I deserve it. I was selfish accepting today's invite, especially because it came from Harley. More than anything, I wish my first time visiting Cat's home was at her request, but instead I'm invading.

But it was Harley's words that had made the decision.

"You can help Cat."

Okay, those weren't her only words. Luckily, I listened to the message she left on my work voicemail when no one else was around.

"What's up, dicknose? If you have time this afternoon to crawl out of your douchebag cave and be an annoying fishy fuckwad in a place of my choosing, I'm offering you a chance to redeem some of your previous assholery. I'm texting your man baby partner in crime an address. Be there at 6. If you're not too squidshit to show up, you can help Cat. Byyyyeee."

Not exactly work-appropriate, but still enticing enough to have me calling Sammy and picking him up after I got off work.

"So is this a pool party?" Sammy flicks his fingers, creating mini water tornados that zoom around the surface of the pool. "I didn't bring my suit, and I'm a proponent of going commando. Gotta let things have space to roam, you know? But I'm happy to skinny dip. Who wants to see the goods?" My friend waggles his brows, and I fight a groan.

Wrong fucking audience.

"Just FYI." Harley tosses her riot of red hair over a shoulder, giving Sammy a smile that promises violence. "The only reason those three-hundred-dollar sunglasses aren't melting off your face right now is because I'm tamping down Cat's power."

This is her stifled?

Sweat puddles in my armpits and traces down my back. My aquarium polo sticks to my skin, and I'm wishing I didn't wear khaki pants to work today. *Get ready for some embarrassing stains.*

With my attention locked on Cat, I watch as she struggles to smooth out her face and hide the level of fury that has her powers overflowing. But before she can cover her emotions, her sister is in front of her, snapping her fingers just short of her nose.

"Stop that," Harley says. "The whole point of this is for you to be angry."

Cat's eyes flick open to glare at her sister. But Harley keeps up with the lecture, fists planted on her generously curving hips. "I didn't bring these Squids here for you to prove you're unaffected. I brought them because they piss you off more than anyone else in the world." Harley clasps Cat's shoulders like she's the coach, and Cat's a prize fighter about to head into the ring. "Lean into that hate."

Her statement hits me like a jab to the gut. Sammy laughs, but the sound lacks the easygoing note from before.

"Cat doesn't *hate* me," he says. "We just snipe at each other because it's fun." The end of his sentence curls up with a hidden, uncertain question mark.

"It's not fun." Cat shoves the words through bared teeth, taking a threatening step toward Sammy. "It's *never* been fun."

The Squid's face goes slack, as if Cat tore away the golden, glittery glasses he always stares through when viewing the world.

"Good." Harley grabs Cat's wrists and holds them up. We all see a glowing, molten substance beading on her skin. Lava seeps from her pores. "You're furious right now. That's fine. Hold onto it. But also hold onto your heat."

The urge to argue surges in me. I want to beg Cat to let her anger go. To forgive me.

"I never meant to hurt you," I say without thinking.

Cat's eyes flash open, the brown now a glowing gold, as if her body is brimming with molten metal. Heat presses against my skin, uncomfortable but not harmful. Yet.

"Don't lie to me," she spits, and I half expect fire to spew from her throat.

I recall a time when I was the last person she'd ever be angry with. We were so close that I was the catalyst for the first time her powers appeared, but not because I was pissing her off. Back then, Cat would only ever get angry on my behalf. I let my mind sink into the memory as a temporary escape from her current hate.

We were young, me fourteen, her twelve. Back then, when the heat of the sun wasn't unbearable, we would walk to a convenience store to use the few dollars from our allowance to buy candy and slushies. One day, we were sitting on the curb outside the store when some older boys from school, dumbasses who wanted to fight everything that moved, started harassing me. Cat yelled at them to stop, but they ignored her. I thought I was going to have to fight four guys at once and have my ass handed to me, until one tripped. Then another. Then, their fancy bikes clattered to the ground, the tires of each having melted into rubber puddles. Just like the soles of their shoes. As the humans tried to figure out how all their shit had melted on a temperate day, Cat and I ran off.

That's when we learned her powers were anger-induced. And now, I'm the one who inspires the heat in the worst way.

"Don't try to suppress the anger, focus on the heat. On the places it's leaking out. Pull it into you. Hold it." Harley, sounding more serious than I've ever heard her, coaches Cat. The instructions are similar to what my mom taught me when I was younger. Though I'll never ask out loud, I wonder why Cat is only going through this now.

Is it my fault?

Her plump lips part, letting out rapid pants that show how hard she's working. Slowly, we watch the lava soak back into her skin until she's glowing red-hot like a brand, but the air around us is normal Phoenix heat.

Cat's eyes widen, and she grins broadly at her sister, letting out a heavy breath. "I think I've got it. How much are you helping?"

"I'm taking about ten percent off the top. But I was doing fifty at the start." Harley shares Cat's excited expression. "Much better."

Cat's attention flicks back to me, and in that moment, her triumph transforms into a glare. "I'm done practicing. Get them out of my yard before I set their pants on fire. On purpose." With an abrupt grab, the glowing Pyro snatches her purse off the lounge chair and stalks into her house, leaving the three of us behind.

Without thought, I step to follow her, panic returning as she disappears, but I stumble to a stop when a wall of flames erupts in front of me. For a second, I'm worried Cat's lost control, but then I see Harley's raised hand, and her smirk that pairs with scowling eyes.

"You've served your purpose."

"I just—"

She flicks her fingers and the wall of fire inches toward me, pushing me to the fence's gate.

"I was there." Harley meets my eyes as she forces me out. "The night you ended it all. I helped her get ready. And then I held her when she came home crying. Now, Cat wants *you* gone. Better fucking believe I'm happy to make you go." With a wave of her hand, Harley gifts Sammy with his own fiery bouncer. He yelps, scrambling away from the pool and scooping up his shoes before jogging after me.

"This is the thanks I get?" my friend calls over the flames, a put-upon pout in his voice.

"Your thanks is Tuesday, eight p.m.," she shouts, then shuts the gate of the privacy fence behind us, all signs of fiery pursuit gone now that we're in view of the street—can't have humans knowing what elementals are getting up to.

On the way to my car, I glance over at Sammy and find him wearing an odd expression. Kind of hopeful. Through my haze of hurt, I wonder what the day and time Harley called out to him meant. But, once we're on the road, Sammy goes through another emotional shift.

"Do you..." Sammy clears his throat, staring out the side window. His trailing question is out of place in his normally confident, exuberant personality.

"Do I...?" I prompt, hearing the sadness in my own voice.

"Do you really think Cat hates me?" He frowns down at his hands, still holding his shoes and socks.

Sammy is an interesting soul. Someone whose wild nature draws other people into him. He's goofy, and cocky, and sometimes obliviously self-involved. But he's also generous with his time and money, and he's always been there for me. We became friends within moments of meeting each other. No doubt he always thought Cat's animosity towards him was just their schtick, but it's obvious to me that his magnetism was not properly calibrated to her. For some reason, she was repelled on sight.

How do I tell a guy that looks like a kicked puppy the hard truth?

"I'm not really the person to ask about Cat's feelings," I hedge. But that's partly a lie.

Because I've *known* for the past twelve years that Cat hates me, even if I prayed to the gods every day that she didn't.

Chapter Fifteen

CAT

Normally, a documentary about sharks and their courtship habits would have me fully engrossed. But I'm stuck in a riptide of social media scrolling, and I barely register what's playing on my TV as I flip through pictures of the past. Quinn is out with her boyfriend, August, which means I don't even have to be circumspect about my unhealthy choice to cyber-stalk a certain Squid.

That's right, on my first night off in four days, I'm stuck on a Rafael binge.

"That mustache looked ridiculous," I mutter, having made it back to high school years. Seventeen-year-old Rafael tried for facial hair and spent months walking around with an embarrassingly small smudge of fuzz on his upper lip.

Aspen was already shaving daily back then. Sometimes, I'd sit on the Petal Pusher's bathroom counter and watch as he lathered up his face, then carefully ran the razor over each surface. Silently, I marveled at how *he*—basically a grown man—would want to be with *me*, a girl who still wasn't tall enough to ride half the rollercoasters at a theme park.

Luckily, senior year, I got a few more inches of height, but soon realized size does not always equate to maturity.

As I sip my Moscow Mule—Mia taught me how to perfectly balance the ginger beer, vodka, mint, and lime—I'm careful to keep a hold on my heat whenever a picture of Rafael and Sammy pops up together. There are a lot, which makes this perfect practice.

Even though I hate to admit it, and still resent Harley for springing them both on me, yesterday's ambush has helped my confidence. I've never done that before: dragged the power back to me while staying angry. Ever since I was twelve, and the heat roared to life under my skin, I've been in a constant battle with my anger instead of my magic.

But maybe *I* wasn't the problem.

With a swirl of my glass, I use the clink of ice cubes as proof that I'm still in control, even though I'm looking at an image of Rafael posing behind the wheel of Sammy's convertible—a car too fancy for any sixteen-year-old to own, but the Reyes parents gave their baby boy anything he liked. Sammy got *everything*.

The hot pulse pounds with more force, but I mentally guide the surge deeper into myself, imagining the fire as a string of flames wrapping tight around my bones. Keeping close to me, not spilling out.

My drink stays cold.

When I click to the next image, I almost drop my glass, but manage to set it down with a thunk on the end table.

Three familiar faces—mine, Rafael's, and Aspen's.

As a hammerhead shark swims across my TV in the background, I lean in closer to my computer, examining every detail of the past scene.

This picture used to be one of my favorites. I think Ms. Aguado took it. I was at their house, sitting on the couch, holding a gaming controller, with Aspen beside me. When she had snapped the candid shot, the Petal Pusher was in the middle of pointing something out to me, both of our focus on the colorful buttons in my hands. Meanwhile, Rafael loomed behind us, pretending like he was about to dump a bowl of popcorn on our heads, grinning wide for the camera.

This was before I went to high school. When Rafael didn't care that I was a couple of years younger than him and still invited me to hang out with his friends.

As I gaze at our three young, innocent faces, a pang of loss goes through me.

This is what we could have been. The three of us, friends.

But you liked Rafael as more than a friend, a teasing voice in the back of my brain reminds me.

And alone in my house, with no one here to read my mind, I can admit that's true. I had a gigantic crush on my best friend, which only meant his rejection had broken my heart in two ways.

But that raises the question, what would have happened if Rafael hadn't ended our friendship? Would Aspen and I still have dated? Or would I have silently pined for the Squid all through high school?

Or...would Rafael had fallen for me too?

The alcohol must be getting to me because suddenly I can't think of anything other than Rafael Aguado showing up on my doorstep, confessing his undying love for me. Begging for a second chance.

This time, I don't get mad.

This time, I drag him inside and strip off all his too-tight clothes off and shove him onto my bed.

"Gods, Cat, I want you. I've always wanted you."

As I conjure the words, I flinch. They hurt too much to even play silently to myself. I want to shut him up, fantasy or no. Luckily, it's my imagination, so a gag is easy enough.

And restraints.

Suddenly, I'm picturing a naked Rafael with his limbs bound to the corners of my bed, a scarf bunched in his mouth, and me straddling him.

I hold all the power.

Rafael's gray eyes sear a trail down my bare body, rabid to touch me. But he can't.

And yet I want to be stroked, and petted, and worshiped.

I guess it's my mind. I can have him bound, but also able to touch me, right? Only, the hands I envision aren't long-fingered with tan skin. Instead, I feel thick digits with calluses and spy a sprinkling of dark hair on pale knuckles.

Aspen's hands.

Aspen's large, hot body at my back, surrounding me, pinching my nipples, whispering in my ear.

Ride him, Red. Show him what he missed. Show him what you and I had.

Gods, what we had.

What Aspen and I had was *so good.*

The Petal Pusher befriended me almost immediately after my falling out with Rafael. A few months later, he asked me to go mini-golfing, and at the last hole, he stuttered out how he'd like to be my boyfriend. When I said yes, a nearby cactus suddenly bloomed with a riot of pink flowers, and we sprinted away before anyone noticed. Aspen and I dated a full year before we went further than kissing. When I realized the football player wasn't going to make the first move, I knew I would have to or else miss out on the chance. A week after my sixteenth birthday, I pretended to go to bed, then snuck out, drove Quinn's car to Aspen's house, climbed up the trellis outside his window, and pushed into his bedroom.

The Petal Pusher was shocked at first, when I tumbled onto the window seat.

"Hey, big oak," I'd whispered with a smile as I climbed onto the foot of his bed. "Do you want to have sex?"

I had thought the answer would be an obvious *yes*, but he was frozen silent for a good minute. Embarrassed, I was halfway back to the window before he launched out of the bed and caught me up in a kiss. Aspen asked me at least ten times if I was sure, and after ten enthusiastic yeses and me pulling out a box of condoms, we stumbled our way back to his bed. At the time, I thought every moment was great. Some discomfort, but mostly heat, and touching, and kissing, and spying the plants around Aspen's room grow extra leaves as I told him I loved him.

Because my driver's license had a midnight curfew, I couldn't linger, shimmying out his window with a large grin and a new soreness between my legs.

The next day at school, I dragged Aspen into the shadows under the stairwell because I *had* to kiss him. Unfortunately, the sprinkler system had gone off a minute later in a false fire alarm, dousing our passionate encounter. But not for long.

Climbing into Aspen's window became a regular occurrence, and we found out how good sex could get with practice. Then, we plotted ways for me to stay the whole night. I'm surprised Aspen didn't get sick of me. But every time I reached for the latch of his window, he was there, dragging me into his room and to his mouth for an eager kiss.

Those days were bliss.

Then graduation came, and I ended everything.

"No, don't think about that," I mutter to myself, instead focusing back on my fantasy. Rafael between my legs, Aspen wrapped around me, every sensitive part of my body kissed and caressed. Rocking and thrusting. I lay back on my couch, pushing a hand into my sleep shorts and sinking two fingers into my wet channel, as I do my best to imagine what Rafael would look like during sex. How the tendons of his neck would strain, and his brow would furrow, almost angry that my pussy could make him feel so good.

I don't need to imagine Aspen's face because I memorized it years ago. All I need to do is add his thick beard around a mouth open with pants, eyes glazed with pleasure.

"A-Aspen," I whimper, pressing harder against my clit. "Rafael," I groan, knowing I'll hate myself later for having his name on my lips as I come. My body tenses, seizes, pleasure pulsing through my muscles, and slickness coating my fingers.

When I blink my eyes open, the TV shines bright in front of me, showing an expanse of azure that seems to stretch endlessly. And in that world of water swims a lone shark.

As the aftershocks of my orgasm recede, loneliness rolls in. I can't help staring at the blue shark, on its own. The creature's large eyes and pouty mouth give it a lost appearance.

Same.

Chapter Sixteen

ASPEN

After two weeks of working at The Jewelry Box, I can tell why Cat is content with her gig as a waitress. The first night was a fluke with the grabby customer. For the most part, patrons seem to know how they're expected to behave themselves.

Of course, the good behavior may result from the fact that I make regular circuits of the floor, doing my best to appear imposing in my tight black T-shirt that reads *Security* across the front and back. When I first pulled it on, I considered asking for a larger size. But then Cat saw me, and her face went slack. She swallowed deep as a blush bloomed over her cheeks.

"You look good in that," she'd said, the slightest squeak in her voice, before hurrying off.

Tight shirts it is then.

I walk through the floor now, my gait slow and steady. I trade off each hour with the other bouncer, one of us patrolling the club, the other working the door. When I asked Yasmin if they ever get into a tight spot, needing more than two muscle men, she just smiled and said if it gets that bad, she starts cutting off the air supply until the police arrive.

Note to self: don't cross an Airhead if I want to keep breathing.

A dancer with the stage name Sapphire is on the main platform. Her blue thong glitters in the spotlights, and a sheer top with strategically placed rhinestones hints at her nipples. I've learned the performers tend to dress in colors related to their faux names, and each one is some sort of gemstone: Ruby, Emerald, Pearl, Diamond, Jade. The list goes on.

The Jewelry Box stays on brand.

Briefly, I watch in fascination as Sapphire climbs up the pole that must be at least fifteen feet, then drops suddenly, catching herself at the last moment using only her thighs. The crowd whoops encouragement, throwing cash on the stage while I calm my racing heart. I don't think I could ever trust a pole or my thigh muscles that much.

"She's really talented," a familiar voice says at my elbow.

Glancing down, I find Cat beside me with an empty drink tray in her hands. She has on a similar outfit to the first night I showed up. A bra-like top fashioned out of metal and black ruffled booty shorts. After two weeks of seeing her in the getup, I shouldn't still be fighting off the twitch in my groin, but I can't help the way she affects me.

"I almost shit my pants in fifth grade when we went on a field trip to the fire house, and the teachers expected us to slide down the pole because they thought it would be fun," I tell her.

Cat snorts then covers her mouth, staring at me with eyes that glitter with humor. "Sorry. I shouldn't laugh."

"You should," I murmur, barely loud enough to be heard over the music. "I love the sound of your laughter."

"Aspen!" She swats a hand against my chest and backs away toward the bar. "When did you get so good at flirting?"

Her grin is pure joy. Cat was never a coy smiler. She's genuine in her happiness. Then she turns away and gives me a view of her gorgeous ass.

Fuck, I want to take a bite out of it.

You're at work. Other people are allowed to be horny here. Not you.

Pulling myself back to the job I'm getting paid to do, I return to the unofficial station by the bar that gives me the best view of the club floor. Here, I can keep an eye on the whole area and look for potential hotspots of trouble. Like all my other shifts, things aren't quiet, but they're well-behaved enough.

And without the distraction of trouble, my eyes seek out Cat repeatedly. My gaze isn't the only thing stuck on the Pyro. After that heavy chat at my nephew's birthday party, my mind never strays far from her too.

She didn't stop loving me.

At least, not back then. Plenty of time has passed, and we're different people now. I doubt she loves me anymore.

But there's a sense of potential. A live seed nestled in the ground, just waiting for some nurturing. Maybe, if Cat's willing, we could try growing that love again in more mature soil.

But she's been quiet since our talk. Contemplative, maybe. I must remind myself that she shared an insecurity, exposed a raw nerve I think might still pain her. At work though, she's been friendly and helpful.

Cat energizes in an interesting way at The Jewelry Box. Her spine straightens, her smiles widen, and she enthusiastically chats with customers and coworkers. I wonder if it's all a customer service facade or if there are parts of this job that give her confidence.

The Pyro in question sets her tray on the far end of the bar and saunters toward me. Since when did Cat start sauntering? And how am I supposed to survive the sight?

"Don't let me distract you." She hops up on a stool near me and leans down to rub her calves, as if they pain her. She doesn't have on the intimidating stripper footwear, but she does wear a set of stilettos that make me wince in sympathy. "I'm just taking my fifteen."

"I'm honored. Using your few minutes off to hang out with me." My stare does another revolution of the room as I respond. Anything to keep my hungry gaze from the sight of her massaging her legs.

A clink of glass on wood has me glancing over to see Mia has set two glasses of water on the bar for us before hurrying off, waving away Cat's thanks.

"So." The Pyro turns her deep brown eyes on me, and I try not to get lost in their depths. "I don't want to pry. But I can't figure out what's going on with you." She watches me, brows raised with innocent curiosity. "I almost sent you an email, hoping you'd open up that way."

My chest tightens under the attention. "Open up about what?"

Cat spreads her arms wide, causing the decorative, delicate chains on her top to sway. "What are you doing in Phoenix, accepting a job at a strip club? No judgment, obviously, but I'm lost. Did you get disbarred?"

My lips twitch. "No."

"Okay." She sips her water before taking another guess. "Does this life change have something to do with Shawna and Ryan?"

My brief amusement fades at the sound of their names. I need a moment to formulate the right answer because it's both "yes" and "no."

In my mind, I can still see the first email I sent to Cat about them, the married couple I'd started dating. We were four months into the relationship at that point, and I was feeling the initial stirrings of love, which automatically had me thinking of Cat, the first girl I'd ever loved. There was an undeniable urge to share with her—because we were corresponding regularly at the time—this new discovery I'd made about myself. That I felt whole in a relationship with multiple partners. I didn't explore the need to have Cat know this about me. All I concerned myself with was worries of how she'd react.

Would she say what I wanted was wrong? That I was wrong? Would she stop talking to me?

Those anxieties made my fingers ache with reluctance as I typed out the email. But I still sent it.

Waiting for her response had me sick enough that Shawna and Ryan asked if I had caught the flu. Then a message appeared in my inbox. Her typed words saying she was happy I found love. There were a few logistic questions that I could tell arose from innocent curiosity, and I answered them gladly. After that, I was candid about my relationship. Not that I sent her emails about our bedroom activities. But when the three of us went on a fun outing or trip, I'd tell Cat about it. When Shawna and Ryan asked me to move in, I told her about it.

When they suggested I go home, on my own, to visit my family for the holidays, I told Cat about it.

When their adult children showed up for a surprise visit, and they told them I was just their renter, I told Cat about it.

Then that final straw, when they planned an international trip for their anniversary without consulting me on the dates, and insisted I take off work because I was their *gift* to each other. I had locked myself in the bathroom, hyperventilating because of the pain.

And I had pulled out my phone to email Cat. Not about my panic attack, but about how I'd become no more than an object in a relationship I'd thought I was an equal partner in.

"After I ended things and moved out, I was okay," I say. "But that's it. I was just okay. So, I thought I might start over somewhere new. Closer to home." *Closer to you.*

It was a bad reason to choose Phoenix. But I convinced myself Cat wasn't the reason. I told myself all I wanted was to be closer to my family.

And the decision *definitely* had nothing to do with Sammy's call, telling me Rafael had accepted a job at the local aquarium.

At least, that's what I told myself. Quitting my job, ending my lease, packing my things, finding a house to rent, loading everything in a moving truck. Over and over during the process, I focused on the fact that I wanted a change, and Phoenix just happened to fit.

I refused to let myself think about Cat and Rafael.

Problem is, ever since that first date with Shawna and Ryan, a fantasy has lived in the furthest corner of my mind. That somehow, if everything lined up just right, the three of us might find ourselves together.

And then we might be...*together.*

It was a wild hope. A dream I shouldn't have had in the first place.

Still, I can't seem to let go of it.

"What's your plan?" Cat asks, confusion wrinkling her brow.

"To stay here." *As long as it doesn't feel like my heart is bleeding in my chest from being in the same city as you and Rafael and not having you both.* "The next bar exam is in February. If I pass, I'll be able to practice law here. Figure this job is a good one to hold me over until then."

Cat slides off her stool, teetering for a moment on her heels. She stares into the middle distance, as if her thoughts have pulled her away from me.

"Cat?"

She blinks. "Sorry. I'm just processing." The Pyro straightens her shorts and chugs the rest of her water. "Do you need to head home after work? Or could you grab a bite with me at the end of the night?"

"Food. Yes. I'm in." The words stutter out, tripped up by my hope.

It's just two friends hanging out. I tell myself. *Not a date.*

"Okay. It's a plan." She steps away, then turns back. "Do you happen to have some on you?"

"Some what?"

A playful smile sparkles under the shifting club lights. "Mint."

The word shocks a laugh out of me, and I reach into my pocket for a tin container. I pop the lid open to reveal a cluster of green leaves inside. Fresh mint.

"I knew it!" With careful fingers, the Pyro reaches out and selects one, placing the spikey leaf on her tongue. I try not to groan at the sight. She was the same in high school, always asking me to share my mint. I carry it instead of gum. Something to chew on, always kept fresh with a small strand of my magic.

Every time Cat snuck one from me, I would get the uncontrollable urge to kiss her, knowing I'd taste the fresh herb on her tongue.

It's all I can do now to simply close the box and slip it back into my pocket. Maybe one day, I'll have the privilege of her lips again. But for now, I have to watch her walk away.

Chapter Seventeen

CAT

A shift has never gone slower in my life. Especially because I don't wear a watch. I'm super friendly with the customers that have ones on in the hopes I'll catch sight of the time and find the hours are passing. But each time, only a few minutes have crawled by.

Everywhere Aspen is, I can feel him. Close, far, doesn't matter. There's a tie between me and him. Probably one-way, but as solid to me as a rope.

He's staying in Phoenix. I had convinced myself that this was just an extended vacation or maybe a temporary stop before a more permanent move to another city, states away.

Not that him staying in Phoenix changes much between us. I had my chance with Aspen, and I pushed him away. Just like those two fools who also let him go. Every time he wrote me an email about another slight against him, I had to walk away from my laptop, so I didn't melt the keys.

How could they treat him as nothing more than a boy toy?

Despite them not being the end-game for him, I can't help seeing the vast differences between us. Shawna owned her own high-end beauty boutique, and Ryan did software engineering that earned him millions. Plus, they were both in their late forties. Successful adults.

Unlike me.

I haven't deluded myself into thinking that Aspen is back here for me. For us. That was a relationship between children, and I was right to end it when I did. But gods, I just want more time with him. Feeling his steady presence near me. Hearing his deep voice. Chewing on his mint leaves. As much as I can get before he finds someone, or multiple someones to fill the romantic space in his life.

Finally, the club closes. As I wipe down the tables and collect stray glasses, Aspen walks the performers out to their cars. I hear a few of them laughing along with his deep chuckle.

Don't compare yourself to Ruby, or Sapphire, or Jade, I tell myself. But it's hard not to. Their bodies are honed into tight, lush curves and muscles from dancing and a few helpful additions from surgeons. Jade's boob job, in particular, is magnificent. She was happy to let me touch them, just to see how they felt. Still soft, and all the more mesmerizing for it.

I bet no one mistakes *her* for a high school student with a fake ID when she goes to a bar.

At least Aspen doesn't ditch me for any of my beautiful coworkers. At the end of the night, it's me he walks with down the street to my favorite food truck. For now, I'm the one who holds his attention.

"Thanks, Terra." I say to the flush-cheeked woman handing me my raspberry cream cheese crepe, and the pulled pork crepe Aspen ordered after I bullied him into letting me pay.

"No problem. Busy night at the club?" She accepts my slightly crinkled cash and hands me change that I immediately stuff in her *Don't tip cows, tip me* jar.

"A little. Made good tips. Has Harley been by?" My sister works at the dungeon down the street and rarely misses a chance to end her night with one of Terra's creations.

"About an hour ago, I think. Said she was heading home."

I wave in thanks before joining Aspen under a nearby streetlight. A part of me is happy I won't run into my sister with Aspen by my side. I love her, but my surprise power training lessons are proof that she is adept at shoving herself into every crevice of my life. If she sees me standing next to the only ex whose guts she didn't hate, there's no telling what mission she would assign herself regarding me.

Memories of standing in my backyard, a living, breathing volcano, twist my stomach.

I know Harley said it's okay to feel my anger, and I'm starting to agree with her on that. The problem is, I don't think I ever realized how angry I've gotten. That emotion should have faded over the years as time and space came between Rafael and me. We were just kids when he hurt me, and an adult should be able to let that go. But if anything, it's festered and grown into a burning sludge monster waiting to consume me.

"Praise the gods," Aspen groans beside me, pulling my mind back to the present moment. His bearded cheeks are puffed out with food. He chews slowly, his eyes closed, before swallowing and gazing at me in wonder. "This is delicious. I've never had a savory crepe."

"Yeah. Terra's the best." I take a bite of my own, reveling in the tartness of the berries, creaminess of the cheese, all held together with a delicate crepe. We're forced to move farther back, a crowd forming with the night clubs closing. Realization hits, and I huff a laugh at myself. "I'm sorry, I should've introduced you." I lean in closer, even though no one is paying attention to us. "She's a Petal Pusher. I think that's part of why her food tastes so good. She has the best herbs and fruits around."

Curiosity sparks in Aspen's gaze, and he leans to the side to get a better look at the woman. At that moment, Terra laughs at something a customer says, showing off her gorgeous white teeth, bright against her umber skin. Her hair, despite the many flyaways caused, no doubt, by a night of frazzled work, is a lustrous black mass only partly tamed by a braid. Then there are her curves. Mountains and valleys of softness that have me glancing down at my own, much flatter, landscape.

I hate this. Hate comparing myself to other women—ones that I like and respect, no less—because my insecurities have me thinking of myself as a child. Again.

Maybe if I'd left on my metal waitress top instead of pulling on a sports bra and loose T-shirt, I wouldn't have so much trouble remembering that most of the time, I'm perfectly happy with how I look.

"Ready to head to your car?" Aspen's voice comes muffled by the last bite of his crepe, and I nod, working to catch up with my own food. For the first block back, we're quiet.

"Everyone at the club seems nice," he volunteers when we pause at a crosswalk, waiting for the light to change.

"Yeah. They're great. Sometimes, there's a guest performer that comes in and is kind of a stuck-up asshole. But all the regulars are friendly. Most of them are like *us*." I nod my head when I catch Aspen's brow raise.

A strip club full of elementals. Not a huge surprise when you remember it's owned by an elemental too.

"Yasmin put out the word to as many of us locals as she could find. Need a job, get in touch with her."

"Is that why you started working there?"

"No. That was Harley. I was going to try getting a waitress gig at a diner or something, but she knew I'd make better money at The Jewelry Box." We've reached the side street where my car is parked, and as we approach, some self-sabotage reaction has me blurting out another fact. "A few of the performers are single. Ruby and Jade. Pearl too, I think. Just...you know...if you wanted to know."

Gods, if only I hadn't already finished my crepe, I could have stuffed the dough in my mouth to cut off my ridiculous words.

Not wanting to see the interest bloom over his face, I busy myself with unlocking my car and tossing my bag onto the passenger seat. When I turn back and lift my chin, I discover a set of hazel eyes locked on me, lips twisted in a small smile that almost appears sad.

"They seem great, but I'm not interested," Aspen says.

My chest clenches with some emotion I refuse to examine closer. Instead, I fall into defensiveness. "Because they strip? It's not a big deal, you know."

The big man's beard twitches as the corners of his mouth curve high, some of the melancholy drifting away. "I have no problem with dating someone who strips. What I meant to say was I'm not interested because..." His hesitation has me leaning toward him. "Because I still have a crush on my first girlfriend."

The world tilts, and I grip my car door to keep steady.

Did he just...is that...could he mean...

"Did you date someone before me?" I rasp. He was seventeen to my fifteen when he first officially asked me on a date. Aspen, member of the varsity football team since his sophomore year, could easily have had a relationship before I got to high school.

He chuckles, and in the dim streetlight I watch a hint of red bloom over his cheeks. His fingers scratching at his beard in a self-conscious tic.

"No. You were my first. And you're still...never mind. I'm sorry, Cat." He shoves his hands in his pockets and shifts his weight, ready to walk away. "We can forget I said anything."

Acting on instinct, I brace my foot on the lip of my car cab, leveraging myself up to put my face level with the Petal Pusher's. Before Aspen can retreat, I fist the collar of his shirt, tug him in, and claim the mouth I haven't tasted since I was sixteen years old.

Chapter Eighteen

RAFAEL

After a long shower, I finally get rid of the dead fish smell. I don't always leave my job smelling like I got on the wrong side of a tuna, but today there was an unfortunate slip while holding a bucket of chum for the shark tank. I wasn't even supposed to be doing the task, but two people called in with the flu, so it was all hands on deck.

And then, it was all fish on my pants.

Now, though, I'm smelling clean and ready for an evening of watching soccer with some Squids. Damien promised homemade lasagna. Much different than the guy who used to think ramen noodles were the height of cuisine back when we were teenagers. Apparently, when he basically adopted his sister, the guy decided to learn how to cook. Sammy was raving that if real estate doesn't work out, Damien could win a whole slew of cooking shows.

The man does have a face for TV. Back when I didn't admit I was into guys, I made every excuse as to why I was fascinated by the older Squid's high cheekbones and long, sooty lashes. *It was just because he was so symmetrical*, I told myself. Or *I wanted to look like him to get as many girls as he did*. Maybe, *I was going to be an artist and thought he'd make a nice study*.

I wish I could've just accepted the truth back then.

Dude, you're bi, and he's hot.

Now, I acknowledge that, and move on because, despite his model-like face, I don't feel anything other than friendship toward Damien. Being near him doesn't heat me up like being near Cat. And that's even without her malfunctioning powers.

The same heat that also cropped up when I saw Aspen.

Damn the Petal Pusher, coming here and complicating an already insurmountable situation. He's putting me in the same predicament I was in during high school, and I fully expect to fuck everything up again.

As I'm climbing into my car, my phone vibrates in my back pocket. When I see Damien's name on the screen I answer.

"Hey, man. I'm about to head over. What's up?"

"Hey." There's the sound of voices in the background, including a very loud shout of "*GOAL!*" The shouter sounded an awful lot like Sammy, and since the game hasn't started yet, I can't imagine what mischief he's already getting into. "Glad I caught you. Would you mind picking Marisol up on your way here? She's at tutoring, and her friend flaked on giving her a lift home. The place is on your way, and I'd rather you grab her than she takes an Uber."

"Of course, but tutoring? It's only September. How long has she even been in school for?"

There's a half-sigh, half-laugh on the other end. "She's taking four AP classes. She wants to make sure she doesn't fall behind."

"Are you sure she's your sister?"

"Fuck off," he says without heat. "I'll text you the address of the place. And thanks, man. I don't like her getting in some stranger's car."

"No problem."

After we hang up, the address immediately dings on my phone, and I plug it into my maps app. Ten minutes later, I'm outside of a shop called Land of Ice Cream and Snow, wondering if Damien sent me to the right place.

When I climb out of my car, I smell the delicious aroma of waffle cones and decide it doesn't hurt to check the place out. Even if this is the wrong destination, I could treat myself to some mint chocolate chip before hunting down Marisol elsewhere.

Aspen tasted like mint...

I shy away from the memory. That was a mistake.

After shoving open the door harder than I meant, I find the search is over. When I step into the shop, out of the heat into cool comfort, I spy a mass of wavy black hair in a booth off to the side. Marisol has her head bent over a pile of papers, scribbling with a pencil as she gnaws on her bottom lip. I don't want to interrupt her mid-study session, but in case she missed a text from Damien, I decide it's best to let her know I'm here.

"Hey, Merry Berry." I pull out the nickname we all called her when Sammy, Damien, and I were younger, when she was only a toddler. Back then, the little Squid would giggle. Now she jerks her head up with a scowl and rolls her eyes, as if I'm an embarrassing uncle making knock-knock jokes. "If you didn't hear, I'm your ride home whenever you're ready."

I say all this as I approach the booth. When I reach the table, I shift to apologize to the tutor—then choke on air when I meet a set of burning brown eyes.

"Rafael." Cat says my name, and even though it's almost a hiss, I love watching her mouth form the letters. "We're still working."

Cat is the tutor. I wonder if Damien realized what he was doing when he sent me here, or if the guy just forgot. He probably has more important things on his plate than keeping up with the people who hate me.

"Hey, Cat." The greeting comes out as a desperate wheeze. *Please stop hating me*, I want to add. The image of her burning like an ember in her fury blares in my mind. I brought on that reaction. *Is she going to go fireball right now?*

"I should be ready to go in like five, maybe ten minutes. Is that okay? I'm finishing a practice test, and Cat's going to grade it." Marisol waves a piece of paper in the air, the fluttering catching my attention enough to break away from the Pyro's simmering animosity.

"Yeah, sure. Take your time." I rock back a step, flicking my gaze to Cat. "I guess I'll grab an ice cream."

Then, she does something odd. Cat Byrne smiles at me.

It's not a good smile. The curve of her lips comes slow and jerky, a drawbridge cranked into place for defense. It's the same creepy doll smile she gave me at the aquarium. A shiver of discomfort travels down my spine, and I force myself to leave them and approach the counter.

Looking for a distraction, I take in more of the shop. Land of Ice Cream and Snow is not a playful ice cream parlor with colorful, delicate furnishings. Everything here is heavy, sturdy, and appears durable in a comfortable way. Like the furnishings in a wooded cabin. This aesthetic would fit better in Denver than Phoenix, but with the slight chill in the air, everything works.

The counter is a slate slab supported by dark wood. Waiting just behind it, at the register, is a mountain of a man. The guy is as large as Aspen but has blonde hair instead of the Petal Pusher's dark brown.

Stop thinking about Aspen.

As I meander up to order, I take in more of the shop worker, as he does the same with me. The guy gives me rugged, cold wilderness vibes. He matches the shop aesthetic, and I wonder if that's why he was hired.

"Hi." I offer my friendliest smile when I reach the good-looking guy about to scoop me ice cream. I may not want to pursue him, but I can still enjoy the experience.

His thick brows dip. "You're Rafael."

"I—" My words stumble. I wasn't expecting that. "Uh, yeah. Yes. That's me. Have we met?" This guy is someone I would remember.

"I was at Damien's party." He keeps going when I only look confused. Damien has a party practically every weekend. "Where Cat pushed you in the pool."

"Oh." That means two things. One, this guy is an elemental of some kind. Two, he's acquainted with Cat.

My gaze flicks over to the table where she and Marisol are still working.

Is the tutoring session happening here because Cat wanted to hang out with this ice cream guy afterwards? Are the two of them dating?

If this is her boyfriend, she obviously has a type. Tall, bulky, hands that could pound a nail into wood better than a hammer.

Meanwhile, I'm five-nine on a good day, lean more than large, and I need a rubber grip most times to unscrew the lid of a pickle jar. Sometimes, I still can't get it, and just live my life without pickles.

Fuck my life, I've got no chance.

"Is that the Squid I think it is?" A familiar voice calls my attention and out from a back hallway, Quinn appears. The third Byrne sister. I brace myself for the same animosity shown by the other two, but Quinn surprises me by strolling up and wrapping me in a tight hug. "How's it going, Rafael? Seems neither of my sisters have murdered you yet, so better than I expected."

Quinn leans back, her hands on my shoulders, a welcoming grin on her freckled face. The woman is drop-dead gorgeous and the same age as me. By all accounts, she should've been the one I fell for in high school. But it was always Cat, for me.

Cat and—

Nope. Not going there.

"Still alive." I nod and try for a carefree smile, but I figure it comes out more like a grimace when Quinn's brows quirk. "Things are good, I guess. Settling in at my job, and I found a good rental."

She gives a friendly squeeze of my upper arms before stepping away and circling behind the counter, heading straight for the ice cream man. That's when I notice how the personified mountain watches the Pyro. As if she's the only dessert in the shop, and he's been starving for a week.

Tension eases from my chest as Quinn slides a possessive arm around the guy's waist. Not dating Cat after all.

"Have you met August?" She waves between us. "August, this is Rafael Aguado. Squid and Cat's former best friend, current nemesis." I try not to wince at the accurate description. At least, accurate on Cat's end. "Rafael, this is August Nord. He's the owner of this fine establishment, and I'm dating him for the endless supply of ice cream."

The man rumbles a chuckle and glances at me with friendlier eyes than before. "I'm a Snow Cone," he says as if the statement makes sense. "Harley came up with the label."

"Ice." Quinn holds up August's palm and kisses the center. When she pulls her mouth away, there's a distinct shape of lips made of frost on his skin.

I feel my face go slack. "Whoa, I never—I mean, I didn't realize there were any...of you." I clear my throat. "Sorry. I mean, I've never met an ice elemental before." I keep my voice at a moderate volume, to keep the few customers on the other side of the shop from hearing. I have no idea if they're elementals or not, so best to be circumspect.

"I didn't either." Quinn grins up at the guy, besotted. "But he's real. Lucky me."

The big man blushes, and her words dislodge a memory. "Wait. You wouldn't happen to be Sammy's cousin, would you?"

August nods. "Don't hold it against me."

"Shit, I thought he was messing with me." At some point, Sammy talked about how he had a cousin who was an ice elemental. But for one, it's not common to have different elementals in the same family. And two, no one I knew, who I took seriously, had ever encountered one. I just assumed he was trying to see how gullible I was. "Guess I owe him a drink."

The shop owner chuckles. "I don't blame you for second-guessing him. So you want some ice cream, or what?"

After browsing the interesting selection of flavors, I opt for one called the Fiery Goddess. Quinn smirks in triumph, informing me that's *her* flavor. A dad with a collection of kids shows up as I'm paying, so Quinn and I stand off to the side while August serves them. I try not to groan at how delicious the intriguing sweet and spicy flavor of my treat is.

After a few licks, I give in to curiosity, hoping I'm not about to blow up a good thing.

"Why are you being nice to me? Aren't I the Byrne sisters' enemy number one?"

Quinn smirks. "No. That would be firemen." Her humor fades with a sigh, and she finger combs her long ruby hair away from her face. "Harley holds grudges like it's her business. She's hard to piss off, but when you accomplish the feat, get ready for long-term derision. That's just how she is. And Cat is the one you hurt, so obviously she's got you on her hit list. Me," she shrugs. "I think I get it."

I pause with my cone halfway to my mouth. "Get what?"

"Why you turned into a douche. Why you kicked Cat out of that party. I mean, I don't condone what you did. Everything you said was extremely shitty. But gods." She leans back against a table, her arms crossed over her chest. "I can't say I wouldn't have done something similar if I'd been there that night." Both Quinn and I watch the booth as we talk about the woman occupying it. "I drove her there, and I was half ready to pass the place by and take her back home. She's just one of those people you want to encase in bubble wrap and protect from the rest of the world, you know? Even now, she's a grown woman, and I still worry I'm going to hurt her feelings. That I'm going to crush her if I lose my temper and say the wrong thing."

Fuck. I don't know how she did it, but Quinn said everything I felt that night.

"That's...exactly it." I somehow manage the words even though my lips are numb.

The Pyro nods absently. "You saw her there and freaked out. But damn it, Rafael." She turns to me, her eyes confused. "Why didn't you *fix* it? You two fought before. Not *that* bad, but still. She would have forgiven you if you'd tried."

Regret plagues me. "It wasn't a fight," I mutter. "It was a decimation. Cat didn't push back. She just left. And when I saw her next—" I cut myself off because it's so petty, and I'm fucking ashamed.

When I saw her next, she was with Aspen.

Not that they were *together*, at that point. The two of them had just been laughing about something, and she was sitting beside him at a desk, walking him through some math issue. Tutoring the guy like she's doing with Marisol now. Jealousy had surged so fast in me that the water fountain in the hallway busted, and I had to spend the entire class concentrating on the liquid in the pipes to keep it from bursting out in a massive fountain that would quickly fill the hallway.

"I didn't know how to fix it," I mutter. "I was a coward."

Quinn doesn't correct me. She just hooks her thumbs in the belt loops of her shorts.

"She still has the shark."

"You mean—"

She nods. "Mr. Murder Fins, or whatever she named it."

"Dr. Bloody Jaws," I correct, feeling a smile tug at my mouth at the memory. On Cat's tenth birthday, I went with the Byrnes to an aquarium. I spent the whole trip making her laugh by making up ridiculous stories about the fish. Her favorite—the one that got her laughing so hard she cried—was about the sand tiger shark. My tale went that he dressed up like a doctor and convinced all the other aquarium residents he could help with their ailments, but the minute he got them into his tank he gobbled them up. Dr. Bloody Jaws. Then, I spent two months' allowance buying her a stuffed shark from the gift shop.

She'd hugged the toy and stared up at me with such joy I thought I might explode from being loved so much.

"She..." I have to clear my throat, no doubt because a chunk of waffle cone got stuck in the back. "She kept him?"

Quinn watches her sister as she talks. "When we moved in together, we went through our stuff and did a big purge. I found the thing and asked if it should go in the donate box. Cat said no. She held it for a while like she was worried I might throw it away when her back was turned." The redhead lets out a weary sigh. "She's mad because she cares. Cares too much. Harley thinks it's okay if Cat's pissed till the day she dies. But I don't think that's good for her."

Could it be true? Could Cat still care about me under all that fury?

"What do I do?" The question is barely above a whisper.

Quinn pushes upright, stepping toward her sister, tilting her chin in a direction for me to follow.

"You could start by not abandoning her again."

Chapter Nineteen

CAT

When Rafael steps away from the table, I am determined not to pay a single iota of attention to him.

That plan fails the moment my sister calls out his name. Something burns in my chest when, from the corner of my eye, I watch them embrace.

That should be us.

Wait, what? No, it shouldn't. We don't hug because he threw me away, and now I hate him.

I hate the way his soft, honey-brown hair swoops in the occasional tasseled wave. I hate how his laugh spills out from a charming smile and sounds almost like it did when we were younger, only a note deeper now. I hate how his clothes fit his body in a way that makes it easy to imagine mapping the shape of him with the palms of my hands.

I hate that I can't get the fantasy of him between my legs out of my mind.

Oh gods, what is happening to me?

"You look like a creepy clown." Marisol's observation has my head jerking toward her, which has me realizing I was staring.

"What?"

"The too-big smile and overly wide eyes." She gestures at my face with her pencil. "Creeping me out big time. Maybe try for stoic instead of pleasant, if you don't want to let on that Rafael's making you hot."

"Hot?" I squeak the word and immediately try to school my features. "I'm not *hot* for him. To be clear, I haven't had a crush on him since I was younger than you."

The lingering romantic feelings belong to Aspen, as demonstrated by the impulsive urge I gave in to kiss him the other night.

His lips were firmer than I remembered. Like a supportive mattress I wanted to spend an entire night on. He tasted like mint and a tease of the BBQ sauce from his crepe. His hands were strong and warm when they rested on my hips, pulling my body into his.

And his beard, that was new. A tickle and rasp against the skin of my face. In my fantasies, I hadn't been sure if I would like it. But I do. I did.

I had panicked when I realized what I was doing. I'd pushed him away, mumbled a quick goodbye, and probably left skid marks in the alley I peeled off so fast. The only reason I'm not still in a whirlwind of regret is the text I read when I got home.

> Aspen: Don't ever apologize for kissing me. Let me take you out.

I'd waited until I was in the safety of my bed, as if my covers would defend me from my irresponsible choices, to respond.

> Cat: You don't have to do that. We're friends, and I'm good with that.

My fingers had stumbled over a few of the words, as if reluctant to type them. A moment later, my phone rang and after hesitating, I answered.

"You're saying you didn't like kissing me?" Aspen's voice was a delicious grumble through the phone.

"No...I did. But I shouldn't have."

"Why not?"

"We're...I mean you—"

"Want you." The way he had growled the words had my nipples

tightening. "I want you, Cat. If you don't want to be with me, that's okay. But you can't kiss me again because it drives me fucking wild." There was a defeated chuckle on the other end of the line. "Scratch that. My mouth is yours. Kiss me whenever the hell you want."

I'd pressed my knuckles into my mouth so hard I worried I'd bruise my lips. The way I had wanted Aspen to.

"Cat?" He asked after I'd been quiet for too long.

"You said you want to go out?"

We had made plans, but I still can't believe it's happening. That I'm only a few hours away from a date. With Aspen.

I just need to get through this suddenly much more stressful tutoring session. Marisol stares across the table at me with a single, skeptical eyebrow raised.

"I meant *magically* hot. You had a crush on Rafael?"

My face floods with an overwhelming flush. *Great, just show my whole ass, why don't I?* Luckily, Marisol doesn't tease me. Instead, she passes her completed practice test my way, giving me an excuse to look at the table rather than meet her eyes.

Grading the thing is easy. Partly because Marisol got almost every answer right, but also because math has always been second nature to me. That's why I chose to major in mathematics in college, just like Quinn. Only, when she graduated, she was excited to start working as an accountant. I, meanwhile, was bored to tears, and opted to work a string of part-time jobs instead of finding a career in my field. I'm still using a chunk of my paycheck to pay off student loans for a degree I never finished. Even these tutoring sessions don't require more math knowledge than what I already had when leaving high school.

"So you had a crush on Rafael when you were my age?" Marisol's question causes me to flinch, and I end up tearing a small fissure in her test. "And Aspen? You dated him, right?"

"Yes." I opt for short, honest answers and the stoic face she suggested. Marisol is too smart for me to try to distract her.

"There's a guy in my Calculus class." A rosy tinge blooms on the apples of her cheeks. "I'm pretty sure he likes me."

Much preferring the focus to be on her, I smile—not creepily this time—and hold up the practice test. "Planning on wowing him with your big brain? You did great, by the way. Just missed a step on problem eight." I slide the paper her way.

"He does like math, so maybe. But..." She drums her fingers on the table, a pout forming on her mouth. "Even if he asks me out, I don't think Damien will let me go. He's gotten super overprotective since my parents left."

I grimace in sympathy, both for the uncomfortable absence of her parents, but also from knowing how bothersome it is when someone treats you like a kid when you're not one anymore. Or when you wish you weren't.

"Your parents let you date when you were my age," Marisol says as if I know a secret password that I could share with her.

I shrug. "They met Aspen a few times before he asked me out. They liked him." My mouth curves in another true smile when I think back on the first time he came over to watch a movie with me when we were officially a couple. He had been nervous and brought my parents a cactus. "And after raising Harley, I guess I seemed easy. Or maybe they were just exhausted."

Marisol snorts, then frowns. "Not sure that helps me. Damien would probably scare anyone off if I invited them over for a date."

I nod. "Maybe go out in a group? At least at first? Working up to it slowly might not be the most fun, but I doubt Damien would object to you hanging out with multiple people."

The young Squid sighs and offers me an exasperated smirk. "Yeah. Maybe." She slides out of the booth. "Thanks for this. It helped."

After a wave, I pretend to look for something in my purse, hoping to appear busy until Marisol and her ride are gone from the shop.

Then, I'll have a scoop of the strawberry shortcake to calm my nerves, before going home to get ready for my date.

And like magic, the exact flavor of ice cream I wanted appears in front of me, a freckled hand offering the delicious treat. I go to smile up at my sister in thanks but get caught halfway when I realize she's not alone.

Rafael is at her side, staring at me with his familiar gray eyes that I wish I didn't know so well.

"Hey." Quinn moves to sit across from me. "I asked Marisol to chill with August for a few minutes."

"Hmm," is the only sound I can get out, as I try to keep a serene expression on my face. If it were Harley here with me, I'd have no problem glaring fiery daggers at Rafael. My oldest sister and I have that kind of relationship, were I can be an emotional mess, and she'll just roll with it.

Quinn—though she's the one closer to me in age—is the sister I tend to worry about when it comes to good opinions. I can't help it. She just seems so elegantly put-together. Especially now that she has fully mastered the control of her powers. But even before she was able to rein in her heat, Quinn's abilities are lust-induced, meaning she only set things on fire when she got horny—which is not exactly a sisterly activity. I saw her lose control very few times in our lives. Other than that, she's this gorgeous, statuesque woman with a full-time job, healthy relationship, and an overall sense of put-togetherness.

I love her, but I feel like she's about to drop me off at my first day of kindergarten half the time.

And now she's gesturing for Rafael to join us, and more than anything, I don't want to lose my shit in front of her.

"Harley told me about your practicing. I figure we can do another round since Rafael is already here."

Shock erases my calm countenance. "Here?" A quick glance around shows there's a family by the front window and a couple at the counter ordering. "But people. And ice cream." Practicing magic in public is a big no-no.

Quinn reaches out to push my ice cream closer. "We'll use this as your barometer. Harley said you kept it under your skin, but you were glowing like a torch. Now you have a reason to suppress that too. And you've got me and August to help if the magic gets away from you."

Try as I might, humiliation infuses my face with heat, and we haven't even begun yet. "Quinn—"

"I believe in you." My sister offers an encouraging smile, and I find I can't admit how pathetic I am. I guess she'll just have to see for herself.

"Fine." I tuck myself into the furthest corner of the booth, glad that the high back shields me from view of the rest of the customers. Finally, I allow myself to meet Rafael's gaze.

As always, there's a thud in my chest simply at the sight of him. When we were younger, it felt like a heavy puzzle piece settling into place. Now, it feels like someone crashing into me with a moped.

Relaxing the stranglehold on my emotions, I allow my anger to rise. At least, I try to.

What comes instead is a sense of exhaustion rather than fury.

Gods, I can't even get angry right.

"Could you talk about something?" I huff.

"What do you want me to talk about?" His voice is careful as he watches me, his attention a touch against my skin.

Why did you throw me away?

No. That is too big and too deep to bring up. Instead, I opt for the tried-and-true method.

"Tell me a story about Sammy."

He hesitates, eyes flicking as if mentally cycling through a whole filing cabinet.

Because they have so many. The first spark of annoyance ignites.

"In college we took a trip to Ireland together," he offers.

Anger, my old, toxic friend, creeps out of a jealous pit. Rafael's smooth voice keeps going, relating how the two of them tried to visit every bar in Dublin, getting drunk off their asses on Guinness that's richer than anything you could get in the States. As the sound of a smile enters his voice, I know he's enjoying revisiting the memories.

Meanwhile, I'm cataloguing how many items of his I could melt.

Watchband, that would make a nice silvery puddle on the table.

Shoe soles, classic, but maybe overdone at this point.

Zipper on his pants, and he'd have to cut himself out of them with scissors.

A pants-less Rafael pops up in my imagination, stifling my anger with a shot of lust. *Gods, I bet he wears boxer briefs that show off his ass to perfection.*

"Then we took a train down the coast and found this amazing beach." He keeps going with his story, unaware of the turn my mind took. "It was too cold for most people to go swimming, but not us, of course."

Of course. Of course not. Two Squids swimming in the waters off the coast of Ireland. I bet they found some gorgeous mermaids and had a supernatural orgy.

What a grand time the two of them had, traveling through a country together. Having adventures that they can reminisce about for years as they meet up for more. Rafael and Sammy. Partners in crime.

It used to be Rafael and Cat. *I* used to be the one in the stories.

We were young, I remind myself as the anger flares in a strong, thumping pulse under my skin. With a mental hand, I guide the pulse back within myself, directing the power toward my heart rather than out my pores.

I'm so angry. So furious.

But not...not with him. Not so much, anymore.

All with myself.

"Cat—" Rafael's voice has my eyes flicking to his face. Staring across the table, I find both watching me. "Is this helping?" he asks, the question hesitant.

Because he cares.

"Damn it," I mutter, the curse directed at myself.

"Sorry, wait. I'll try something else." Rafael leans forward, storm cloud gaze latching onto mine. "Have you ever heard of fractions?"

Despite the anger and disappointment and shame burning in my chest, that question, asked so earnestly, as if he needs my permission to mansplain math to me, sets off a surprisingly pleasant fizz in my chest.

And I laugh.

Damn him. How did he do that?

Now there's an expression of wonder on his face, and I need to leave before he realizes the same thing that I just figured out.

That I'm not mad at Rafael. Not anymore.

I'm mad at the version of myself I can't ignore when he's around.

With a quick glance down, I examine my skin for the glow that would reveal my magic. There's nothing but my normal, paper-pale skin. Heat pools in a heavy, steady thrum, but I've tucked it into the hidden compartment of my heart. Fuel if I need it.

The anger is there. The power is controlled.

My ice cream sits in front of me, unmelted.

"How much did you help?" I ask Quinn, ignoring Rafael's hopeful stare.

"I didn't have to." Quinn watches me with an expression that mixes curiosity and concern.

"Well, I was super pissed." *At myself.* "But practice makes perfect." With a smooth move, like I'm confident I'm not a mess inside, I grab my cup of ice cream and stand, meeting Rafael's eyes at the last moment. "Thanks. Looks like I don't need you anymore."

And you definitely do not need me, I silently add.

Despite the heat so recently coursing through my body, as I leave the shop, my insides feel cold.

Chapter Twenty

ASPEN

I wipe my hands on my pants, my palms sweaty as if I'm a kid going on my first date again. With a bracing breath, I knock on the front door of the address she sent me.

There's nothing to be nervous about. This is Cat.

That doesn't help because her being Cat is the whole reason I'm on edge. I can't imagine I'll get another chance after this one to make things work.

With a loud squeak, the front door wrenches open. The Pyro smiles up at me, her cheeks flushed from the effort. "Sorry. It sticks sometimes." Stepping back, she waves for me to enter. "Come in. I just need to put on my shoes and grab my bag."

I do as I'm told, closing the door behind me and trying not to appear too lecherous as I watch every slight movement she makes while buckling the straps of her sandals, then grabbing a purse and a duffle bag. The second probably has her work gear. I'm dropping her off after the date because this is my night off.

My eyes hungrily devour her current outfit. She's wearing a sundress. But more than that, it's patterned with tiny cacti. A miniature field of them on the fabric. Does she know what seeing her covered in growing things does to me?

"You look amazing." Somehow, I keep the groan out of my voice.

Her cheeks plump with a smile as she smooths her hands over the skirt. Teasing me. "I thought you'd appreciate this pattern. But wait!" She whirls around, snatching up another piece of clothing. Then, despite the warm evening, Cat slides on a loosely knit, emerald-colored cover up. She strikes a pose I think is meant to be sultry, but only works because of how adorable she is.

"Is that a new sexy cardigan?" I ask, thinking back on high school Cat, and how she waxed poetic about another chunky piece of clothing I mainly found hot because it smelled like her. And, sometimes, she'd wear it when she would climb in my window at night.

"Exactly!" Then, it's Cat's turn to look her fill. She drags her gaze from the top of my head, over my neatly trimmed beard, down my chest that contains a heart beating heavy for her and settles south of my belt buckle.

Lust twines inside me, needy vines wanting to wrap around her.

My happiness threatens to make that a reality, and I tuck my tingling hands in my pockets, so I don't double the size of the pothos plant she has on a nearby shelf.

"How's it going?" I ask in a gruff voice, hoping she'll talk about her day and give me something to think about other than what her cactus dress covers.

"Actually," Cat leans a shoulder against the wall, as if standing has suddenly become hard, "stressful."

That cools my libido and replaces my happiness with worry as I trace the pucker between her brows. Stepping toward the Pyro, I hold her gaze with mine. "What happened? Can I help?"

She shrugs, reaching out to fiddle with a button on my shirt. My cock leaps at the familiar gesture. Cat used to do the same thing when we were younger, before slowly unbuttoning whatever I was wearing. Her fingers are always curious.

"I had a power training session with Quinn. I've had a few with my sisters since I found out I'm not as in control of my magic as I thought I was." She grimaces and lets her hand drop. "I know how that sounds."

"How?"

"Like I'm...immature. Dangerous." Cat fusses with her short bangs. "I mean, how could I not have mastered them by now?"

"Didn't you say Quinn only recently got hers under control?"

Cat twists a short lock of hair, and I want to lace my fingers with her fidgeting digits. "She's lust-induced. Lust and fire, it's a hard combo to deal with."

"And you're anger. I don't know about you, but I don't enjoy getting angry." Moving forward, I let my hands settle on her waist. "You're a kind person, Cat. My guess is, you didn't get enough practice because you didn't like getting pissed off. Am I right?"

"I..." She stares up at me, and I wish I could stay forever in her eyes. "I feel like you see more of me than anyone else."

My heart is hers in that moment. I'm fucking gone for this woman. Before I can think better of it, I'm kissing her. Tasting her hot mouth as my fingers fist in her tempting dress and soft cardigan. She opens for me, eager licks dancing against my tongue until I'm panting.

"Do you want me to help you destress?" I gasp out the question as a selfish idea enters my mind.

"Help how?" She blinks up at me, her brown eyes dazed.

In answer, I kneel so my face, my mouth, hovers near her lower belly. My hands cup the back of her knees, thumbs running over the soft skin before creeping upward. "Let me kiss you here."

"Aspen," she moans out my name, but then, praise the gods, she nods before bracing her shoulders against the wall.

With fingers that shake, I drag my hands up the warm stretch of her thighs until I find a set of cotton panties. When I slip them off, I find they're thin, green silk with lacy edges. I would love to have her sprawled in a bed wearing nothing but this scrap of fabric. For now, though, I'm glad they're gone. Especially when I lift her skirt and find her mound, covered in neatly trimmed red curls.

"Yes," I rasp the word out as my thumbs part the soft, glistening petals of her lips to reveal the warm pink underneath. She smells earthy, like a woman should. Leaning forward, I swipe my tongue along her folds.

Cat's hips jerk forward, seeking my mouth out. Her hands fall to my shoulders then delve into my hair, nails scraping along my skull. Encouraging me forward.

This is what I've been craving for what feels like years. To be here, between her legs again. We didn't start hooking up immediately when we got together in high school, but once we did, I never wanted to stop. Later, when I was an adult and in a long-term relationship, I found my sexual appetite fluctuated day to day. I figured the ravenous longing I felt for my Pyro was something to do with puberty. I was just an overly horny kid who always wanted someone to touch his dick.

But now I'm here again, and the craving for her arises full force, matching my magic. My powers aren't lust-induced like Quinn's. They come with my happiness. And how could I be anything else with Cat's taste on my tongue? Earth magic builds a pressure in my hands, begging to be set free. My growing ability doesn't have the same detrimental effect as fire, so I let some spread out from my fingertips, just for the boost in pleasure.

Then, I refocus on the small nub of nerves I find under her hood. The seed sits perfectly on my tongue, and every time I lick and suck, Cat makes such beautiful, needy noises. When I feel her body quivering, I grasp one of her legs and guide it over my shoulder. I'm tempted to collapse back on the ground, dragging her with me so she can fully sit on my face and ride me like a bike. But the hallway is too narrow, and I don't want space coming between me and her vulva for even the briefest second.

"I think—I think—" Cat starts kneading my scalp, her fingers involuntarily curling in a pre-orgasm muscle spasm I remember. Gods, the first time I got her to come—when I figured out just the right way to tease and touch her—you would've thought I won a million-dollar jackpot. One more reason I wanted to fuck her twenty-four seven. I learned how to make her come, how to get her to pant my name as if she needed to breathe in the sound to survive.

That's what my younger self wanted to hear every second of every day.

"Aspen...Aspen..."

My eyes close in ecstasy as the present moment matches the memory. I slip my finger into her pussy just in time to catch the pulses of her inner muscles as an orgasm claims her. The sensation of her pleasure, mixed with the magic that lives in the joints of my fingers, has me feeling like the most powerful elemental on the planet as I kneel in front of my fire goddess. My erection presses against the front of my pants, begging for attention, for relief, but I couldn't care less about myself in this moment. Everything is for her.

But as the lust onslaught clears from my mind, the full situation clarifies around me. Before even taking her out once, I'm already bringing sex into this.

Is this all Cat is going to think I want from her?

"Fuck," I mutter, standing slowly. "I shouldn't have done that."

At a small gasp, I meet Cat's gaze, and her wide, wounded eyes have me cursing myself.

"I just mean, I don't want this to be a hookup." My mind tries to reorder itself, which is hard to do when her chest is still flushed and heaving, and I can feel her slickness on my fingers. "It's supposed to go relationship talk, *then* give you all the orgasms."

The worry that creased her brow smooths away, and Cat lets out a hesitant, adorable chuckle. "Oh. Okay. Well, I didn't mind this order so much."

Pride glows in me. "But we're still on for our date, right?"

"Right." She straightens her skirt and resettles her cardigan, then glances around the space before narrowing her eyes in suspicion. "Did you...?" Fast as a snake, she lunges forward and plunges her hand into my back pocket, recovering her underwear from where I tucked them away. Cat lets the delicate material dangle from her finger as she gives me a mock glare. "Are you still trying to pull this BS? No stealing my panties." With her free hand, she jabs a finger into my chest, then carefully steps back into the undergarments and shimmies them into place. I have to bite back a groan.

"I wasn't stealing them." I try to defend myself, but it's no use. In high school, half the time we hooked up I'd nab her underwear when she wasn't looking and keep it like a perverted souvenir. She knew though, and often caught me in the act, giving me hell right before kissing me with a ravenous passion that told me she wasn't too mad. Sometimes, she'd sneak into my bedroom while I was at football practice and steal them all back.

Now, she slips her hand into mine, tugging me toward the door. "Don't lie. I know you." Then she stumbles to a stop, and I follow her gaze.

Cat stares at her pothos plant. The things are low-maintenance and have large, glossy leaves that add a soothing spot of green to the entryway.

Only this plant isn't a small accent piece anymore.

Not since it grew by ten. Vines snake over the sides of the pot, dripping onto the floor, ready to trip whoever next enters the house.

Cat turns to me, eyes wide.

Okay, so maybe I let off a *little* more power than I should have. With a sheepish smile, I shrug. "Guess you're not the only one who needs a refresher on control."

A grin splits her face, and her joyful laugh ricochets around my chest. This moment—us together—is so close to perfect. I could be happy, just like this.

But there's a shadow around us. One that's always lingered on the edge of our relationship, and it takes the shape of a man.

Chapter Twenty-One

RAFAEL

The nature documentary playing on my TV could be about monsters from the hell dimension planning to invade Earth for all I've grasped of it. Colors and words flick across the screen, but my thoughts drift elsewhere, just like they have all afternoon. Ever since that trip to the ice cream shop.

For a handful of seconds, I had hope. Cat laughed—a genuine spark of amusement, and not at my expense. But her parting words put me in my place.

"Looks like I don't need you anymore."

Cat might as well have taken an ice cream scooper to my heart with that comment. Afterwards, I couldn't be around anyone. I dropped Marisol off at her house and told her to let the others know I wasn't up for hanging out. Instead, I've been slowly sinking further into my couch, letting the cushions consume me in my misery.

I waited too long. She won't ever forgive me.

A knock on the door makes me jump in my seat, then grimace. I bet Sammy decided to come over and pester me until I'm in a good mood again. Maybe he could do it, but right now I kind of want to be miserable. I feel like I deserve it.

Still, with all my lights on, there's no hiding from him.

I'll only open the door an inch, not enough room for him to shove in, then tell him I'm headed for bed. He'll have to leave. The words are already forming, half out my mouth, when I open the door and find a completely different unwelcome guest.

"Aspen?"

The Petal Pusher stands on my front stoop, looking fine as hell in a button up shirt and black pants that fit his thighs too well.

"Hey. I brought booze." He holds up a six pack as proof. "Can we talk?"

Talk to Aspen? Is there anything in this world I dread more?

"Please, Rafe." His voice rasps over the nickname. "I want a truce."

I don't even know what that means, but something has my muscles moving to push the door wide enough for him to slip his broad shoulders inside. The guy makes me feel small next to him. Like he could easily manhandle me if he wanted to.

No need to dwell on how my pulse quickens at the thought.

Heading into my living room, I gesture for him to take a seat and mute the TV. He settles his large form on the end of the couch, the exact spot I'd occupied a moment ago, then cracks open a beer and passes the can to me.

Only, I realize a moment later it's a cider. When I sip, fruitiness mixes with alcohol and carbonation on my tongue, and I stifle a sigh of contentment.

I am not content. Not with him *here.*

"What kind of truce do you want?" I take a larger pull of my drink.

"One where you don't pretend like that party never happened."

I choke on the cider, some of the bubbles going up my nose. After clearing my throat and sinuses with a cough, I glare at him and blink away watery eyes. "What party?"

Aspen shakes his head, annoyance in the pinch of his lips. Lips I know all too well. Or did at one time, anyway.

"The one at Sammy's house. We made out. We dry humped until we came in our pants. You freaked out. *That* party." He leans forward, his hands hanging loose between his knees. "But you're out now, right? Bi? So, I don't get it. Why are you still pissed at me?"

Of course, he doesn't understand. Aspen is the honest, stand-up one. Not like me, hiding away my selfish desires.

"Fine. It happened. I admit it. We good?"

"Better. But not good. Not yet." The Petal Pusher watches me, his thick brows dipping. "Are you still attracted to me?"

I burst up from my seat before I realize what I'm doing. "Why the hell are you asking that when you're back in town for *her?*" My voice breaks on the last word, and we both know who I'm referring to. Jealousy stirs my magic, the subtle force rocking me back and forth on my heels. The can in my hand rattles as the liquid inside moves with my rhythm.

Stop it. You have no right to be jealous.

Aspen stands slowly, approaching me cautiously. "We're not talking about Cat right now. We're talking about you and me."

My heart thunders in my chest at his words. *Him and me? Like the two of us could be an* us?

Fuck my body, and my heart, and my mind for how much I remember wanting that. How easily I could fall for Aspen Baumann again.

So many nights, I spent mapping his face in my mind while I gripped myself. Imagined that it was his strong hand stroking me until I was coming hard, my hips thrusting into empty air when I wanted his massive body there.

But his body wasn't the only one I wanted. Whenever I built a fictional relationship in my mind starring Aspen, there was a gap. An empty hole I wanted filled with another.

Because I'm greedy. Unsatisfied with one amazing person.

I'm fucked up.

As I try to swim through the whirlpool of thoughts, Aspen comes to stand in front of me. Wide, rough palms cup my face, thumbs mapping my cheekbones. Minty breath filling the air between us until I'm sure all that's in my lungs is him.

"You and me," he murmurs. "I want you. Do you want me?"

"Yes," I groan out the reluctant confession.

Aspen takes me. His lips on mine, firmer than I remember. All of him is more than he was that night when we were just teenagers, fooling around. My cock rises, twitching with each flick of his tongue against the seam of my mouth. I open for him, drag him inside as I grasp his waist and press his hips to mine. Next thing I know, the wall is at my back, and Aspen is grinding into me as he plunders my mouth.

The demand for his body roars through me, stronger than any romantic connection I've tried to establish over the years. Aspen is what I've wanted, all this time. The taste I had, that no one could match.

Maybe one could, but I never got to sample her.

As if hearing the stray thought about another, Aspen pulls back enough to whisper one, world-shattering sentence.

"I want both of you."

"Huh?" The unintelligible question sneaks out of me as I try to clear my head enough to understand the implication of his words.

He leans back farther, eyes boring into mine. "Can you taste her on me?"

"What?"

Aspen swipes a thick thumb over his lower lip, drawing my eyes to where I just was. "Cat."

His words take a moment to register, but when they do, I jerk back, my shoulders slamming into the wall.

"Are you fucking kidding me?" Realizing I have nowhere to go, I shove him away.

Aspen steps back, giving me some, but nowhere near enough, space.

"No." His face is that stoic mask he's so good at, while I'm over here reeling and showing every wild thought on my face.

"You were with her? Tonight?" Pain lances through me at the thought. Them together. Without me. He *tasted* her. The pipes in the walls of my house groan, the water straining. "Why the fuck are you doing this?" I close my eyes and focus on the magic, plugging up the leaks in my control. If I flood this house, I will *not* get my security deposit back.

"I'm being honest with you. I'm laying out exactly what I want." Aspen steps in close again, holding my eyes with his so I can't escape. "Imagine it. The three of us. Together."

I have. Too many times.

"You're out of your mind." Tearing my stare from his, I pace away, my chest heaving, my dick still aching, my powers pushing at the flimsy dams I've constructed. "You can't say shit like that."

"Sure I can." Aspen leans a shoulder against the wall, crossing his arms. "Just admit it. You're attracted to me *and* Cat. You want us both."

"But I can't have both!" I shout. "And even if we lived in some perfect world where I could, Cat *hates* me." I whirl on him, no longer jealous. Just pissed. "And you're trying to convince her to, what? Take part in a threesome?"

Aspen frowns, the expression pronounced with his glorious beard. "This isn't a hook-up for me."

A harsh laugh expels from my chest. "Could've fooled me." Gods, I wish I had more clothes on. Like a parka. That way he wouldn't be able to see how his kiss and words are affecting me. "You show up here and start making out with me, when we've barely talked to each other for years."

Aspen digs his fingers into his hair, finally showing agitation. Revealing that he's not the cool, calm, collected one in this shit show of an exchange.

"And whose decision was that?" he growls.

Mine. The word blares through my mind, but I clamp my teeth down on it. So what if I kept my distance because I couldn't stand the sight of him and Cat together? He doesn't have the right to know that.

"You cut us both out," Aspen says. "But it's been years. High school drama. I want to move forward." Now there's a note in the Petal Pusher's voice. Hunger and hope. "The three of us could be something, if we tried."

Am I dreaming? Is this a hallucination? It must be. There is no way that Aspen Baumann is standing in my living room, trying to convince me to date both him and Cat. I must have fallen asleep with porn on, or something.

Still, I keep arguing with dream Aspen.

"That's not how these things work."

"They can." He spreads his arms wide, putting his drool-worthy mountain man body on display. "I've done it before."

Chapter Twenty-Two

ASPEN

From the slack look on Rafael's face, he was not expecting that. He wasn't expecting any of this.

Neither was I, really.

The fantasy of having a polyamorous relationship with Cat and Rafael is not new for me. Plenty of times I've fantasized about how that would play out. The three of us tangled up in bed all night, then eating breakfast together. Us watching a movie piled on top of each other on the couch. Cat and Rafael coming to me with their little life problems and me bringing mine to them. Houses. Pets. Rings. Sharing our lives together.

A future with a passionate Pyro and a charismatic Squid.

But I have no true game plan for the approach. All I've had is a hope that planted when I found out Rafael came out as bi. Of course, not all bisexuals are open to polyamorous relationships, but some spectrum of that sexuality is kind of a requirement when you want someone to fall for both a man and a woman.

That still leaves the problem that the three of us haven't been in the same room since high school. Groundwork would do us all good. Strengthen the foundation. Clear away any lingering bad feelings. Then,

I can work on bringing the two of them back together like they should be.

Anyone who saw Cat and Rafael together would know that the gods had a hand in their relationship. They were destined. I know this in my bones.

Maybe it's selfish, or misguided, that I want so badly to be a part of that partnership along with them.

So I came over here to start mending fences. I never intended to kiss him.

This looks shitty from the outside. Going on a date with one person earlier in the night, then making out with someone else just an hour later.

Please don't let this explode in my face. I send the prayer to the gods. All of them.

"What do you mean you've done it before? Like you, Cat, and—"

"No," I wave that idea away. It seems wrong somehow, Cat and I being with a third person that wasn't Rafael. "I dated a couple before. It worked for a while."

"A while." The Squid wrinkles his nose and shifts farther away from me as if I smell, which I know for a fact I don't because I showered and put on cologne before my date. "But it imploded, right? Because that's not how relationships work."

I want to grab him by the shoulders and shake him. This is what he wants. I know it is. But for some reason, he's balking.

"They weren't the right people for me. You and Cat are. And if you'd get your head out of your ass and apologize to her, we might have a chance at this."

"I have apologized!" Rafael stalks around his living space in agitated yet graceful movements, the guy's limbs always flowing like water. "She hates me. She won't even eat ice cream near me anymore."

I'm trying to pay attention to his pissy argument, but I can't help how my attention drifts lower, to the bulge in his gray sweatpants. Thank the gods for those.

"Hey." Fingers snap in my face. "My eyes are up here." Following his gesture, I find his slate gaze burning into mine, and not all that heat is frustration.

I need to leave. If I give into my attraction again, there's no telling how far the two of us will go tonight. And I couldn't do that to Cat. There's a thin line between encouraging behind the scenes and outright lying to her.

Abandoning my drink, I head toward the door, pausing at the threshold.

"Think about it, Rafe. Really think about it. The three of us."

"She *hates* me." There's a small tilt up at the end of the sentence, almost turning it into a question. I bet he'd be overjoyed if I could present concrete evidence that she doesn't. But all I have is a gut feeling. A sensation that might be born from my own wants or might be an urging from a higher power.

And I'm cradling a small hint of triumph that he's not arguing against us. Him and me. That's one third of the equation already solved.

"Then fix it," I tell him.

Please.

Chapter Twenty-Three

RAFAEL

"This is exactly what you need." Sammy grins at me as he makes declarations about my life based on no factual evidence.

"I'm kind of over the club scene, man. Everything is loud, and sweaty, and overpriced." I shrug, knowing I sound like an old man. "I'm just not in the mood."

"I swear, it'll be worth it."

I'd like to trust my friend, but I don't know what his motivations are. Sometimes, Sammy wants to make everyone around him happy. Sometimes, Sammy just wants to make Sammy happy. At least the music leaking out from the cracks between the doors sounds decent and waiting in a line after dark in Phoenix isn't entirely uncomfortable. The air has a touch of coolness without the sun burning an angry hole in the top of my head.

As I casually scan the other club-goers waiting for entry, I don't notice anything off at first. Belatedly, a connection registers, and I do a second scan.

I was right. Most of the people in the line are men.

Is Sammy taking me to a gay bar?

My best friend knows I'm into any gender, but he usually opts for a place that serves him too. I try to suppress a sigh. Men or women, I'm not looking to flirt or hook up with anyone. Not when I still have Cat's dismissive words and the hot press of Aspen's mouth on my mind.

Gods, that kiss. In high school, we were just fumbling virgins. But when he took my mouth this time, every swipe of his tongue promised expert-level pleasure. And I was ready to melt for him.

"I want you both."

And I thought *I* was the only greedy one. Aspen made it sound so easy.

You want two people? Sure! Go ahead and fill your plate.

Exactly something my dad would do.

Hating the mixture of thoughts about Aspen and my dad, I shake my head and follow my friend as we approach the bouncer.

"Hey, Sammy." The massive wall of muscle greets my friend with a familiar tone, which throws me off.

Since when did Sammy become a regular at a gay bar?

"Hey, Trevor. Brought some new blood tonight." My friend claps a hand on my shoulder and the doorman gives me a nod that lacks the enthusiasm of his previous greeting.

"ID, and twenty-dollar cover." Sammy pays the man for both of us, and I hand my card over. When the bouncer gives it back, he holds my eyes. "No touching without an invite. We're a one-strike place, so don't fuck it up. Tip your waitress."

"Don't worry. I'll keep him in line. And he'll tip our waitress *generously*." Sammy pushes me forward as I try to understand the instructions. Not that it's a bad thing to remind club goers to be decent human beings, but it's unusual.

When we move past the coat check, I'm pleasantly surprised. There's not a giant mass of writhing dancers, and even though the music is loud, it's at a volume where I can still hold a conversation. Plus, there seems to be plenty of seating...

Wait a minute.

That's when I notice why there's so much seating. Men fill the plush chairs and low tables, that all tend to face the center of the room where a stage holds court. And on that stage is a gorgeous woman spinning around a pole. In addition to her, there are women dispersed throughout, chatting with customers, grinding on their laps, and serving them drinks.

"Sammy!" I grab my friend's arm before he can move any further into the building. "This is a strip club!"

He affects a shocked face, staring around with wide eyes and a gaping mouth before bringing his attention back to me. "It is? How can you tell?"

"Fuck you," I mutter lower than the volume of the music, but no doubt he reads it on my lips and my entire face. "I'm leaving."

That gets his slightly less goofy face to appear. "Come on, Rafe. It's a great place. Seriously. The dancers work the stage like Vegas show pros, the drinks are the best in town, and I've spent enough for entry into the VIP section." He waves toward a roped-off area with leather chairs and low lighting that somehow looks comfortable as opposed to seedy or gaudy. In fact, the whole strip club is several notches above the few I've stumbled into with Sammy in the past.

"I'm concerned about your money spending habits."

He either hears or sees my resolve weakening, because the next moment my friend has his arm around my shoulders and is leading me across the room. "These are hard-working women, and I appreciate the view of a scantily clad body. Everybody wins. I'm supporting the economy."

Damn him for making me smile. The ridiculous Squid always seems to manage that, no matter how pissed off I am at him.

Maybe I should take notes from Sammy to get Cat to forgive me.

Quickly, I push thoughts of the Pyro away. They don't belong in a place like this.

Besides, his charm never worked on Cat, either.

"Hey, Sammy," a honey voice purrs, and I find a tall woman with long braids and midnight skin draped in light green silk and crystals has approached my friend's other side.

"Jade. My gorgeous darling! How are you tonight?" Despite talking to the entrancing stripper, Sammy keeps his hold on me. Suddenly, I'm worried the guy is going to try to hire her to entertain the both of us. The prospect is too like what Aspen was proposing for me to have any interest in it. And though Sammy is an objectively good-looking guy, I've never seen him that way. Then, there's the fact that Jade is working, which is fine, but I'd rather have my partner's true interest.

"It's a busy night, so I'm good. Pearl isn't here though, so I thought I might keep you and your friend company instead." She trails a sharp acrylic nail down Sammy's chest.

"That is an offer I hate to refuse, but I'm afraid we're just here for some drinks and voyeurism. However..." Sammy presses his palm to hers, passing a bill over. "I would be grateful if you could ask Red to swing by our table with a bottle of—"

"Not tequila." I cut him off before he can destroy my liver again.

Sammy smirks. "Fine. Have Red get us two top-shelf whiskeys. We'll be in the VIP section."

She glances at the bill, which I see is a hundred, flashes Sammy a broad smile, and saunters away.

"Generous, aren't you?"

My friend shrugs with a distracted smile, and keeps us moving. His family is flush with cash. What's odd is that Sammy's personality would lead many to believe he'd simply live off his trust fund. Instead, he got a degree in architecture and is making a decent living on his own merit. He even volunteers time into designing and constructing affordable housing. The guy is hard to fit into a single box.

"Who's Pearl?" I ask as we settle into the plush chairs of the VIP section.

Sammy's smile goes dreamy. "A goddess among men."

Well, that sounds like my buddy thinks he's in love with a stripper.

"And does this goddess make a lot of money off you?" He's a smart guy in a lot of areas, but I could also see him getting swindled out of a fortune because a canny woman notes him as an easy mark.

Sammy's smile melts into a frown, an uncommon expression on his face. "I wish."

"What is that supposed to mean?"

He waves off my question. "Never mind Pearl. What do you think of the place?"

With a sigh, I let the subject drop and shrug. "Nice for a strip club. Nice for a club in general. Still not really my scene."

He nods as if he doesn't mind my lack of enthusiasm. "I've been trying to convince the owner to let me invest, but she won't hear it. Says she can't trust me. More like she knows this is a cash cow and doesn't want to share a bit of it with anyone." Sammy pinches his lower lip, eyes unfocused as he ponders his business roadblock. Meanwhile, I sink lower into my chair and wonder if I can take a nap.

I couldn't get any sleep last night after Aspen left. My whole body was horned up, my mind was fucked up, and I couldn't stop following his instructions. Imagining Cat, him, and me together, living our lives as if three was a normal relationship number.

Three of us eating dinner in a nice restaurant. Would we get a table or a booth? A booth, but then who would sit where? Maybe Cat next to me, and I could tuck her into my side and inch my hand up her skirt where the waitstaff couldn't see. Then Aspen would watch, eyes hot knowing what I was doing to our Pyro just a few feet from him. Maybe he'd stretch out a long leg, tease the toe of his shoe under my pant leg. A gentle, yet sensual caress.

Three of us flying on an international trip together. Who would sit in the middle seat? Logic might say Cat because she's the smallest of us. But Cat would want to gaze out the window, so I'd take the middle, and I'd book us the emergency exit row so Aspen could stretch out his long legs. I'm almost happy none of us make enough money for first class seats, because those are usually two-by-two.

Maybe it could work, a voice in the back of my brain would agree with me. Then, another piece of input would barge into the discussion.

"You can't expect a man to be with only one woman."

The voice of my father had effectively curdled my hope, until I wanted to be sick.

Now, I'm functioning on maybe three hours of sleep. I had a full day at work with two field trips of screaming children that all wanted to jump into the fish tanks. One almost figured out a way to. My bet is, I won't make it through half my glass of whiskey before I start nodding off.

I shouldn't have agreed to come out tonight. Matter of fact, I didn't. Sammy just showed up at my place, picked out an outfit for me—which felt awfully domestic for a man who's not my partner—and herded me into his car.

"Here we go," Sammy murmurs, and I almost miss it over the thump of a new song, but there's an edge of anticipation that catches my attention. A new dancer, maybe? Someone my friend brought me here to see?

Then, I notice the cocky smirk on the guy's face and realize he's not looking toward the main stage, but instead over my shoulder.

"I told you to stop asking for me as your server." The familiar voice drags along my nerve endings and practically squeezes my cock to life. "If you do it again, I'm going to melt your belt buckle. You'll never be able to get your pants off."

My body sits frozen, as if August showed up and decided to demo his ice elemental abilities for the room.

"Oh, Red." My friend—if I still want to call him that—grins like the kid who almost made it into the stingray tank this morning. "You know how I love a challenge."

"I'll also tell Pearl I saw you kick a dog." A teasing of heat presses against my side as a body moves into my peripheral vision. "She *loves* dogs."

Sammy's playful smile falls into a truly unhappy pout. "Don't do that."

"You've been warned." Pale hands set two glasses of amber liquid on the table between us. Then, the waitress turns, and I meet a set of familiar brown eyes.

"Cat?"

Chapter Twenty-Four

RAFAEL

"Did you slip me LSD?" I hurl the question at Sammy, mentally cycling through all the minutes between him sweeping me up at my house to now, when I'm staring at the woman I'm still in love with, wearing shorts that show off her tight ass and what amounts to a chainmail bra.

I must be on drugs. That's the only explanation.

"Of course not!" Sammy scoffs. "I don't secretly drug my friends. I kindly offer them mind-altering substances, like a decent person." He relaxes back in his seat, sipping his whiskey, flicking his gleeful expression between me and the being of utter erotic torment.

Cat is dressed like some BDSM fantasy I never allowed myself to have but will probably engrave in my mind so I can revisit the memory every day until the gods smite me from this earthly dimension.

"You look..." There are no words in this language, so I make up a few that sound like a man drowning.

Cat gives me a look that's part anger, part exasperation, and if I'm not mistaken, part concern. Well, I do sound—and feel—as if I'm dying. Then her dagger eyes spear Sammy. "It's official. I'm telling Pearl you *murder* dogs."

The Squid across from me sputters on his expensive drink as the redhead stalks away. As if magnetized, I levitate out of my chair to jog after her.

"Cat!" My voice floats over the music. I slam to a stop when my chest hits a hard, flat surface. Belatedly, I realize Cat whirled at the sound of her name and whacked my chest with her serving tray.

"Shut up," she hisses. In her eyes, I spy the flickering of angry heat, and hate myself for once again sparking the fuse. "Do not use my real name here. Even Sammy is smart enough to know that."

"Sorry." Scrambling for the right moniker, I remember the few comments he made. "Red. You go by Red."

Jaw tight, she nods then turns to leave me again.

"Fix it," I hear, as if Aspen is standing next to me. The command rings through my bones, and without thought I reach out to clasp her hand.

My entire body vibrates at the contact. Immediately, my fingers lace through hers, just like they used to. The sensation of her warm palm against mine mixes familiar memories and the indicators of years past. Her fingers are a touch longer, with a few more calluses.

But the heat, pulsing just under the surface, is the same.

"Please," my voice—raw from wanting and lonely misery because she's been gone from my life for so long—begs her to stay still. Stay with me.

A gasp catches in Cat's throat, and I watch her lips part with surprise. And she stays.

"I was an asshole. I *am* an asshole. But I need you. I've always needed you." The honest words spill out of me, riding the heavy beat of the music.

Cat's red brows dip, and I watch the sparks continue to lighten her irises. Her hand becomes almost too hot to hold. I don't let go.

"You don't need me," she declares, but I think I pick up the subtlest hint of question.

Could this be it? Have I finally found the smallest crack in her wall of anger?

The pure hope brings a smile to my face.

Mistake. Something about my expression hurts my standing, rather than helps. Her glare turns fierce, a sharp blade of flame. However, she doesn't super-heat the air around us, and as she steps in close to me and I rock back on my heels, I note that the soles of my shoes aren't melted to the club's floor.

"You don't." This time she sounds certain.

Gods, I want to kiss her. Sink into the closest chair and pull her with me until she's straddling my lap.

"Don't tell me what I need," I say, a hint of my own temper in my voice. She keeps pulling herself away from me, and I'm done with it. My other hand stretches out, ready to clasp her bare midriff. More of my skin against hers. More of her heat scorching my nerve endings.

"Ca—Red?" The gruff voice calls her attention over my shoulder, and I could howl at the distraction. "You good?"

"Aspen," she says, then steps hurriedly back, untangling her fingers from mine.

When the name and tone finally register in my mind, I stay still, as if a Stoner encased me in granite. The Petal Pusher comes into view, blinking in surprise when his eyes meet mine.

"Rafe?" Aspen moves his attention from me to Cat, then back. "What's going on?"

"Just serving a customer," Cat grits out.

My eyes drag over both of them, trying to make sense of this picture. Then, I notice the indecently tight black T-shirt Aspen wears has a word printed on the lapel.

Security.

"You work here?" I choke out the question. "Both of you?"

His heavy brows drop, and he nods. Then, in the most casually instinctual move, Aspen sets his large hand in the exact spot at Cat's waist I'd been aiming for as he arrived. The Pyro raises her gaze to his, and they share a look.

I don't know what passes between them in that moment. All I know is the message is theirs. Not mine. It's not the three of us. It's just two. The two of them and never me.

We might as well be in high school again, with me skulking in the stairwell as they dry hump in the shadows.

Jealousy forces a thick, toxic wave of magic in a rocking current that sets me tipping forward, then back on my feet.

"Shit," I hiss, trying to stem the flow, but I haven't dealt with this level of emotion in a long time, and the power takes me by surprise.

There's a tingling noise, a series of loud pops, then the rushing pound of a sudden rainstorm. Shouts of surprise go up as the club experiences a torrential downpour.

All the sprinklers coming to life at once.

Chapter Twenty-Five

CAT

As water soaks the scant amount of fabric I have on, I try to figure out where I went wrong. I was mad, there's no doubt of that. Sammy ambushed me, bringing Rafael to my strip club job where he'll probably judge me.

But I thought I kept the heat inside.

Am I so oblivious to my powers that I heat up enough to set off the sprinkler system without knowing?

"I thought I had it controlled this time." My defeat must show on my face as I glance up at Aspen because he cups my cheeks in a comforting embrace. But his attention drifts to the third in our little group, and I can't help following his direction.

Rafael stands looking like a dejected puppy that fell into a puddle. Water streams over his sun-kissed skin and drips insistently from the ends of his hair, all the curls plastered to his face. The Squid's eyes flit to mine, then land on the floor.

"It's my fault," he announces, as patrons streaming by us toward the club exit jostle against him. Meanwhile, Aspen's sturdy body protects me as we stand, an island among the river of fleeing customers.

Rafael set off the sprinklers?

It was a water elemental error. Not fire. Not *me*.

"It wasn't me!" Jubilation buzzes through my limbs, and despite my workplace descending into chaos, I can't help a dancing shimmy of celebration. "I'm not the fuck-up this time!"

When I grin up at Aspen, he returns the expression, reaching out to cup my cheek again and swiping at the droplets coating my face, as if that'll be enough to stop the continuous downpour soaking me. But I'm wet through and through at this point, and I don't care, because it's *not my fault*.

It's Rafael's.

Through the joy that's snuffed out my anger and completely removed any risk, a fact niggles in the back of my brain. A discovery young Cat and Rafael made one day when my dad drove us to a park to play soccer, using his fire magic to keep the heat of the day bearable. We ran and kicked that beat-up ball until the sun sank low in the sky. At one point, after I made a very impressive headbutt goal, my dad had scooped me up, swung me around, and proclaimed how proud he was until I was giggling so hard I couldn't breathe.

Then, our water bottles exploded.

My dad's bushy brows had dipped as he studied a red-faced Rafael. He told me to practice dribbling while he took my friend to the side for a quick chat. I didn't mind. Rafael's dad never took us to the park, or to get ice cream, or to see a movie in the theaters. His dad wasn't around much at all, so I was happy to share mine because back then, I thought of Rafael more like a brother than anything.

But when my friend came back, he looked an awful lot like he'd been crying. When I asked my dad about it later, he said Rafael just got a little jealous of how much fun we were having, and it turns out that's what fuels his power.

After that, I always made sure my best friend was included in all my fun.

When I got older, I realized it wasn't so much about the fun, but *who* I was having it with.

Sometimes, even though he tried real hard not to—Rafael got jealous of me and my dad. When that happened, juice in a nearby cup might spill over the edge, or a puddle would turn into a whirlpool, or water might spray from the faucet.

He'd apologize, and I would hug him and tell him he was my best friend and would silently wish I could make his father a better man.

Until this moment, I'd forgotten about those times. Or, more like, I'd actively chosen not to remember them.

Rafael set off the sprinklers because he was jealous.

I stare at the grown man in front of me, who looks as ashamed as that little boy used to.

"Why are you jealous, Rafael?" Gods, it feels like centuries since I've spoken his name out loud. I fully expect to garble the letters. Instead, they flow out of me as if I've spoken them every day of my life.

The sprinklers shut off. It's unclear if Rafael halted the deluge, or if someone reset the system when it became obvious there was no fire.

"I'm sorry." He apologizes instead of answering, before stepping into the mass exodus, following the flow of people out of the building.

And I stare after his retreating form, not angry in the slightest.

Chapter Twenty-Six

CAT

When a strip club has multiple elementals on staff, it doesn't take long to mitigate water damage. One of the dancers is a Squid, and she focuses on directing the largest puddles toward drains. Yasmin, Mia, Jade, and I partner up on drying. The Airheads draw out a steady stream of air, while us Pyros fill the gust with heat. A giant blow-dryer.

Aspen's Petal Pusher nature doesn't have too much to contribute, but he finds some dry towels and goes to work wiping down the hard surfaces.

"That's as good as we can expect," Yasmin announces after two hours of damage control. "I'll cover what you normally would have made in tips." The Airhead is a good boss like that. Firm, but always looks out for us.

As I slip the strap of my bag over my shoulder, I try not to wince as it weighs down on my tender skin. This is always how I feel when I use my magic without the fuel of emotion. Like I have a sunburn, or a bruise, and my skin just needs time to recover.

Aspen must see something on my face because he immediately snags my bag, carrying it for me as we walk to my car.

Despite the aftereffects of my power, I'm riding high on the knowledge that I didn't let my heat get away from me earlier when I got pissed. Tonight was a big step—I'm finally gaining control, and I want to celebrate.

My gaze tracks over to Aspen, with his broad shoulders and a mouth whose talent I haven't been able to forget. I'm brainstorming how to entice him over to my house for some wild sex when he asks a gruff question that shoves away all my lighthearted excitement.

"Why do you hate Rafael?"

I flinch at the word *hate*.

Do I hate Rafael?

At one point, I thought I did, but now I'm not so sure. Still, I'm not ready to admit a possible change of heart out loud.

"You know why." Everyone who went to our school knew, whether or not they were at the party. Gossip spreads fast.

And for me, the event sticks around. A cast-in-iron memory that always weighs down the back of my skull.

Just over a month into my freshman year of high school, I could tell something was wrong between Rafael and me. He was distant and often busy with his older friends. I tried not to resent the changes and instead brainstormed how I could change too. Rafael was obviously growing up, and I wanted to grow with him, instead of forcing him back into our childish version of friendship.

Then, Quinn told me about the party happening at Sammy's house one weekend. She, a classmate their age, was invited, but she wasn't going. My sister worried about any situation with cute boys where her guard might fall. She didn't want to burn a house down just because her crush flirted with her. But since Rafael was going to be there, she figured it would be okay if I went.

Harley was in town for the weekend, home from college and keeping an eye on us while our parents were away for their anniversary. My sisters helped me pick out a cute outfit that I thought made me look a few years older. They curled my long hair and lectured me about not drinking anything unless I saw where it was poured and by who.

"Better yet, pour everything yourself," Harley had said. "Don't trust anyone at a party."

I can trust Rafael. I'd kept the thought to myself, even as I was sure it was true.

How naive I'd been.

That night, getting ready, for the first time I didn't feel so much like the baby of the family.

Quinn drove me over and gave me her cell phone to call when I wanted to leave. Mom and Dad were planning on buying me one for my fifteenth birthday the next month, and I couldn't wait to have my own. I promised to cherish Quinn's, and my sister laughed and poked my arm before staring longingly at the mansion Sammy's parents owned. Even in the car, we could hear thumping music and see colored lights flashing in the windows.

The party was loud and energizing. As I walked into the house, I pushed away my initial urge to wrap my arms around myself, to become smaller than I already was. Instead, I let my body sway with the music and wore a smile. Luckily, I was ahead in a number of my classes, so some upperclassmen faces were familiar. A few people even waved, or nodded, or said "Hey, Cat."

I felt like a celebrity—or at least like I belonged.

Naturally, I gravitated toward the kitchen, seeking a cup to occupy my hands to keep them from nervous fidgeting. That's where Sammy found me.

"Little Cat!" He sidled up to me, looking both handsome and annoying, which was his usual look. I fought a grimace at his condescending nickname. Part of tonight was showing Rafael that I could fit there, and that meant accepting his new friends.

"Hey, Sammy." The greeting almost sounded pleasant.

The Squid grinned and threw an arm around my shoulders. "I know a party newbie when I see one. Let me be your guide. You looking for a drink?"

The buddy-buddy situation was a little too much, so I slipped out of his hold but stayed by his side. "Yeah. But I need to pour it myself."

"Smart girl. This house is teeming with unsavory characters." He opened a massive refrigerator to display a whole collection of beer, wine, and sparkling water. "I hope you know my name is at the top of the list."

The Squid almost earned a smile from me at his self-mockery. I took a sparkling water, not quite ready to try alcohol. At least, not until I had someone I trusted completely at my side. For some reason, Sammy seemed interested in occupying that space, at least for a stretch. After filling his red solo cup with mystery juice I'm sure neither of my sisters would approve of, he waved for me to follow him. Sammy really did live in a mansion. And biggest shocker of all, his parents knew he was throwing a party. They were oddly lax in the rules department.

After snorting at Sammy's attempt to moonwalk across the dance floor, we came upon an open door with a stairwell leading down. I peered into the shadowy depths.

"What's going on down there?"

Sammy leaned a casual shoulder against the door frame and wore a mischievous grin as he took a deep gulp from his cup before answering.

"That's where some of the naughtier activities take place." His blonde brows waggled.

"Like...spin the bottle?" I tried not to blush too hard when Sammy barked out a laugh.

"Oh, Little Cat. Sure. Spin the bottle and other things." He stood up and moved to head down the hall that led back toward the kitchen.

The dismissal irked. "Wait!" My call halted his retreat. "I thought you were giving me a tour. So," I waved down the stairs, "give me a tour."

The Squid ran his eyes over me, but the examination didn't come off as suggestive. And even though I had negative one million interest in Sammy romantically, I couldn't help being offended the guy couldn't even show an iota of interest, or at least acknowledge I might have a reason for wanting to know what other things are.

"Sorry, Little Cat." Sammy held up a hand shoulder height. "You need to be this tall to ride those rides."

Anger burned my cheeks and tingled in my blood. "My height doesn't matter."

"I'm talking about your metaphorical height. When it comes to experience." The Squid gave me a cheeky grin. "Are you a virgin?" he asked.

I didn't even have time to sputter at the blunt question when a hard hand clasped my arm and spun me around.

Rafael.

But he didn't look like my Rafael in that moment. He didn't even look like the distant Rafael who'd been fading away from me.

He just looked furious.

"What the hell are you doing here?" His words hit me like a slap, so I could only stare up at him, slack-jawed. "Are you drinking?" He snatched the can out of my hand.

"No," I managed to gasp.

"Doesn't matter." He started towing me toward the front door. "You need to

leave." His grip didn't hurt, exactly, but his hand felt like iron. An unbreakable manacle dragging me out of his life.

Panicked that this was my last chance to grab hold of him, I wrenched free.

"I don't need to leave!" I waved at Sammy, who watched the exchange between my best friend and me with a fascinated smile. "Sammy knows I'm here, and it's his party."

With a quick step, I got around Rafael and beelined for the basement. Determined to show him that I was fine in this group of older people. That if I walked downstairs and saw...sex, or whatever, that it wouldn't phase me. That I was just as mature and worldly as his new friends.

"Cat!" He barked my name, and next thing I knew, he was in front of me, a barricade. "Get the fuck out of this house!"

At his curse, I flinched back.

But he didn't calm down and apologize. Rafael just took another menacing step toward me.

"Go home and watch cartoons or whatever the hell you normally do on a weekend. You're just an immature kid, and no one wants you here." He spread his arms wide, and I flicked my eyes around to realize a good portion of the partygoers were watching him scold me. The handful of people who had greeted me now watched my humiliation at the hands of the boy I loved most in the world.

"Raf—" I choked on his name, scared in that moment. Not of him, never him, but of what this meant. Of what he was doing to our friendship.

"Just stop." He cut me off with a swipe of his hand. "I don't need you following me around like some clingy little sister. Go hang out with people your own age. I'm not your babysitter."

In that moment, there was no fight in me. No anger to melt his shoes to the floor, or scorch the ends of his perfect, honey-brown hair.

There was just me. A little girl playing dress up in her sisters' clothes, losing her best friend because he finally saw her for what she was and what she wasn't.

So, I left.

"I know why you hated him in high school," Aspen's soothing voice brings me out of the memory. "He was an asshole that night. But that was one night, over a decade ago. And before that, you two were everything to each other."

I shake my head, not wanting to remember the time before. The time when Rafael was my world.

Still, the Petal Pusher won't leave it alone. "And he's a different man now. Maybe one you would like, if you gave him a chance. Is there anything he could do to fix things? To help you get over your anger toward him?"

I want to climb into my car and drive away from this conversation. To drive into the night and pretend like all my reactions are completely logical and justified.

But I've made it a habit to be honest with Aspen. And I'm also trying to be honest with myself.

With a groan, I bury my face in my hands, mumbling my confession.

"What was that?" Strong fingers encircle my wrists, uncovering my face with a gentle tug.

Trying not to cringe, I meet his understanding eyes. "I said...I don't think I'm mad at *him* anymore."

"What do you mean?"

"I'm mad at *me*." The self-disgust weighs heavy in my gut. "That night, Rafael brought up all my insecurities and rejected me because of them. I felt like a child. I felt immature. I felt like everyone around me belonged, and I didn't. And the fact that the person I loved mocked me for it hurt even more." Half of me wants Aspen to let me go so I can turn away from his gentle gaze, while the other half wants to sink into him. "Now that he's back, I'm just...I'm bracing myself for him to do it all over again. And I'm mad because he *could*." Rafael is not the object of my anger. He's merely the trigger. "A lot of the time, I feel exactly how I did that night. I'm twenty-six, and I still don't have anything about my life figured out. Nothing to point to and say, 'Look, I'm grown.' And that pisses me off, which sets my powers off, so I try to be sweet, and nice, and calm to get rid of the heat. But then that makes me look and sound even more like a kid, which makes me angry all over again. It's a vicious cycle. And Rafael...he sets me off every time I see him, without trying."

"Cat," Aspen sighs my name, but not as if I exasperate him. There's a deeper note. One of longing, or maybe understanding. Carefully, he lowers our hands to my sides, then he leans in to press a brief, gentle kiss to my mouth. When he pulls away, the lingering scent of mint soothes me. "For what it's worth, I think you're a strong, independent woman. And I'm honored you give me the time of day."

Blood flushes hot in my face.

"And," he presses on, "I want to be honest with you, so we stand on equal footing."

"Okay," I hedge, unsure of where he's leading with this.

"I think you should give Rafael another chance."

My body tightens on instinct, even though I might—maybe—agree with him. "Why does this matter so much to you?"

The earth elemental holds me immobile with the weight of his gaze. "Because I never stopped believing you two would end up together."

My breath stutters, and confusion roars through me. "What...are you...if..." I suck in a deep breath and blink away the threat of tears. "You don't want to be with me?"

A muscle twitches in Aspen's jaw, and he lets his lids shut slowly. "I always thought you and Rafael were destined for each other. That I wouldn't have a chance."

So many thoughts zing through my mind and body. *Rafael and me together? Aspen not having a chance?* "But you do. Right now. I want to be with you." I fist my hands in the cotton that stretches tight over his chest, as if I can keep him close to me forever. "Maybe wanting you is selfish because I have zero of my shit together. But gods, Aspen, I want you so badly." My voice has a desperate edge because this conversation is starting to feel like the prelude to a breakup.

"Shh." He soothes me, wrapping his arms around me. "You have me. Never doubt that. But Cat..." He hesitates, pulling in a deep breath I feel as his chest expands. "I never thought I would have a chance with *either* of you."

One of the things I pride myself on is my intelligence, and yet it still takes me a full minute to comprehend what Aspen is saying.

"You and Rafael?"

His beard brushes the top of my head with his nod. "You know about the relationship I just had." Aspen's heavy palm strokes up and down my back, comforting as my thoughts continue to tangle and reform with this new information. "I don't need to be in a polyamorous relationship. But I'd like the chance to love all the people I love. And I want them to love me." His lips press against the top of my head. "And I want you to love each other because deep down, I think you do. Or, at least, you could."

"But Rafael doesn't...with me...he wouldn't...not like *that*." I struggle to make sense of what Aspen is saying while also pointing out the obvious.

Just because Rafael wants me to forgive him, doesn't mean he wants to *be* with me.

"Cat." Aspen rests his forehead on mine, gazing deep into my eyes. "Rafael has wanted you like that as long as I have. Maybe longer."

No words immediately present themselves, so I stay quiet, reorganizing how I look at Rafael. And Aspen. And the three of us, together.

The comforting circle of the Petal Pusher's arms fall away, and he steps back, heavy hands resting on my shoulders.

"Sorry. This night has been stressful. Didn't mean to pile more on you." He leans in to press a quick kiss to my cheek. "Just think about it."

Aspen moves to leave. But that would ruin the plan that's started forming in my mind. A wild, unconventional plan.

Something that could be beautiful. Or an utter disaster.

With so much already messed up, tonight suddenly seems like the perfect time to test a world-altering plan.

"Aspen, wait." I let my nervous smile show when he glances back. "Follow me in your car. We have somewhere to be."

Chapter Twenty-Seven

RAFAEL

I laid down an hour ago and still haven't figured out how to fall asleep. Doesn't help that my shoulders ache like I've been lifting a hippo over my head. That's what overexerting myself trying to reverse my magical fuck-up did.

Images from the night keep playing on repeat in my head. Cat in her sexy waitress get-up. Aspen in his tight security shirt. The two people I want more than anything in the world touching in a casual, intimate way that speaks to their rekindled relationship.

The water pouring down on them only making them hotter.

"Fuck," I groan, flipping over on my stomach to smash my face into my pillows and hopefully smother myself enough to pass out for the night. Instead, I end up rocking my hips, pressing my half-hard cock into the mattress in a pathetic attempt to assuage my horniness.

I'm suddenly distracted from my self-pity when I hear a thump, and a curse, and a chuckle. Raising my head from my pillow, I glance around my dark bedroom, but see nothing. There's another thunk, and I realize the noise is from a room over.

Ghosts?

Am I getting robbed?

The latter is more likely. With scrambling movements, I hurry out of bed and locate a baseball bat propped up in my closet. With quiet feet, I step into the hallway and carefully nudge the door of my guest bedroom open. Then, I need a moment to understand what I'm seeing.

"Cat?"

At the sound of her name, the redhead tilts her chin over her shoulder, but she doesn't let go of the arm of the Petal Pusher currently halfway through the window.

"Rafael! Help me. Aspen is stuck."

I obey her command, even as I reel in confusion.

"Hey, Rafe." He mumbles with an embarrassed grin. "Think my belt is caught on something."

"What in all the gods..." I mutter while examining his waist and finding that, yes, there's a stray nail head hooked in one of his belt loops. With deft fingers, I slip the denim free and the guy slides forward. Cat squeaks as Aspen essentially bowls her over. Luckily, he's quick enough to snake a hand under her head to keep her from bashing her skull on the hardwood floor. I kneel beside them, wondering if I'm dreaming as they dissolve into laughter.

"We used to be so much better at this," Cat claims through a series of chuckles, wiping tears from the corners of her eyes.

"We're losing our flexibility in our old age." Aspen meets my eyes. "Is this your bedroom?"

Silently, I shake my head and point to the wall beside us.

"Hah!" Cat fist pumps in the air. "I was right. You were wrong." Lightning fast, she presses a kiss to Aspen's chin, then slips out from underneath him.

The affectionate move shocks me enough into speech.

"Uh, what the hell is going on?"

When Cat is free, Aspen settles fully sprawled out on the floor, looking ready to take a nap. The Pyro sits cross-legged beside his prone form, and the humorous expression on her face sobers as she meets me stare for stare.

"What's going on is I'm trying to be more mature." Cat's voice softens as Aspen reaches out to grasp her ankle in a show of support. "I'm letting you talk. This is your chance to explain what happened that night at Sammy's party." Her pale fingers rub against her chest as if there's a pain that needs soothing. "I can't move on from it. I need to know why you flipped out on me. What changed?"

Embarrassment consumes me, and I shy away from revealing the messed-up logic of my teenaged mind.

"Can't I just tell you I'm truly sorry for what I said?" I ask. "I didn't mean any of it. Not a word."

Cat's face falls, and I mutter a curse at the obvious "no" that implies. Silence stretches between us as I try to work up the nerve to lay myself bare.

"How about," Aspen speaks from his spot on the ground, "every insight you share, Cat and I will take off a piece of clothing?"

My tongue gets thick in my mouth, but I force a word past it. "Naked?"

Smooth. Used to be, people thought I was charming and charismatic. But now, I'm a bumbling mess at the idea that both of these people are here, offering to strip for me.

Cat studies me. "Do you want to see me naked?"

The question isn't coy. No flirtatious air.

She truly doesn't know how fucking gorgeous I think she is.

"Hell yes," I breathe out, my throat ragged.

Cat's disquiet disappears with a spark in her eyes, and she gives a stern nod. "Deal. Spill it, Rafe."

The nickname on her lips hits deeper than most anything else could. The affection, a hint of possibility.

Could Aspen be on to something?

It's dangerous to hope, but still, I do.

"Okay, truth. Yeah, I can do that." I wipe my sweaty palms on the athletic shorts I sleep in and try to think how my vulnerable words will mean I get to see more of them. Both of them. Bare.

"My dad cheated on my mom. A lot."

Raise your hand if you're bad at dirty talk.

I watch as Cat and Aspen share a look. Next thing I know, Cat is tugging off the tennis shoes she must have been happy to put on after those heels she was working in. Aspen stays lying on the floor but toes off his shoes as well.

"That's it?" I mutter. "You'd think I'd get a little more than shoes for that tidbit."

Cat leans forward, surprising me when she captures one of my hands between hers. Warmth spills from her palms, sinking into my skin in a soothing caress.

"Keep going."

Chapter Twenty-Eight

CAT

When I touch him, for a moment I forget any time has passed. In that instant, we are the friends we used to be. Maybe more, always with that hope. But all traces of my anger disappear as I stare into that vulnerable, stormy gray gaze.

Rafael sucks in a ragged breath. "You know he was a pilot. The guy had someone in every hub city."

Even though this is the oddest stripping situation, a promise is a promise. I slip off my socks and Aspen does the same. Rafael tries to smirk, but the expression looks more like a grimace as he contemplates whatever drove him to push me away.

When he's quiet for a stretch, I decide to help. "How did you find out?"

The Squid lets out a strangled laugh. "That's what's so fucked up—he *told* me. Gods, he bragged about it. Just to me, not to Mom. He put in some effort to hide the affairs from her, but not enough. Every time she found out..." Rafael shakes his head, tangling his free hand in his hair. "She was crushed."

And on that note, there goes my shirt.

Rafael's gaze flares as it passes between me and a now shirtless Aspen. It's interesting to realize, in that moment, he and I share an attraction to the Petal Pusher. I...like it. A lot. The connection of mutual longing for another. It makes me want to dig deeper into the good stuff.

"So what does this have to do with me?" I prompt when Rafael seems more interested in admiring our bodies than opening up.

The Squid drops his eyes. "Dad told me because he wanted me to be like him. I dunno if he was just craving someone to tell him he wasn't a complete asshole, or what. But he was always saying I should take what I want, when I wanted." He meets my eyes. "And I started to want you."

I swallow heavy, his words affecting me deep in my chest. He doesn't wait for us to strip off more clothes before charging on.

"But you were two years younger than me. And I know it annoyed you, but yeah, I thought of you as innocent. In the best way. What we had between us was easy, like childhood friendships are. I didn't want to ruin that. I didn't want to push you to grow up faster than you had to. And that night..."

Again, he trails off, but I can't let him fade away when I'm so close to understanding. "I knew you were pulling away, but that night you blew up. Why?"

"Because Sammy was talking to you about sex and leading you to the basement."

"Gods!" I jerk back. "You didn't think I was going to sleep with Sammy, did you?"

"No," he holds out staying hands. "Not that."

"Then what?"

Rafael glances to the side, and I watch him exchange a meaningful look with Aspen.

The Petal Pusher is the one to respond. "A few weeks before, Sammy had another party. I was at it. So was Rafe. We were playing stupid games like suck-and-blow. We made out. Then, we hooked up."

My mouth bobs open at this new discovery. Obviously, since we're here, I know that Aspen is attracted to Rafael and Rafael might feel the same back. *But they were already together?*

I wait for a rush of jealousy. Instead, lust infuses my muscles.

I want to see them together now.

Rafael, on the other hand, hangs his head. "After that, I realized I wanted Aspen. But I also wanted you. And I kept hearing my dad's voice saying I should take what I want. Then you were there, looking so gorgeous in your party outfit, and I freaked out because I couldn't take what I wanted from you. Not when I might hurt you." He buries his face in his hands. "But then, I did hurt you. And the next day, you were talking to Aspen. You two were laughing and looked so good together. I got jealous. And you know what happened then." He opens his palm and a slim trail of water flows into the room from somewhere else in the house. Rafael makes the liquid into a mini fountain in his palm.

As he confesses and makes little water displays, I shimmy out of my shorts because I promised. Plus, he's so raw in this moment, I don't want him to be the only one exposed. Aspen rolls to his back and unzips his fly. At the sound Rafael lifts his head.

"You don't need to—"

"So you didn't apologize because Aspen and I became friends?" I press, wanting every piece of truth laid bare between us.

The Squid lets the water trickle through his fingers as he runs his eyes over my bare legs and up my stomach, to where a bra cups my half a handful of breasts. As encouragement, I nudge one of the straps to slip off my shoulder. *This is the next to go* is the silent message. I try not to feel guilty about how giddy I am that my body distracts him. In this moment, I don't feel childish. In this moment, I'm a tempting woman in a room with two gorgeous men who want me.

"Every time I saw you two together," Rafael rasps, "my powers threatened to break loose. I thought I was going to flood the school. I had to stay away from you."

The confession sparks a memory, and my fingers pause in the act of undoing my bra clasp. I glance over at Aspen. His hazel eyes hold mine, and the corner of his mouth quirks up as he hooks his thumbs in the waistband of his briefs.

"The stairwell," I whisper, then turn to Rafael and find him red-faced. "You saw us kissing in the stairwell that day, didn't you? That's why the sprinklers when off."

He scratches the back of his neck. "Can you blame me? Aspen was dry humping you. I practically came in my pants just from the sight."

"You peeping Tom!" I sweep off my bra and chuck it at his bare chest.

Rafael offers a wicked grin, and I love seeing the discomfort leave his face. Then, I shiver as he focuses on my breasts and licks his lips. Without warning, he leans forward and scoops me into his arms. Next moment, I find myself pressed hard against his chest as he drags in a shuddering breath.

"I never thought I'd get to touch you like this."

Despite my lack of clothes, the embrace doesn't start off as sexual. Rafael just holds me close, burying his nose in my hair and kneading his fingers into the bare skin of my shoulders. Without thought, I twine my arms around his torso, sinking into him.

So much time has passed, but even when we were friends, Rafael and I never held each other. I'd always thought, at some point, he would be my first kiss. But that ended up being Aspen, and I've had a whole string of mediocre kisses after breaking things off with the Petal Pusher.

Now though, I tilt my chin, raising my mouth to linger just in front of his. An invitation to make up for the lost opportunity. His cool palm cradles my face, thumb tracing over the curve of my cheek.

"Can I kiss you, Cat?"

Finally. "Yes."

Rafael tastes like water after a drought. Life-sustaining and crisp. He maps my mouth in gentle, exploring nips and kisses, before pressing fully flush and plundering until I'm gasping and wondering how I can drink him in deeper.

So good. Delicious and invigorating. My fingers delve into his hair, holding him closer. Locking him against me.

This is better than anything we could have managed when we were teenagers. No doubt my younger self would have enjoyed it just the same because I would have been kissing Rafael, but now I earn a promise from his skilled kiss.

That this is only a hint of the pleasure he's capable of.

At some point, Rafael deviates from my lips, tracing teasing licks to the lobes of my ears, then down my neck. Eyes hazy, I manage to find Aspen next to us. The Petal Pusher reclines on his elbow and rests a hand on Rafael's thigh, petting the man.

When I take in his expression, I find him grinning broadly.

Chapter Twenty-Nine

ASPEN

Finally. It's as if the air around them shifts, settling into the proper course. All this time, there's been an unbalance in the world with Cat and Rafael on the outs. But now they're here, twined around each other, each with lips plump from kissing.

Gods, I want to taste both of their mouths.

Just as I begin to wonder if I might be an intruder on this moment, rather than a part of it, Rafael reaches out the hand not occupied with stroking Cat's bare back. His fingers find mine, lacing our hold together. Anchoring me to them.

"You did this," Rafael rasps, and Cat nods while holding my eyes.

Heat flushes under my skin, and I'm grateful for the beard that hides the blush. "I just cleared the way. Got everything out in the open."

The mischievous Pyro smirks and tugs at Rafael's waistband. "Not everything is out."

Rafael uses one hand to clasp both her wrists, staying her sneaky fingers. "Can you forgive me? For what I said back then? And how much of an ass I was afterward?"

I watch emotions play over the precious woman's face, too fast for me to catalogue them. Luckily, she ends with a soft smile. "Lately, I've been madder with myself. Mad at the idea that I'm still the child you called me back then. And I..." she hesitates, then presses on. "I still struggle with that insecurity. But that's my problem, not yours. "

We both love you, so it is our problem, I think to myself and find Rafael glancing at me as if in agreement.

"So, yes," Cat continues. "I forgive you. Now that I know why you freaked out the way you did, it helps. And I'm done with letting a mistake made when we were young stop us from being happy now. I want to be with you, Rafe." Again, she uses the nickname that makes his eyes sparkle with a smile.

The Pyro reaches out to clasp my shoulder, holding my eyes.

"The three of us...how do we do this?" Cat's question could mean different things. *This* could refer to an entire relationship, or just this one night. Maybe it would be better to focus on sex, moving past the raw emotions left by Rafael's confession. But I'm also naked, and hard, and possibly too horny to make rational decisions, so it's best to put it up to the room before taking the lead.

I eye the two elementals waiting for my answer. Cat, naked except for her panties, vibrating with an excited energy that has my pulse responding by picking up a rapid beat. Rafael, all tan and taut with tension, his eyes hungry. Both linger on the edge, ready to delve into this passion between us.

"The first thing..." Keeping my voice steady becomes difficult, as Cat pets my chest like she can't keep from touching me, "...is finding out what everyone is comfortable with."

Before I can define anything further, Rafael has his body tilted forward, bringing both himself and Cat closer to me.

"Everything," he growls.

Chapter Thirty

CAT

At Rafael's lusty proclamation, I let out an involuntary squeak.

"Okay. Cool. For you. I-I'm not at the *everything* level yet," I stutter. The confident woman from a moment ago has disappeared. "Umm... because...my butt."

Goddess save me! The blush doesn't stay at my face, but instead consumes my entire body. Both men stare at me, and I wonder how I went from sex vixen, freely stripping off my clothes, to scaredy cat.

It's just, there's *two* of them. When Aspen first told me about his polyamorous relationship, I spent time fantasizing about that kind of setup. But I've never actually done it before, and I'm just realizing how little I know.

A comforting caress of my cheeks has me meeting Aspen's understanding hazel eyes. He's gentle, letting me know I'm supported. "Why don't you explain what you mean?"

With a thick swallow, I try to be more articulate. "I've never done anal. And I'm not sure I want to. At least, not right now." When I flick my gaze to Rafael, I find his expression slack in shock, and a defensive spark ignites in my chest.

"What?" I snap, glaring his way.

His face clears of the surprise, and he smiles ruefully. "Sorry. It's just,

I started this night miserable and alone, and it's just hitting me that I'm here with two sexy-as-fuck people, and you're talking like you're already imagining us inside you." As he speaks, Rafael hardens beneath me, and his hips give an involuntary rock. "I'm just trying to take it all in." The last bit almost wheezes out of him, and humor creeps in to replace my embarrassment.

Shifting my body, I lean back against Aspen's bare chest that is now close enough to act as a chair, and I gaze at Rafael with my legs draped over his lap, contemplating all the ways I want him. Aspen's heavy hands settle on my shoulders, smoothing up and down my biceps in a soothing, yet erotic caress.

"Noted." His chest rumbles against me as he speaks. "Cat's ass is a no-go zone."

"Well," I hedge, "not entirely a no-go zone. You can grab it. Maybe give it a gentle slap or two."

By the time I finish my caveats, Rafael is staring over my head, sharing some kind of silent communication with Aspen. Still, I can see his pupils dilating to the point his eyes appear black.

"Any other no-go zones?" Rafael rasps.

I shake my head, and Aspen adds a "no" as his hands slide from shoulders to cup my breasts, tweaking my nipples in a gentle pinch that has me gasping, hips rocking. The Squid grasps my thighs, rearranging my legs so they split around his hips. Even while wearing shorts, his dick thrusts upward between us, a lewd picture as I stare down my body.

Gods, I can't wait to feel him inside me.

Over the years, even while I was holding on to my anger toward my former best friend, I could never completely keep him out of my fantasies. When I accepted that fact, I would craft scenarios where he came crawling to me, begging for a chance to taste me. To spend the night in my bed. And in my mind, I would let him. I would ride him until he was worn out, wrung dry. Then, I'd leave him as he begged for me to stay. I'd stroll off, satisfied and in control, while he craved another taste.

Now, I don't have the urge to torture him. I just want to experience Rafael in the throes of passion while Aspen holds me steady. The Petal Pusher's hard length presses against my back as he cradles me in his body, hands kneading my breast. Rafael shifts forward, looming over me, then bends to press a hot kiss against my collarbone. Or maybe I'm the one producing the heat. What does it matter, when he slides me off his lap only to draw a path down my stomach with his sinful mouth?

By the time he reaches the edge of my panties, I'm writhing, only held in check by Aspen's strong arms.

"Can I taste you?" Rafael breathes the question against the thin, damp material of my underwear.

"Please," I gasp, spreading my thighs wider, only to have him press them closed so he can slip the underwear down my legs. Then, I'm allowed to part as wide as I want. He helps by laying his palms on the sensitive skin of my inner legs.

"Gods, I'm hungry for you." He moans, leaning down to kiss my mound. "Do you know how often I imagined this?" As Rafael's thumbs draw my slick lips apart, Aspen continues to tweak my hard nipples. With one arm, I reach behind me to clasp my hand on the back of Aspen's neck, and the other I extend down, combing through Rafael's soft curls and encouraging him forward. His breath comes initially, a cool puff of air against my overheated clit. At the first drag of his tongue, I whimper. At the second, I shout. And every one after that, my muscles tighten, and I call out whatever desperate words come to my mind.

"Two fingers in her," Aspen directs. "Completely circle her clit with your lips, then flick with your tongue."

Oh, hell. He's giving lessons in my pleasure.

Rafael shoots us a quick grin, his lips wet with my arousal, then he follows the instructions exactly, and suddenly I'm pulsing, and crying out, and losing the small amount of control I have as pleasure scorches through me.

"That's our girl," Aspen whispers, pressing his heavy hand against my lower belly, which keeps the fire burning a few moments longer. Rafael sits back on his heels, panting as his eyes stay locked on my core. Like he can't believe I'm drenched for him.

"Nice way to start," Aspen announces, his deep voice filling the room and vibrating against my sensitive skin. "But now, I think it's time for Rafael to find out just how fucking glorious it is to be inside you."

My breath stutters out as needy gray eyes meet mine.

Chapter Thirty-One

RAFAEL

Inside her.

My muscles tense in pleasure merely at the thought. That, and the authoritative way Aspen talks about Cat's body.

They must have hooked up plenty of times in high school. I'm surprised to realize the idea doesn't prick at my jealousy anymore. Instead, I drag my gaze over her flushed, aroused form, framed by Aspen's massive, strong body, and think how we've never all been together. This will be a first for us all. Even if Aspen did have a relationship with multiple people in the past, they weren't Cat and me.

"Yes," I agree. "But we need condoms. And a bed."

A smile overtakes my face when our little Pyro grumbles a protest about moving. Next second, Aspen is standing with her cradled in his arms, a smirk crinkling his beard.

"Next door?" He tilts his brow with the question. I nod, and the big man steps out of the guest room and down the hall. I follow close behind, my stare falling to the taut globes of his ass. Unable to help myself, I reach out and cup one, grinning as they clench in response.

Once we reach the bedroom, Aspen tosses Cat onto my mussed bed. She bounces on her landing, giggling all the while. The joyous sound fills the room, lightening every corner. An unopened box of condoms sits in my top dresser drawer. I slide my fingers under the cardboard flap, breaking the seal and pulling out one of the foil squares before joining Aspen at the foot of the bed to admire Cat, as she stretches in an erotic arch that thrusts her tits out.

Does she know what she does to me? To us? Because no doubt Aspen is as turned on as I am.

Even her sensual moves seem unplanned. Cat is naturally seductive. It boggles my mind this fierce, beautiful woman thinks the world could ever view her as childish.

I'm going to be inside her. I groan at the thought. Aspen lets his hand settle on my lower back, stroking his thumb along my spine.

The Pyro props herself up on her elbows. "Are you two just going to stand there?" Her core glistens from her previous orgasm as she moves, and the wetness calls to my body. I rarely try to manipulate any liquid other than water, but an idea suddenly strikes me.

Since I'm not jealous at the moment, it takes more concentration to pull on my magic. But I find the inner current and encourage the flow, enough to coax the slickness at her center to move in firm waves over her sensitive lips. Cat gasps, and Aspen eyes the subtle motions I make with my hands. A grin unfurls over his face as he makes the connection.

His hand drops lower to my ass and squeezes. The Petal Pusher leans over to nibble my neck, almost breaking my concentration. "You said you're open to everything?" Aspen asks, voice husky.

"Mm-hmm," I manage as he drags off my shorts. My erection bobs up to slap my stomach when I'm freed from the fabric. He steps back, and I kick the piece of clothing away. As I watch, Aspen grabs his own condom from the box, then opens the drawer again, searching until he finds the bottle of lube I forgot to take out.

My ass clenches with the knowledge of what's coming next.

"You take care of our Pyro." Aspen returns to stand by the bed. "And I'll take care of you."

That's it—I'm dreaming. Or maybe I died and ended up in a pleasure dimension because this is too much of exactly what I want.

Who the fuck cares how you got here? Take advantage of it before you wake up!

With fingers that shake, I roll my condom on. Cat watches the movement, her focus on my cock. As I approach her, I palm my balls, cupping and tugging them, panting in anticipation.

She's beautiful, sprawled out before me. Grabbing her ankles, I pull Cat toward my spot at the end of the bed, glad my mattress sits at the perfect height for me to match my hips to the apex of her thighs.

"You ready for this?" I try to sound confident, put-together. But I gasp the question with desperate starvation. All these years of wanting, longing, and she's *here*. They're both here.

"Yes. Goddess, Rafael, I want you."

My name, her voice, that tone. We're lucky if I last at all. I might as well be a virgin again, with the edge I'm already on. Trying to keep from immediately spilling, I gently arrange my cock at her entrance and slowly sink into her slick heat.

Cat sobs out the gods' names at my invasion, a beautiful red flush tracing down her throat and over the surface of her breasts. I lean forward to suck on a taut nipple just as my length settles fully cradled inside her.

When heavy hands rest on my waist, I let Cat's nipple go with a pop and straighten, staying buried deep. Aspen hovers at my back, his beard brushing my shoulder. Turning my head slightly, I find his mouth waiting. My cock pulses in time with his kisses, my hips giving gentle thrusts whenever his tongue slides into my mouth. Cat whimpers as her inner walls flutter in a tease of what's to come.

Aspen breaks the kiss first, his large palm pressing between my shoulder blades, directing me to bend forward. My hands land on either side of Cat's head, our eyes locking as I feel him slick lube on the crease of my ass.

The Petal Pusher massages the lubrication along the edges of my tight entrance, drawing a gasp from me as he presses the tip of his finger inside. I've been with men before and fucked in multiple positions. But there's only ever been one partner.

And there's never been love.

Now, I stare with rapt fixation at the woman I fell for more than a decade ago, experiencing the welcoming clench of her, as the man I never let myself love readies to delve into me. My body tenses, begging for release, but I breathe through the pleasure, needing to last. If only I could draw this out forever.

"You ready for this?" Aspen repeats the question I asked Cat. He snakes his hand around my front, sliding his touch over the base of my cock right where I disappear inside our Pyro. She moans and rocks her hips, and I need to shut my eyes and drag in a few shuddering breaths to keep from coming.

"Yes." The word is a plea.

Aspen doesn't enter me as easily as I sank into Cat. My body pushes back, but he claims each inch with gentle persistence that threatens to undo me. Aspen mutters encouragements all the while, telling me how I'm better than his fantasies. He tells me how he's going to go deep, and I'll feel him tomorrow.

That last one has my lids blinking open, only to be met with the heart-wrenching sight of Cat's joyous grin. She reaches up to stroke her hands down my chest, as if I need comforting from the overwhelming wave of erotic words.

"Aspen loves talking in bed," Cat informs me, and the big man chuckles, which sends a whole wave of new pleasurable sensations through me, and I moan from deep in my chest.

"That's it. That's my man." The praise comes as strong legs press against the back of my thighs. He's fully seated, and I'm a wave of cresting desire. There's no stopping the crash. All I can do is brace for the inevitable ecstasy.

Even as my dick keeps Cat pinned to the bed, she props herself up enough to press a kiss to my jaw.

"You weren't there, the first time we did this." Her warm fingers trail over my neck in another soothing pet. "But now you know how we both felt. Filling someone and being filled."

All I can manage is a grunt because her words urge the wave taller, faster.

"Now," Aspen's voice vibrates through his cock. "Take her, Rafael. I'm not going anywhere." As if to prove his point, heavy hands grasp my hips and hold me tight to him.

When I rock, he shifts with me, and Cat lets out the sweetest noise of needy surprise.

By all the gods, help me get through this and give them both the pleasure they're bringing me.

As I continue to stroke forward, my eyes threaten to roll back in my head at the delicious grip of Cat's body paired with the fullness of Aspen buried in me. I have enough mental capacity to sneak my fingers to the Pyro's hard nub above where I slide in and out. Her knees bend as I circle her clit with firm pressure, the stroking as relentless as my thrusting.

When Cat starts muttering my name and pinches her own nipples, my rhythm stutters, but I force myself to stay the course. I need her to come before me.

Our Pyro sobs out a plea to the gods, and her whole body convulses around my cock, promising to milk me dry.

"I'm close," I grit out, getting the sense Aspen would want to know. "Stop."

Chapter Thirty-Two

ASPEN

Rafael isn't the only one about to bust. Watching the Squid drive into our Pyro until she breaks apart is the most erotic visual I've ever had the luck to set my eyes upon. And with my dick clenched in his tight ass the entire time?

My lust practically overwhelms me. And with it, my magic.

Because damn it, I've never been happier.

The power of the earth thrums heavy in my palms. I try to spare some brain space to keep the urge contained, but these two are too distracting. A small amount leaks out, and I hope no damage is done. Maybe Rafael will simply find a few extra cacti in his front yard tomorrow.

Whatever the consequences, there's no way, in all the godly dimensions, I would ever be willing to pause this.

"Stay deep in her," I command, my voice hoarse with need as I watch Cat shake from the aftershocks of her orgasm. The dreamy smile curving over her lips has me wanting to kiss her.

Later. Now is Rafael's time.

"I'm going to fuck you, Rafe." I take a handful of his ass, digging my fingers into the meaty muscle. "I'm going to take you the rest of the way."

Rafael lets out a grunt of agreement.

My first thrust is a slow retreat and a gradual entry, the sound of suction from the lube filling the bedroom.

Every day. I'm going to need this every day.

On the entry, he grits my name, and I bite my lip and siphon off some more power as it presses heavy in my palms. From the noises my water elemental makes, I can guess I've found his sweet spot. With gentle, quick thrusts, I massage the pleasure point until he's choking on curses, hands fisted in the sheets. Only when he gasps my name again and half collapses on our Pyro do I turn my attention to myself.

Eyes on where I slide in and out, hypnotized by the sight of my length disappearing into Rafael, brings me to the point of agonizing ecstasy. Cat combs her fingers through Rafael's hair, then trails her touch down his side to cover my hand where I grip his hip. In that moment, I feel as though I'm entering them both simultaneously.

Using all my self-control, I hold onto the sensation as long as possible. Just in case this is a dream. A vivid fantasy I've built in my unconscious mind of the perfect moment. I have both of them, and I don't want to let them go.

But then Rafael turns his head, pressing a kiss to Cat's neck and then grinning at me over his shoulder. The sight is too much. I plunge as deep as I can while my body shudders out the most intense orgasm I've ever experienced. A noise like an animal rips from my throat. A beast claiming what's his and warning all others off.

Cat and Rafael are mine.

Finally.

Chapter Thirty-Three

RAFAEL

If we'd chosen sleeping arrangements based off size, Cat would've been the little spoon, Aspen the big spoon, and me cradled between them. Instead, Cat claimed since she didn't have her body pillow here, she needed to "octopus herself" around someone—that was the exact descriptor she used. I, meanwhile, sweat an uncomfortable amount if I'm cuddling when I fall asleep. Aspen immediately laid down and dragged Cat against his back, wrapping her arms, then legs, around his torso.

The two looked ridiculous and adorable. After coaxing water from the bathroom and giving everyone their own glass-less refreshment, I flopped down beside them and stretched out a hand, which Aspen claimed and pressed a kiss to the back of.

That's how we slept. Spent and deliriously happy.

I wake up terrified none of it was real. Luckily, both elementals are still beside me, Cat's leg slung over Aspen's hip so far that her purple painted toes brush my thigh.

This is what happiness is.

Wanting to do something nice for them, I slide off the mattress and quietly use the bathroom before heading to the kitchen. My intention is to make a delicious breakfast. But when I get down the hall, all thoughts of salsa-covered omelets and banana pancakes disappear.

"What the hell?" My question bursts out loud, echoing around my kitchen. At least, it used to be a kitchen.

Heavy footsteps pound toward me and a nude Aspen appears, soon followed by Cat, who's made herself a toga dress from my sheets. Both stop and stare at the odd sight.

"Are those..." Cat tilts her head, and at any other time I'd be distracted by her messy bed head, wanting to drag my fingers through the short, wild locks. But my brain is busy trying to figure out what happened in my house.

"Flowers," I wheeze. "Everywhere."

My kitchen counter is covered in crimson blooms. And not as though someone dropped off a surprise floral arrangement. More like a green thumb decided to transform the place into a greenhouse.

"You didn't happen to have some seeds on the counter?" The question comes in a deep rumble, and I shift my focus to Aspen. The Petal Pusher.

"No." I rack my brain. "Well, I mean, I had poppy seed bagels."

"Ah." The skin above his beard flushes a dark red.

"Ah? What does *ah* mean?"

In an uncharacteristic display of self-consciousness, he shifts his weight from foot to foot, then sighs deep. "They're poppy plants."

Poppy plants?

"They're very pretty," Cat offers before covering her mouth and suppressing what sounds suspiciously like a giggle.

Understanding hits me. "You're *lust*-induced, aren't you?" Last night was the hottest sex of my life. If Aspen was affected anywhere near the amount I was, I'm surprised I don't have Jack's beanstalk in the middle of my house.

He clears his throat. "Happiness."

Even as the confession squeezes my heart, I can't help giving him some shit. Especially after the sprinkler incident.

"Aren't these used to make opium?" I prod an accusing finger into his bare, tempting chest. "Did you turn my kitchen into a drug den?"

Aspen grimaces, and the expression somehow makes him more handsome. Meanwhile, Cat has fully buried her face in the sheet to try to stifle her laughter.

"Yes and no. They could be used for that, but I think as long as you don't make drugs, they're perfectly legal." The Petal Pusher runs his gaze over the blooms, suddenly thoughtful. "But a kitchen counter isn't the best place to grow them."

Cat chokes, and I can't fight my grin any longer. "Really? Never would've guessed."

"You're not mad?" There's enough waver of uncertainty in the question that I leave off my teasing.

"Not if you help me clear them out of the way. I can't make breakfast with a garden on my stovetop."

After pulling on pants, Aspen carefully transfers the blooms to his trunk, claiming he knows a few of his kind who'd be happy for some poppy plants. Then, he and Cat end up helping me cook, the three of us navigating the kitchen together with only a few stumbles, and a lot of suggestive hand-brushing. When we find ourselves at the table, Cat asks the question that's been on my mind since the two started kissing me.

"Can we have the official relationship talk?"

Both Aspen and I freeze, and despite a flush taking over her cheeks, she holds both of our eyes in turn.

"Okay." I wipe sweaty hands on my shorts. "I'm down for that."

Aspen gives a curt nod.

Cat seems to realize we're waiting for her to take the lead. I watch her chest rise on a deep, bracing breath. "I think, Aspen, you made it clear you want both of us. My question is, is this just the three of us sleeping together, or more?"

"More." The word escapes me before I can think it through. But I don't need to think. I already know. The three of us. I want it, and I've been telling myself I'm not allowed to have it. But here they are, so close.

Is it selfish? Maybe. But...maybe not if they want it too.

Cat's smile starts small, then crashes across her face like a great wave. In that moment, she and I connect. There's an *us*.

But is there an *all* of us?

"Aspen?" I turn to the big man, trying to be as brave as Cat was when she brought the topic up. The Petal Pusher's elbows rest on the table, his face cradled in his big hands as his fingers massage his temples.

Shit. Cat and I share a panicked glance. *Does he not want this? Does he not want any more of us than what happened last night?*

"Nothing," he huffs out, "would make me happier than being with you both. In a relationship."

Cat scoops up his hand and sinks her teeth into the meaty part of his thumb until he hisses, even as he wears a smile. "Don't do that," she growls. "You gave me a panic attack."

"So this is real. This is a thing." My mind whirls and mixes us together in a beautiful concoction. "Ratpen."

They both stare at me with dipped brows.

"Did you just say *Ratpen?*" Cat asks.

"Yeah. It's our names. Rafael, Cat, Aspen. *Ratpen.*" I grin at them both.

"I move that Rafael doesn't get to choose our relationship name." Cat knocks her knuckles on the table like a gavel.

"I second that motion," Aspen agrees.

"Motion passed." The little Pyro smirks my way.

"And I use the veto powers of supreme sex appeal to strike down your motion," I declare with a triumphant smirk. "Ratpen it is."

The two of them groan, and then Cat climbs from her chair only to straddle my lap and kiss the hell out of me. Obviously, because I'm irresistible, and not at all because Aspen told her to find a way to shut me up.

Chapter Thirty-Four

CAT

When I invited my two new boyfriends over for a pool party a few days after our first night together, I didn't plan on my sisters crashing it. My mind was too horned up with the idea of sex on a lounge chair while the sun warmed my skin, then us all cooling off in the water afterwards, to remember the house I live in isn't mine alone.

But I'd only just started suggestively rubbing sunscreen on myself when the sound of the gate latch clicking alerts me to the fact our alone time is over.

As first Quinn, then Harley step through the gate, I anxiously eye Aspen where he's leisurely floating in the pool, then Rafael, sitting at the end of my chair with my feet cradled in his lap.

We'd only agreed on this relationship dynamic a handful of days ago. Work and family obligations have kept us from much more than late night hook-ups when Aspen and I finish at the club. Rafael then has to leave in the morning for his job, so this is our first day we all have off together.

And I haven't found the best time to explain to my sisters what's going on. As they pause with matching expressions of astonishment, I realize I should've at least sent a group text to start the ball rolling.

"What in all the divine dimensions am I seeing right now?" Harley stalks forward, head swinging back and forth between my intimate position with Rafael, and Aspen's presence and obvious lack of concern about the arrangement as he leisurely strokes up to the side of the pool.

"Hey there!" My voice comes out way too chipper, and I belatedly realize I've never greeted my sisters with a "hey there" before, so now they're definitely going to think something is wrong. I clear my throat and try again. "Hey, um. Harley, Quinn. You know Aspen and Rafael." *Duh. What in all the gods' names am I saying?* "So, Aspen is back in town. And Rafael is back in town. And I...uh...never left town." *Come on, girl! Start making sense!* "We talked. Them. Me. The three of us. Dating now."

Oh no, panic is sending my words to weird places, and I can see the fiery wreckage approaching, but I can't stop myself. "I'm sleeping with both of them! They're my boyfriends! We're Ratpen!"

That is not how an adult tells people about her relationship.

Aspen, the traitor, smooths a hand over his mouth, but I still see the way his beard twitches in a grin. Rafael grips my foot in a reassuring hold, then resumes his massaging, which is totally inappropriate but feels too good for me to ask him to stop.

"Do you have a head injury? Is that how this happened?" Harley extends her hands. "How many fingers am I holding up?"

"Two," I sigh. "And please stop giving Rafael double middle fingers."

"Ratpen?" Quinn asks.

"Rafael, Cat, Aspen. Ratpen," the Squid explains, as if it makes any more sense than when he came up with it.

Sucking in a deep breath, I remind myself that I'm a grown woman who can date whoever she wants, and that I don't need my sisters' approval. But still, I love them, and they deserve at least a basic understanding of my choices.

Leaving out the sexy details, I explain how Rafael and I talked and worked through my anger toward him. Then how Aspen had previously been in a throuple and had brought up the idea of us three dating. And lastly, I emphasize how much I care for both men, praying they hear the hope and excitement in my voice. How much I *want* this to work.

"Assfat!" Quinn shouts when I pause, and we all turn to stare. "Aspen, Rafael, Cat. *Assfat.*"

"Nice one." Rafael holds out a fist, and my sister bumps it with an evil grin.

"Stop giving him ideas," I hiss at her, then throw Aspen a pleading look. He just chuckles and shrugs, eyes flicking between Quinn and Rafael. On a delay, I comprehend his message.

Quinn approves.

Well, that's one down.

"You need to make a trip to Denver," Harley says, her comment almost as confusing as Quinn's.

Attempting to sus out the track her brain has veered off on, I hazard a guess. "Are you saying you want to take a vacation? Like, with me?"

My oldest sister rolls her eyes. "No. I mean, sure, we can do a vacay sometime soon. Maybe go to Iceland and see some northern lights. Then, I could find myself a Snow Cone to fuck underneath them." She takes on an eager distracted grin, then shakes the expression away to refocus on me. "Denver for birth control. There's a witch there. She can do a type of binding spell. One hundred percent protection."

"Wow. Um, thanks?" Working at a strip club, and knowing Harley is one of Phoenix's most popular dominatrixes, still hasn't fully smoothed the ground for me to discuss my sex life with her. "But we've got condoms. And the pill—"

"Doesn't work as well for us." She grimaces. "Believe me."

"What?" Quinn yelps, slapping a hand to her flat stomach. "Since when?"

Harley pulls a bottle of tanning oil out of her bag as she shrugs one flippant shoulder. "Since probably forever. You want good birth control? Talk to a witch."

"And you didn't think to tell *me* this?" Quinn digs her fingers into her hair, expression harassed.

Harley adjusts her sunglasses. "Honestly, I forgot. The fact that Cat is getting doubly dicked-down reminded me."

"That's a very unromantic way to describe my relationship," I grumble. Then, I bite my bottom lip to hold back a groan as Rafael digs his knuckles into the arch of my foot in a delicious way.

Quinn rifles through her purse with frantic movements, finally coming up with her phone. "You better fucking hope I'm not knocked up." She presses the screen so hard I'm worried the glass might crack, then holds it to her ear. "Hey, babe." She must have called August. "Are you on your way over? Okay, I'm going to ask you to do something, and I need you to not freak out. Harley just decided to share some *pertinent* information." Quinn stomps toward the house, a bundle of rage and annoyance. "You're going to stop at the next drug store and buy a pregnancy test. Scratch that, buy ten tests." She shoots a glare over her shoulder at our older sister. "Just in case they're as ineffective as hormonal birth control apparently is."

"Poor August." Rafael grins, not looking sympathetic at all. I press my free foot against his chest, which shows how pale I am compared to his sun-drenched skin.

"Poor you and Aspen, more like. I hope you realize this means there's a new no-go zone until I meet with this witch."

Rafael pouts, Aspen grunts, and Harley slips her sunglasses down her nose. "What are the other no-go zones?"

In a fit of playfulness, I chuck a fireball at her instead of answering. She catches it, pops it in her mouth, and swallows the flame whole.

"Ouch." Rafael winces as he digs his clever fingers into my calf.

"Remember that, Squid." Harley directs a pointed glare at my partner, and I sit up fast in case she decides to belch the flames back up and direct the fiery breath his way. "I'm not going to tell Cat who she can and can't date," she keeps going. "But if you hurt her again, I will set inconvenient parts of your life on fire."

What parts? Visions of the aquarium come to my mind. All those precious, innocent fish. Even if Rafael did betray me in some way, I'd never want those creatures to suffer. I can't say my sister would be equally as discerning.

"Harley," I snap her name, and she meets my eyes with raised brows. "I can take care of myself. Promise me you won't burn anything related to Rafael. Even if he hurts me."

"Cat." There's a broken note in the Squid's voice, but I just clasp his hand, hoping he'll realize this isn't really about him. It's about me.

Her lips twist, and she flips some curls off her shoulder. But she doesn't promise.

"Harley," I speak her name softly, but with steel. "I'm not fourteen anymore."

"What?" she barks in an uncharacteristic display of temper. "So you don't *need* me anymore?"

I detect a hint of vulnerability in the question, and that's what keeps my anger from flaring to life in return. "I love you," I press. "But I *need* you to stop treating me like a child. I *need* you to trust me."

The heat of her gaze snuffs out as quick as it flared. Harley is not a woman made to be angry. "Fine. I won't hurt your precious Squid, even if he fucks up." She slides her sunglasses up her nose and lays back against the lounge chair. "But let the record show, I still don't like him."

When I look to Rafael, he offers a small smile and keeps massaging my foot. Acceptance is clear in his relaxed posture and content expression. He knew when starting this relationship that she wouldn't accept him.

The knowledge hurts my heart, but I can't force Harley to forgive him. That's something she'll have to do on her own.

Aspen heaves himself out of the pool, water running in teasing streams down his barrel of a torso. Both Rafael and I watch him with rapt gazes. When he reaches the chair, Aspen leans down to give us both a quick kiss.

Once again, I'm sulky that we're not alone because I want to peel those wet swim trunks off him.

"Dry me off?" he asks with a gentle smile.

Rafael and I grin at each other. The Squid removes the excess water with a flick of his hand, sending the droplets back to the pool. I send heated air through the strands of his hair, the curls of his beard, and the fabric of his swimsuit. And I may let a little extra heat linger between his legs.

The Petal Pusher stares down at me with hungry eyes and moves to cup his hands over his crotch.

Just then the back gate bursts open and a harried August strolls in, a plastic bag swinging from his arm.

"Where's Quinn?" He doesn't stop to hear the answer, jogging past us to the door.

Sharing a look with my partners, I come to an important conclusion. *I need to go to Denver, ASAP.*

Chapter Thirty-Five

CAT

"Birth control road trip!" Geneva pumps her arms in the air as she hops out of her car in front of my house.

Aspen grimaces at his sister. "You didn't get T-shirts made, did you?"

The Petal Pusher's eyes widen in delight. "That is a genius idea. Maybe I can get a printer to have them done by the time we reach Denver. I mean, it's thirteen hours give or take. Plenty of time."

Aspen groans, covering his eyes with his hand as his sister starts swiping on her phone.

"I want mine to say, 'I've got magic in my dick,'" Sammy announces, throwing an arm around both my and Rafael's shoulders. My partner grins, but I fight off a scowl.

I did not want to invite Sammy on this trip. Unfortunately, with Geneva, Aspen, Rafael, Quinn, August, and me going, he's the only one with an SUV big enough to comfortably fit us all. Plus, he owns a condo in Denver, so we don't have to rent a place for the trip.

So he's here, and I'm trying not to let on about my remaining animosity. Even though his shoes are looking awfully melt-able...

Bad Cat. No melting today. Learn to get along with him, I tell myself. *He's Rafael's best friend.*

But that's the entire problem.

As if sensing my discontent, Aspen draws me away from Sammy's hold and leans down to press a quick kiss to my tight lips.

"You can always singe his eyebrows off if he bothers you too much." His beard tickles my ear as he whispers the suggestion. The offer and the sensation cause me to giggle, and my sour mood improves. Sammy is just one person I dislike in a group of people I love.

"Deal." If Aspen says it's okay, then that's all the go-ahead I need. Turning to the rest of the group, I speak up. "I'm going to use the bathroom one more time, then lock up."

Quinn waves me off as she and August load our overnight bags in the trunk, and Rafael palms my ass as I walk by. I'm in a much better mood when I come out and head to the car. Everyone already seems to be inside, so I step up to the open door and freeze.

"Looks like you and I are seat buddies!" Sammy grins wide and pats the empty cushion next to him. Staring desperately around the vehicle, I find Rafael behind the wheel and Aspen in the passenger seat. August, Quinn, and Geneva are snug in the back row. No one meets my eyes, and I suspect foul play.

Betrayal!

"If I melt the tires off this car," I mutter as I climb in and slam the door shut behind me, "it's all your faults."

An hour into the trip, I'm cautiously hopeful that this won't be the most annoying experience of my life. Again, no thanks to any of the other passengers. My sister immediately falls asleep, August reads a book, Geneva has her headphones in, and Aspen and Rafael are fully immersed in a debate of football vs. soccer. Perfect situation for Sammy to annoy me until I break all my hard-won self-control. But he stays to his side of the seat and looks to be busy writing in some kind of journal.

Sammy journals? Never would have guessed.

I'm reading about the second murder in my thriller novel when a piece of folded paper lands in the middle of my book page, jarring me out of the story. My head jerks back, and I glance around, but none of the other passengers are looking at me. I pluck the unexpected missive off my pages and unfold the thing.

I want to be friends. -S

Sammy. Of course.

I couldn't truly believe he'd leave me alone for this trip, could I?

I'm about to crumble the piece of paper into a ball and chuck it at his head, when I glance up and lock gazes with Rafael in the rearview mirror. The skin at the corner of his eyes wrinkles with a smile, and warmth envelopes my heart. Enough that I'm willing to push away the spark of angry heat, pick up the pen Sammy rolls across the seat to me, and write a short answer.

I tolerate you now. Isn't that enough?

Intent on not watching him read my response, I refocus on my book. I've re-read the same sentence ten times when the paper obscures my vision again.

It's never been enough. I've always wanted to be your friend.

Annoyance heats my cheeks, and the tip of my pen digs deeper into the paper this time.

No, you haven't. You constantly tease me and give me shit. And in high school you shoved yourself in between me and Rafael so you could be his best friend. You're a big part of the reason we fell apart for so long.

I flick the paper like a throwing star, hoping it gives him a paper cut on impact.

"Wha—" Sammy cuts of the question, and from the corner my eye I see him shake his head, lips pinched together. Determined to read my book and not think about the man baby next to me, I drop my chin.

Then, the paper returns, and I practically tear it open, feeling my fiery pulse pounding to life, preparing to snap back at whatever excuse he tries to sell me. Luckily, I have a firm grip on the magic, and I make sure to keep it under my skin.

You're right.

The words have me choking on my breath.
You're right.
Air stutters back into my lungs on a wave of relief because, finally, here it is, in writing.
You're right.
I fully expected him to keep denying—to make me doubt and question the things I felt back then until the only explanation was that I was an insecure child who couldn't handle her friend getting along with someone else.
But here it is—the proof—and I can breathe easier as I keep reading.

> *You're right. I was jealous. Rafael talked about you all the time, and I wondered what it would be like to have that kind of loyalty. What it meant to inspire that level of devotion. That's why I poked and prodded you. Not because I wanted to cut you out completely, though. I just wanted to figure out how to get what you two had. But I helped mess it all up.*
> *I'm sorry. I'm really, truly, fucking sorry.*

My throat tightens this time around, and I have trouble swallowing. Then my eyes alight on the last line.

> *That's why I'm doing everything I can to fix it.*

Fix it? I guess apologizing and mending bridges with me is a good way to start.
Another piece of paper flutters into my lap.

> *P.S. I'm giving you three the master suite. Nice big bed.*

When I hit him with a side eye, the Squid offers a hopeful smile, and for the first time in maybe ever, I think I catch a hint of vulnerability. Then, Sammy holds up a staying finger and scribbles out another note, folds it into a paper airplane, and glides it my way. I catch the projectile in midair.

P.P.S. I tease all my friends. Half the time I'm talking to R and A, I'm giving them shit. But I promise to stop if it bothers you.

His claim has me reconsidering our recent interactions, compared to the ones when we were younger. Back in high school, I felt like his comments had a sharp edge to them, as if he was testing me in some way. That's what I hated so much about them. But now when Sammy wheedles, the tone is all good humor. No ulterior motive.

Surprised at the realization, I scratch out a response.

Apology accepted. And I'm not giving you permission to tease me. But I'm also not not saying you can.

Sammy's vibrant blue eyes track over the note then find mine. He grins wide, his whole expression glowing with joy.

Could my decent opinion of him really mean that much?

I'm definitely not blushing as I return my focus to my book.

"Did we just become best friends?" he whispers, though I'm sure everyone in the car can still hear him.

"Don't make me burn off your eyebrows," I mutter. This time though, there's no true heat behind the idea, and I find myself fighting a smile as Sammy lets out a bark of laughter.

Aspen reaches behind his seat, broad hand finding my knee and giving a squeeze of approval.

Chapter Thirty-Six

CAT

My ass still stings, and I try not to wince as I sit on the hard bench at the brewery.

"How you doing?" Rafael settles beside me, wrapping his arm around my waist before pressing a kiss to my neck.

"Good," I respond, breathless at the casual affection I'm still not used to but completely love getting from him. The Squid grins at me, his lips curving more as his eyes focus past my shoulder. A heavy presence settles on my right, and I don't need to turn to know both my men now surround me.

"I don't see how people cover their bodies in the stuff. That shit hurt," the Petal Pusher grumps, gingerly adjusting his pants. The waistband is sitting on the exact wrong spot, pressing down on the sensitive flesh where Aspen just got his new birth control tattoo. All four men opted for their hips, while Geneva, Quinn, and I chose to get the magical symbol on our butts. The witch, who was covered almost head to toe in beautiful ink designs, instructed us to select a spot near our pelvic region. Before starting on any, she made clear that this spell was permanent unless removed by the witch that created the spell. She had us all provide contact information in the event she ever decided to relocate. She also gave the morbid warning that if she were to unexpectedly die, there's no known reversal. Not that she had any plans to perish, but the warning needed to be said nonetheless.

All seven of us went ahead with the procedure.

Now I'm magicked up and dating two handsome, attentive men. Could life get any better?

"Sammy bought the first round!" Geneva settles across from us with only a slight cringe and sets three beers on the table. Quinn, August, and Sammy soon follow, carrying extras themselves until everyone has a drink.

I spoke too soon. Friends and alcohol, now life is complete.

"I would like to raise a toast." Rafael stands beside me and lifts his beer to the table. "To safe sex. Cheers."

We all heartily agree and clink glasses, even as my face flushes. When the water elemental resumes his seat, he returns his arm to my waist. Aspen sets a heavy palm on my thigh, his thumb rubbing against the material of my jeans, and I start counting down the minutes until I can get them both alone.

The conversation turns to Sammy's latest architecture project. I wonder if he had a hand in designing the space we're staying in here. We only got to stop at the condo long enough to drop off our bags, but the place was beautiful.

"Are you interested in the Denver market?" Geneva asks between sips of her beer.

"Nah. Just like to visit. But I am branching out from Phoenix into Tucson," he says. This eventually leads to Quinn talking about the reach of her accounting business, and Geneva chimes in about her marketing firm. Apparently, even the aquarium has a branch in Tucson, which leads the table to ask Rafael about how different aquatic life is chosen for aquariums. I find the topic fascinating, as I've always loved the aquarium, but when there's a break because Rafael returns to the bar for more beer, Sammy focuses on Aspen.

"I bet you're looking forward to taking the bar exam again." The Squid is all smirks, and Aspen lets out a grunt.

"Gods, no. That test is like stepping into a hell dimension. But I've got until February to prepare. And to stress about it." There's a genuine note of trepidation in Aspen's voice that has me leaning into his side and giving his arm an encouraging squeeze. I remember a stretch of time where his emails tapered off. I'd worried we were officially losing touch, but then a few months later he started writing regularly again, apologizing for the radio silence during the time leading up to the bar exam. Apparently, the studying engulfs your life.

"And you're going back into copyright law when you pass?" Sammy asks the question with sincere interest, and as Aspen responds, I realize with apprehension the realm this conversation has slid into.

Careers.

Everyone at the table has shared some detail of their job. Work that they're all passionate about and gives their life purpose and meaning.

What if they ask me the same questions?

I'll have nothing to add.

Want to know a funny story about customers at a strip club? I've got you covered. Want to know the best spots to host a tutoring session? Sure, I can give you some suggestions.

But want to hear about my future plans and the exciting ways I'm expanding on my career?

The slate is blank. Like always, I have no idea what I want to do with my professional life, and I get the sudden sense that I'm a kid who snuck her way into a seat at the adult's table.

When my muscles tense as if in defense of a blow, I know I need a moment to myself. These people are too perceptive. They'll realize something is wrong just by looking at my shifty eyes. Then, if they get the truth out of me, it'll be a whole round of pity for Cat. That is *not* something I can handle. Not when I'm finally feeling like a badass in other areas of my life.

"I'll be right back," I murmur to Aspen. "Bathroom."

He nods and gives the back of my hand a kiss before I walk away. That's all I want to think about. The beautiful, casual intimacy between me, and Aspen, and Rafael. How I've let my past hurts go so I can pursue a healthy—if unconventional—relationship.

But my mind only wants to focus on my failings.

When I'm alone in a bathroom stall, I shake out my hands then hold them flat in front of me, palms up. Without anger, my power sits dormant unless I call on it. This was the skill my father taught me well.

How to manipulate and manage the heat when I'm fully in control of the fire.

Now, I coax the second pulse. The magic thrums to life under the surface of my skin, and I pull at the flames until they gather in two little fireballs in my palms. The sight of the flickering orange, red, and even sparks of blue sooth me.

"You are a strong, independent, *grown* woman," I tell myself, focusing on the fire in my hands. The magic that I now have full control over even when I'm pissed off. "A career does not define you." Speaking the words aloud helps. So does working magic.

When I am confident my insecurities aren't forming into an obvious smoke signal around my head, I snuff out the flames and run my hands under cool water. Fire could never burn me, but my skin always feels sensitive after a use.

Back at the table, talk has turned to travel destinations, with Quinn talking about her trip to Alaska with August. I slip into my space between Rafael and Aspen, once again experiencing a pinch of pain when my tattoo presses against the seat.

Despite the lingering ache, I'm determined to reopen a no-go zone tonight. The witch claimed the magic goes into effect immediately.

Aspen and Rafael better be ready to test that out.

Chapter Thirty-Seven

ASPEN

Rafael starfishes in the middle of our massive bed, looking like a sacrifice on a cushiony alter.

"This might be the most comfortable mattress in the world," he groans before rolling over to press his face into the covers. The new position gives me a delicious view of his ass in boxer briefs, and I have to readjust myself as I flash back to the memory of sinking into that juicy behind.

"Well, don't fall asleep yet." The sweet voice comes from over my shoulder, and I swallow a moan at the sight of our Pyro. She locks the bedroom door then faces us, strolling across the floor as if she's the one who owns this room instead of Sammy. A lacy nighty hugs her chest, the sheer fabric doing nothing to cover her nipples. The fabric falls to the tops of her thighs, leaving little to the imagination. That's especially true when she inches the skirt up to show the clear bandage the witch pasted over the birth control tattoo. The magical tattoo artist called it "second skin," and told us we're supposed to keep it on for a few days while things heal.

The sight only has me growing harder, knowing we have one less thing to worry about in the bedroom.

"Are we going to test this out, or what?" Her lips curve in a playful smile, and the next moment I've scooped her up and fused my mouth to hers in a passionate kiss. Cat wraps her legs around my waist, kissing back with equal gusto. We hit the bed, her pressed into the mattress as I bear my weigh down on her, my hips already rocking in the approximation of being inside her.

A set of cool, strong hands grip the waistband of my sleep pants and tug them down. Rafael must have climbed off the bed to help me out. Good man. With my cock free, the head seeks out her slick core, almost driving deep when I make contact.

"Cat—" I groan against her mouth.

"Yes." Her heels dig into my backside, urging me forward. With a beast-like moan, I slide inside her hot channel, working deeper as her wetness coats me and makes the passage easy. She lets out panting whimpers the whole time that threaten to have me coming before I'm fully buried. But the moment my hips hit her thighs, I've reached nirvana.

"By all the gods," I mutter, my brain a bowl of mush as I brace myself on my arms and stare down our bodies to the place where we join. In fascination, I pull out slow, admiring the slick coat of her pleasure on my cock. Then I plow in deep again, over and over as my fingers seek out her clit.

As amazing as this connection to Cat is, I need more. I need *him*. Glancing to the side, I find Rafael reclined on the bed, watching as I fuck our Pyro. His tanned hand has a firm grip on his own cock, and he jerks himself, gaze lusty as he watches.

"I'm next," he says with a cheeky grin.

His playful tone, and the idea of Rafael planning to take Cat right after me has excitement twining with lust, growing into pure happiness. My magic rushes forward, seeking release into the world. I fist my hands in the bedding to hold the mystical energy back.

"Touch yourself," I command Cat. As she slips her fingers south, rolling her clit between middle and ring finger, I jack my hips forward, grunting with each thrust.

Cat sobs out a curse just as her pussy spasms and clenches around me, the skin of her chest flushing a blotchy red. The sight sends me soaring, and with a groan I spill inside her, thankful for the magical tattoo that aches on my hip and lets me experience the connection of skin-to-skin.

My initial urge is to collapse forward, spent. Rafael crawls across the bed toward us, his hard cock bobbing as he approaches, panther-like.

"My turn," he rasps.

I allow myself to slide free, and Rafael grasps Cat's hips to pull her toward him. She's easy to maneuver, pliant in her post-orgasm haze. With gentle hands, Rafael rolls Cat onto her stomach, then positions a pillow under her hips to angle her up for him. The Squid drapes his now naked body over hers, lips coming to her ear.

"You okay, Red?" he whispers, still loud enough for me to hear.

She nods.

"Ready for me?"

Another nod.

I climb onto the bed and relax against the headboard just in time to watch Rafael straighten, grasp the base of his cock, and guide himself into Cat's already soaked pussy. She moans, her hips rocking and rotating, her head turning to the side so I can see her mouth open and panting.

"That's it," Rafael smooths his hand up her spine coming to grasp her shoulder, holding her in place for a more demanding thrust. Cat squeaks, eyes flying open, then they find mine, and she smiles.

Her happiness fuels mine, and I rub my hands together to contain the tingling surge of magic. My palms sting and my knuckles ache as the power demands to be set free.

Let's hope Sammy doesn't have any poppy seed bagels in the kitchen.

The Squid is relentless, stroking into her, dirty, loving words spilling out of his mouth until I'm hard again, and Cat's begging to come once more. Rafael meets my eyes, his half-lidded as he slides his hand between the pillow and her hips, seeking out that perfect little bud of pleasure. When her entire body goes rigid, I know he's found it. Then next moment, Cat spasms as she calls out his name.

With our eyes locked, Rafael loses the last hint of control, slackening into an almost disbelieving expression as he orgasms in our Pyro. Knowing exactly how mind-blowing that pleasure is, I grin wide and lazily stroke myself.

Never could I have imagined being this lucky.

In a deep dark corner of my mind, a voice whispers that I can't be. That there can't be a perfect balance between three.

A touch on my ankle pulls me away from the doubt, and I spy small, strong fingers wrapping around my leg. A set of liquid brown eyes meet mine despite their lust-induced haziness. Even with Rafael still inside her, Cat reaches for me, bringing me into the experience.

This can work.

Later, when we're spent and getting comfortable under the covers, a shout comes from the other room.

"Where the fuck did this come from?" A second later, Sammy bursts into our bedroom. "Aspen! I love avocados, but I don't need a whole tree's worth. Get a hold of yourself man."

Then, he tosses a sapling with drooping green leaves onto our bed and strolls off.

Rafael scoops the spindly plant up with a grin. "That's one hell of a souvenir."

Chapter Thirty-Eight

ASPEN

"Is that a gold member pass?"

The card in Cat's hand reflects like precious metal as she hands it to the ticket desk worker.

The aquarium employee beams at Cat, then me. "You bet! Cat is one of our premium members. You're in here at least once a week, am I right?"

The Pyro shrugs, with a small smile. "I like aquatic life."

The woman in a Saltwater Oasis polo chuckles as she hands back the card. "No charge for you, sir. Premium members get one free guest per month. A map of the displays is on your right when you walk in. Enjoy your time at the aquarium!"

Cat laces her fingers with mine and tugs me forward, as my mind traces back over our younger years. Now that I think about it, Cat and I did go on a few dates to the aquarium. I was always happy to go because the dim, watery lighting made my girlfriend look like some fantasy princess, and there were a few dark corners where she'd let me sneak a kiss.

But now, I recall the way she'd stare endlessly at the different creatures. The same as she's doing now, in front of a glass window behind which swims a spiky-looking fish.

"That's a red lionfish," she tells me. "Those fin spines are venomous. Not usually fatal, though."

"Is this one your favorite?" I ask, bending closer to get a better look.

Cat snorts. "Oh, I don't think I'll ever be able to pick a *favorite*. That changes minute to minute."

On my own, I've never found fish particularly interesting. Maybe it's the fact that there's always glass between me and them, a barrier that keeps me from fully immersing myself in the beauty. Now plants, that's a whole other story. Take me to a botanical garden, and I'll have the same fascinated joy that blooms across Cat's face now.

But as the Pyro guides me through the aquarium, pointing out the differences between the creatures and plying me with fun, random facts, I find myself wanting to know more. All I want is for Cat to keep talking with this passion in her voice and eager sparkle in her eyes.

Why aren't you working here? The question lingers on the edge of my tongue when I spot a familiar face across the room.

"There's our man," I say instead, placing my hands on Cat's shoulders to bodily turn her away from the bright orange clownfish that always reminds me of that kids' movie—which, come to think of it, is a film Cat and I watched together when we were younger too. Maybe even in theaters.

How dense am I? Dots start to connect in my mind as Rafael makes his way over to us.

The aquarium dates. The fish-themed movies and documentaries she always watches. The first Halloween when we were dating, Cat made an octopus costume and asked me to dress as a scuba diver to match.

And there was that shark stuffed animal she always kept on her bed.

"Excuse me." Rafael comes to a stop in front of us, pulling me away from my revelation. "Who let you two in here? I specifically told the front staff *no* sexy people. It's too distracting when I'm trying to get work done."

From the way he's devouring us with his eyes, maybe the guy should actually implement the policy.

"We're too sneaky to keep out." Cat goes up on her toes to press a kiss to his cheek. She's able to manage the maneuver because Rafael is only a few inches taller than she is. When I want a cheek kiss, I have to bend halfway to meet her. Not that I mind. I also like picking her up so she can wrap her legs around my waist to kiss me properly for as long as she wants.

"I have first-hand experience of you two trying to be stealthy, and let me tell you, the conclusion is not good." Rafael's grin morphs into a pout when he looks at me. "Where's my sugar?"

There's a warm clench in my chest, and I lean forward to give the man a firm kiss on his jaw. In my past relationship, Shawna and Ryan only wanted affection from me in certain spaces—definitely not at either of their workplaces. They both maintained an appearance of a couple, and I was most often introduced as a friend. Sometimes only a roommate. One time, I think Shawna even referred to me as their gardener.

"To what do I owe the pleasure of your distracting presence?" The Squid eyes us both, pinching his lower lip between thumb and forefinger, as if he's imagining doing something else with his mouth.

"We felt bad about our off-kilter work schedules." Cat bumps her shoulder against mine. "We see each other all the time, but you're here all by your lonesome."

"And we're always crawling into your bed at four a.m. like you're a booty call," I offer, then cringe at how that sounded.

Rafael barks a laugh as his eyes flare. "To be clear, I don't mind what you do with my booty first thing in the morning." He shifts to the side and makes a flourishing gesture. "How's a tour sound?"

"Perfect." Cat hooks her arm through mine, then her other through Rafael's.

"Surprised you need a tour, Ms. Premium Membership," I tease as Rafael guides us through an entrance that leaves us in a tunnel surrounded by water. The sight is equally eerie and mesmerizing. I comfort myself that, if the glass were to break and engulf us in thousands of gallons of water, Rafael would be able to keep the two of us non-Squids alive.

"Premium member? I didn't know you came that often." Rafael waggles his brows. "Glad to see you opted for no wig today." He tugs on one of her short red strands.

"Wig?" I have trouble imagining her as anything other than a redhead.

The Squid smirks and Cat's face flushes a delightfully dark shade as she answers. "I may have tried to be sneaky another time. Back when I was avoiding Rafael but still wanted to come even though I knew he worked here. You know," she turns her attention to our partner, "the staff here is loyal. I asked one desk attendant what your schedule was, and she politely refused to tell me. She probably thought I was a stalker, but really, I was just trying to avoid you."

I tighten my lips to hide a smile, thinking of how Mia shot me down in the same way, only I *was* trying to find Cat at the time.

"Ah." Rafael smirks. "I'm glad you failed."

The three of us traverse the aquarium with Rafael giving us behind the scenes information and Cat plugging in random facts about the creatures kept within the tanks. I might as well be with two employees rather than one. When we reach the stingray display, Cat goes on such a long, joyous tangent about how the creatures use electrical impulses to find prey that Rafael and I have time to exchange glances over her head and hold a silent conversation.

I didn't realize she knew so much about this, his bewildered expression tells me.

She loves it here, I agree with a fond smile and a nod.

The Squid grows thoughtful, and I wonder if he might be wondering the same thing I am.

If Cat adores marine life so much, why is she working odd part-time jobs instead of pursuing her passion?

Chapter Thirty-Nine

RAFAEL

When I enter the diner, I immediately spot my boyfriend and girlfriend in the far back booth. As I make my way over to them, I can't help the excited pressure swirling in my chest, knowing they're both mine. That I'm seconds from touching them, hearing their voices, just *being* with them.

The desperate longing doesn't make sense. They left the aquarium only a few hours ago, instructing me to meet them for dinner since they both have off work tonight. But maybe it's the fact that I've been separate from them for years that makes me anxious when they're not around. That has me worried I'll wake up and this will turn out to be a fantasy I created in my head.

The need for them jitters through me so strongly that I don't bother with a hello. The moment I reach their seats, I loom over Cat, cradling the back of her head so I can dive in for a hard, unforgiving kiss. One that claims her as mine and leaves her panting when I straighten. As she recovers, I circle the table to give Aspen the same treatment, the guy grinning against my mouth because he knew what was coming.

"Good day at work?" he rumbles when I break away.

"The best." I settle beside Cat, figuring with Aspen's big build, he'd appreciate more room to stretch out. As I breathe in my Pyro's rose scent, my fingers lace with hers as if her hand is a glove stitched to fit mine perfectly. Under the table, I lightly press the sole of my loafer on top of Aspen's boot, which earns me a smile as he tugs on the bottom of his beard. "What did you two get up to the rest of the day?"

When they detail a trip to Land of Ice Cream and Snow, then a stop further down the strip mall for pedicures—apparently, Aspen appreciates a thorough pumice scrub as much as I do—I try not to be jealous of their time together without me. I don't want them to stay apart when I can't be around, but my hope is that, soon, we can figure out a way to mesh our schedules better.

Besides, I'm here with the both of them now. And we'll have tonight together too.

"Hi there. I'm Kira." A waitress with honey blonde hair in a high ponytail pauses at the end of our table to set glasses of water in front of the three of us. Her eyes alight on Cat and my intertwined hands, and her customer service smile grows into an almost eager grin as she shifts her attention to Aspen—the apparent third wheel to our couple. "Have you gotten a chance to look at the menu? See anything you like?"

That second question has a purr lurking underneath, and I try not to bristle. When I turn to Cat, she rolls her eyes, obviously aware of the flirtation but not seeming concerned. Aspen, meanwhile, offers the woman one of his kind smiles that is sure to liquify her panties.

Does the man not know his effect on straight women, gay men, and they/thems looking for a mountain man to summit?

"A cheeseburger with fries sounds good to me." He hands off his menu, and I can practically hear the waitress ovulating as his deep voice rolls over her. I might be able to forgive her the reaction if she didn't intentionally stroke her hand over his as she accepts the menu.

With discernible reluctance, she transfers her gaze to Cat and me, wearing an almost apologetic smile. Like, *Sorry, but you've got to know your friend is super hot so I'm obviously going to shoot my shot, right?*

He's not just our friend, I want to growl at her. Instead, I order a burrito and attempt a tight smile as I offer my menu to her. Cat places her order for a BLT, and I look forward to Kira leaving the table.

"I'll be right back," she says, fully facing Aspen again, her voice husky like a promise.

When she finally saunters off, I last about two seconds before I break.

"Yeah, no. Not going to have that." After pressing a quick apology kiss to Cat's cheek, I shimmy off my seat, and slide into the space beside Aspen, becoming a full body barrier between him and the overly friendly waitress.

"Somebody is jealous," Cat sings with a wicked grin, then taps the edge of her water glass. "Why don't you take a few deep breaths, Rafe?"

Only then do I notice how our waters have turned into mini swirling whirlpools, agitated by my jealousy. Taking her advice, I suck air in deep through my nose and let it slowly stream out of my mouth. The green monster still sits on my shoulder, but at least my magic only rocks back and forth within my chest.

Aspen's gaze lingers on the drinking glasses then finds mine, his thick brows dipping. "What's up?"

I scoff at the Petal Pusher's oblivious expression. "That waitress was flirting with you."

The big man is all bemusement. "No, she wasn't."

Cat snorts. "She totally was." The Pyro stirs her straw in her drink, approximating the whirlpool I just did away with and shoots me a conspiratorial grin. "It was the same in high school. Half the time they thought I was his kid sister and would go all gooey." She affects a breathy, Jessica Rabbit voice. "Oh, look at the big, buff, kindhearted football player taking out his baby sister! So sweet. Do you want me to get her a milk shake and then suck you off in the bathroom?"

Aspen, part way through taking a drink of his water, breathes the liquid in instead, then coughs and spews the mouthful across the table, a good portion coating Cat. We all sit temporarily speechless, the Pyro gaping as water and saliva cling to her skin and white tank top.

"Shit," Aspen croaks, using his forearm to wipe droplets off his beard. "Cat, I'm sorry."

Her face crumples, but with laughter, not tears. The only water that drips off her lashes was in Aspen's mouth a minute ago. Which, in an odd way, is kind of hot...

"I *have* always been more of a spit than swallow man myself," I offer, which only makes Cat giggle harder.

"Gods!" Aspen tugs fistfuls of napkins from the dispenser. "I can't take you two anywhere."

"Aspen," I growl low in my throat, "believe me when I say you can—and should—*take* me anywhere." I accompany this offer with a firm grip to his thigh. At a small gasp, I turn my head and realize Kira was passing by just as I made my suggestive comment. The waitress's eyes flick from me to Aspen to Cat, then back to me, then take another trip to Aspen, then once again land on me. I give her a cocky smile and shallow nod that says, *You heard that right. Have a nice day.*

She hurries away as Aspen tries to dry off Cat across the table. Our Pyro keeps laughing and batting his hands away as little rivulets of steam rise from her skin, showing she can dry herself. With a subtle wave of my fingers, I gather the water that's pooled on the table and send it in a sneaky stream to a nearby potted plant. I figure Aspen would approve of the use.

We trade a few more suggestive, joking comments about being wet until Aspen finally joins in with a reluctant smile. When our food comes out, Kira addresses the table as a whole and is back to her customer service smile. Silently, I decide to leave a hefty tip, feeling a sudden kinship with the woman and her brief crush on Aspen that can never be. Not that her minutes-long hope was anywhere near my years-long pining for these two, but still.

When we're mostly through eating, Aspen gives me a significant look before turning his attention on Cat. "Couldn't help noticing, you seemed to know as much about the aquarium as Rafael."

"I love it there." Cat smiles wide as she bites into a fry.

The Petal Pusher nods. "I can tell. You fit there. You should work there."

Her brows creep up. A massive thigh presses mine under the table, passing me the baton, which I'm happy to pick up.

"You said you left college because mathematics bored you." I was surprised to learn Cat felt that way, having always thought she liked the subject she excelled in. "But have you ever considered studying marine biology? Maybe working in an aquarium?"

For a moment, raw hope and wistfulness dance in Cat's eyes, but then she drops her stare to the table.

"I can't."

"Why not?" Aspen voices my same thought.

"Because I'm a Pyro who can't control her powers." She leans back in the booth seat, arms crossed, stare on her food. "If I got pissed off at work just once, I could kill everything around me. Boil all those innocent creatures."

The day I first ran into Cat at the aquarium returns to my memory. How she'd gotten mad, but then looked terrified. No wonder she's stifled what is clearly her dream.

"Correction: you *were* a Pyro who couldn't control her powers." There are a few empty booths between us and the other customers, and I'm keeping an eye out for Kira's return, so we don't have to whisper to discuss our magic. "But you're doing better, aren't you? The temperature barely changed in the car when Sammy was bothering you."

"We patched things up. I wasn't mad at him," she argues.

As much as I like the idea of Cat getting along with my best friend, I wish she wouldn't dismiss the point so easily.

"But you didn't set off the sprinklers in the club," I press. "I did."

"And maybe I would have if you didn't beat me to the punch." She shrugs, not meeting my eyes.

"Cat." I use every cajoling bone in my body to entice her gaze upward. Something in how I say her name works, and she cautiously meets my eyes. "Are you getting better at controlling your powers?"

She pinches her lips between her teeth, then sighs and nods, the corner of her mouth ticking up in a reluctant smile. And that's something I remember about the Pyro.

She's good at arguing, but not at lying.

"Then you'll *keep* getting better. And in the meantime, maybe work on earning a degree in a field you're passionate about." I let the statement rest between us and go back to my food, Aspen following suit. We stay quiet as she fiddles with her fries, mulling the idea over.

"Do you think any of the universities in Arizona have a Marine Biology program?" She asks.

Triumph floods my chest, and I lean forward eagerly. "I'm sure one of them does. I'm happy to help you look into it." When Cat offers a hopeful smile, I could fucking explode with joy and anticipation.

"Yeah. Okay." She nods. "I want to look into it. I want to apply."

Under the table Aspen gives my knee a squeeze in a silent *good job*. "That's great, Cat. You're going to rock it," he tells her, and an adorable blush steals over her cheeks.

"Seriously, you are." My hands are shaking, I'm so pumped about this. All I want is to take out my phone and start researching. "And I know a bunch of people in the field. I can introduce you around."

She chuckles, eyes dancing at my enthusiasm. "That would be great."

"Oh, and scholarships!" By time I was a senior in college, I was kicking myself for not applying to every single one I was even remotely eligible for. "There are a ton. I'll make a list. I bet you could have the whole degree paid for and money left over for living expenses. Maybe still tutor on the side, but you could quit the club." I'm adding up dollar amounts of the ones I know, and the math works out so Cat could be a full-time student.

"Why would I quit my job at The Jewelry Box?" Her question distracts me from my mental mathematics, and I meet her confused eyes across the table.

Aspen's fingers dig hard into my leg, which I take as his agreement to push on this. "Because you won't need to do it anymore. Wouldn't you rather focus on classes than serving horny guys drinks?"

The excited flush from a moment ago pools high on Cat's cheeks. "That's an oversimplification of my job."

"Come on, Cat." I offer a conciliatory smile even as my fingers comb through my hair in frustration. "You don't want to be out all night waitressing in booty shorts, do you? You're better than that."

Aspen releases my thigh as a strange, choked noise bursts from his throat. I glance over to find his elbow on the table, hand over his eyes as if he can't bear to see what's about to happen. The pose sets off a warning in the back of my head to recalibrate my argument.

Unfortunately, it's too late to listen. Cat is already scooting her way out of the booth, tossing a twenty on the table as she stands.

"Better not touch that," she warns, pointing at the money. "I got it while at my pathetic excuse for a job. Some horny man probably gave it to me." The Pyro glares my way, and even though I see embers in her eyes, not an ounce of her delicious heat touches my skin. "Well, look at that. You were right." She raises her hands as if putting herself on display. "I'm fucking livid, and nothing is on fire. Guess it's time to follow my dreams." Cat whirls on her heel and stalks away, a gorgeous, furious, frustrating woman I want to kiss the hell out of and shake sense into.

When she's gone, I turn to Aspen, searching for an ally.

"What the hell?" I wave at the door where Cat disappeared. "She *wants* to be a marine biologist. Why am I the bad guy here?" My voice breaks on the last question in a flare of panic.

What did I do?

Aspen raises his head with a sigh and fishes his wallet out of his back pocket.

"Think about it, Rafe." The Petal Pusher lays out his own cash for the meal. "You insulted her."

"I told her I believe in her dream," I push back.

He holds my stare, and I find myself wanting to duck under the table and hide.

"And if her dream was to work at The Jewelry Box? If she loved serving drinks there, and wearing her cute outfits, and chatting with customers, would that make her less than to you?"

All my food turns into a noxious swamp in my stomach. "Of course not," I mutter. "But that's not what she *wants*."

Aspen continues to gaze at me. "But it's what she's doing right now. What she's been doing for a while. And you made her feel like..." He trails off, shaking his head and giving a shooing gesture that clearly says *let me out of this booth.*

Kira comes over, smiling as she clears the plates. I fish out payment too as I stand, and she thanks us for the generous tips. Aspen and I walk out to the curb together, where the heat of the day fades as the sun dips below the horizon. I was so looking forward to the next few hours. A whole evening with Aspen and Cat.

"She's not coming over tonight, is she?" I ask, unable to keep the hope out of my voice. *Please tell me I'm wrong.*

Aspen shakes his head. "She'll need some time to cool off. And I think you need some time to formulate an apology."

"So, you're...?" I leave the question open.

"Going to check in on my house. Feel like I haven't been there in an age." He leans in to give me a swift kiss then heads off, hands deep in his pockets, shoulders bowed, obviously as disappointed with this turn of events as I am.

Fuck. Gods damn it to all the hell dimensions.

I screwed up.

Chapter Forty

CAT

When dressing for work the next night, I put on my tightest pair of ruffled shorts and the most revealing metal top I own. The set is as close as I can get to lingerie. Mia's eyebrows rise in appreciation when I walk out of the dressing room, and I flash her a confident smile before heading to the floor. The club won't open for another hour, so I work on prep. I've just finished wiping down tables and lighting candles in wall alcoves when Trevor waves me toward the entrance.

"Hey, there's a guy outside asking for you. Says he's your boyfriend."

Since Trevor knows Aspen, the person outside is either a liar or...

"Rafael?"

The man nods, a relieved smile on his face. "Thought it might be a creep. He's not, right?"

A small, evil part of me wants to say "*yes*," but I immediately dismiss that.

"No. We're dating. I'll go see what he wants." Luckily, I haven't put my heels on yet, so it's easy to jog to the front of the club. Pushing open the door that locks from the inside, I find the handsome Squid lingering on the sidewalk in the fading twilight. I barely stifle my triumphant smirk when his eyes go wide, dragging over every inch of my scantily clad body.

"Rafael." My greeting holds a simmer of yesterday's anger, but I keep my magic temper in check.

"Cat," his voice breaks on my name, and he clears his throat before continuing. "You look—"

"Hot, I know. Is that why you're here?"

"No. I mean, yes, agreed, you are the fucking hottest woman I've ever seen." The truth is in his desperate eyes, but I refuse to preen under the compliment. "But I wanted to talk to you."

Annoyance itches along my nerve endings, especially when I see a group of people strolling down the sidewalk. No way do I want to stand on the street in this get-up, so I wave for him to move his ass inside. Rafael ducks through the door, pausing in the entryway. Once I pull the front door closed and hear the lock latch, I whirl on him and wrap a clawed grasp around his upper arm, dragging him into the dim coat room. The racks are mostly empty except for a collection of jackets left when their owners forgot them. The Jewelry Box has a one-month policy where we wait for the owners to return and claim them. After that, they're up for grabs. I got myself a cool paisley suit jacket that way.

Pushing Rafael behind the forgotten garments, I afford us as much privacy as possible without going to a champagne room.

"Why are you here? At my *job*?" I hiss. "You have my cell number. You also know where I live."

The Squid cringes, hand mussing his soft, honey-brown curls in agitation. "You're right. Sorry. In my head, this played out as an obvious gesture of 'Hey, look, I'm totally cool with you working here!'"

"So you thought I was looking for your approval to keep this job?" I clasp my hands in front of my chest and bat my eyelashes. "Well thank you, kind sir, for your permission."

"I'm fucking up this apology," Rafael mutters.

"Correct."

"Maybe...shit. I'm sorry. I'll leave. And I'll text you."

As he steps toward the exit, I find myself reaching for his arm. I don't know why, but I can't stand the idea of him walking out of this room with this anger hovering between us.

"You're already here, so say what you came to say."

Rafael's gaze rests on my hand, and when I let him go his stare traces up to my face. His jaw tightens as he releases a sharp breath through his nose.

"Okay, here I go. Round two." The Squid spreads his arms wide. "I was a dick. Obviously, being a waitress at a strip club is a real job—a hard one too. I trivialized it because I'm selfish."

"You mean you're *jealous*." If he's going to set off the sprinklers every time I get a compliment at this job, I'm going to have to ban him from the club.

"What? No." He drags fingers through his hair again, threatening to distract me. "Well, maybe a little. But I can manage that. I'm trying to say I'm selfish about your *time*."

"What do you mean?"

Rafael leans his shoulders back against the wall, and I realize for the first time that the coat room is painted a rich sapphire blue. The color looks good as his backdrop.

"When Aspen passes the bar, he's probably going to get a day job at some law firm. Hopefully, one that doesn't work him ragged, so he has free time. But he'll be working during the day like I do." He waves toward the front door, and my mind brings up the image of the darkening sky. "A degree, even if you've already fulfilled some credits, is going to take years to earn. That means school during the day, working the club at night, and seeing me, seeing *us*, barely ever." Rafael's eyes soften with pleading. "But I get it. You've got to hustle for a while so you can do what makes you happy. I'm sorry I wasn't more supportive. And if all you have for me is five minutes a day, then I'll take it. Because I've lived a decade without you in my life, and it's pure hell."

My entire perspective shifts as I rewind through what Rafael said at the diner and use this different lens. Yeah, some of his words were still bad, but I understand his urge to cling to the chance of us. This relationship is too much of all I never admitted I wanted. It doesn't seem real when the two of them aren't in front of me.

Stepping forward, I set my hands on Rafael's chest, enjoying the heavy pound of his heart against my palm. "I don't only want just five minutes with you either." My touch slides upward tracing over his collarbone. "I promise we'll figure this out. Okay?"

"Yes." He sighs out the word, his entire body relaxing, bowing toward me. "Fuck, thank you. Can I...I know we're at your job, but can I kiss you?"

I nod, and the next moment Rafael captures my mouth in a gentle kiss. At least, it starts out that way. But the moment I have the savory taste of him on my tongue, I'm drawing him in closer, lacing my arms around his neck until we're plastered together. My hips press against a hard ridge.

Rafael moans deep in his chest, the noise passing through our kiss into my body. His hands drop to the bare skin of my ass cheeks, boosting me high so I can sling my legs around his hips, and there's suddenly the hard press of a wall at my back. He breaks the kiss, burying his face in my neck even as his hips continue to dry hump the sensitive apex of my thighs.

"Tell me to stop," he rasps against my overly sensitive skin.

"I need you," I gasp back, the confession raw. Gods, do I need this man. I always have. Not to tell me how to live my life, but to be a part of it with his dirty jokes, playful touches, easy smiles, and loyal support.

Rafael mutters a string of curses, and I let out a whimper of protest when he sets me down. But the next moment, he's turning me around, guiding my hands to brace against the wall, dragging my shorts and panties down my thighs, unzipping his pants, stroking his cock head over my swollen pussy lips, and pressing inside.

"Rafael," I moan his name as he wraps an arm around my waist, holding me in place for his steady, relentless thrusts. So close to perfect. I only wish my fingers were digging into the chest of our Petal Pusher rather than drywall.

"I'm never letting you go again, Cat. Got it?" There's an undeniable force in Rafael's voice. A massive wave that can't be stopped, just like the intense pleasure building in the center of my body. "You're mine." His hips jut forward, seating him deep. "Mine." His fingers strum my clit. "Say it."

Even though I'm not sure I can speak, I somehow manage the words. "I'm yours."

My orgasm hits just as the coat rack shakes, dislodging half of the garments that shield us. I'm gasping through an unstoppable wave of ecstasy as I meet a set of wide eyes.

Chapter Forty-One

ASPEN

"Hey, I'm sorry man. I was rooting for you." Trevor gives me a sad smile and a clap on the shoulder when I step through the back door of The Jewelry Box.

"What's that?"

He grimaces. "You and Red. You were trying to get with her, right? Sorry it didn't work out."

My gut bottoms out, but I manage to keep the reaction off my face. "Did she say something to you?"

Trevor's mouth twists. "Nah, just her man showed up out front. She said he's her boyfriend. Tough break. You want me to rough him up?"

Relief eases through me, and I chuckle. "No, it's fine. You're good."

The security guard relaxes at my easy acceptance of the news, and since Cat and I haven't talked about how to handle our relationship at work, I don't hand out any more info. Not yet, anyway. Hopefully, we can tell everyone about her, Rafael, and me at some point soon.

But we are not calling ourselves Ratpen.

I stride out of the back rooms and across the empty club floor, wondering why Rafael is here. I thought he might have talked to me about showing up at the club to apologize to Cat, but the guy is impulsive, so maybe he just didn't think it through. The front entry is empty, and when I push the door open there's no one on the sidewalk.

Confused, I wait until the front door shuts fully before I head back into the club, but my feet pause when I hear a gasp from the coat room. They must have ducked into the space to have it out in private. Stepping around the desk, I wonder what my role should be in this conversation. I want to make peace, support them both without taking sides.

The sound of steady slapping throws me off enough that I pause.

"You're mine." Rafael's voice, colored with lust, is unmistakable. There's another clear sound of skin hitting skin followed by a moan I recognize, too. "Mine." A needy gasp. "Say it."

Don't. The word blares from a desperate, injured part of my chest. *Don't say it.*

"I'm yours."

When I hear those words from Cat, spoken in secret, just for Rafael, something inside me crumbles, setting free a fear I'd done my best to lock away.

They don't need me.

I could've spent the night with Rafael last night, the two of us tangled up together, fucking. But it hadn't felt right to me without Cat.

The same doesn't apply with them.

Why should I be surprised?

They're soulmates. I'm the add-on.

The knowledge has me unsteady as I turn, trying to escape the glaring evidence of my unnecessary presence. My too-broad shoulder knocks against the coat rack, sending jackets sliding off their hangers and revealing an erotic, devastating scene.

Rafael, pants loose around his thighs, bare ass taught, his arm pining Cat tight to him. The little Pyro is gorgeous bent over, her fingers clawing at the wall, her eyes liquid as they meet mine and she melts into her orgasm.

"Fuck," Rafael mutters, so absorbed in Cat that he hasn't even noticed me standing here. Instead, the Squid lets out a choked groan, and I can practically feel him spilling inside her as his body curls over hers.

My feet root into the ground, unable to leave off staring at them.

They're so glorious and yet unreachable. I was deluding myself into thinking I could be part of what they have.

"Aspen!" Cat gasps my name when she regains the ability to speak. Rafael lifts his head, glancing around as he blinks the post-orgasm haze from his eyes. When his gaze meets mine, I watch a charming grin spread across his tempting mouth.

"Thank the gods you're the one who found us. Sorry, Red." He leans down to press a kiss to Cat's shoulder before easing himself out of her. "Could have gotten you in trouble."

She shimmies her shorts up her smooth, toned thighs, then turns to give Rafael a teasing smile. "I'm sure I'm not the first to be debauched in the coat room."

"I'll watch the door." I push the words out of my tight throat, finally turning my back on the scene that will lead to my eventual heartbreak. As I step out to the coat desk, I wonder if I should end things before they go any deeper.

When I left Shawna and Ryan, disengaging from their lives wasn't easy. They didn't want me to go, and I had to pack up all my shit while they tried to cajole me into staying. Maybe it would have worked if they'd said any of the right words.

But all their offers, of dirtier sex, and gifts, and vacations, weren't what I needed from them. In the end, I'd asked for a single thing. They'd balked, so I left.

I'd thought my heart was broken that day, but really, Shawna and Ryan just cracked it. Cat and Rafael could shatter this fragile organ in my chest if I give them the chance.

A touch on my shoulder has me glancing down to see Cat's apologetic gaze. "I know we shouldn't have done that at work. Promise it won't happen again."

Rafael offers a sheepish grin of his own, like they thought I was going to scold them for being naughty children.

"Sounds like you're forgiven." I'm proud that my voice sounds like a close approximation to normal.

If I have to leave these two, I can't do it here. Not when I'll surely break down in the process. I'm going to need a quick escape afterwards.

And then, there's the part of me that wants to stay no matter what.

Even if all I get from them is the crumbs they have left over after feeding each other.

"Tentatively," Rafael agrees before pulling Cat in for a hard lingering kiss that I'd normally love to watch. Now, the intimacy builds a sheet of glass between us, with me the one gazing in on a scene I cannot have.

"Are you heading out or staying?" Cat's question is breathless as she recovers from the passionate affection.

"I'm going to head home and start researching the local marine biology offerings. See if I recognize any of the professors. Maybe I can introduce you if I do." Rafael earns himself another quick kiss from Cat for that, and my masochistic mind points out how they have one more thing to share that doesn't include me.

And then guilt twists my stomach at the selfish thought.

This is another problem with the third-wheel status. I start to grow resentful of things I should be supportive of and excited about. I don't want to become the surly anchor of the relationship, either.

"See you later, Aspen." Rafael brushes a fleeting kiss across my lips before he heads out the front door.

"I'm going to go clean myself up." Cat blushes as she waves to her lower half, no doubt still slick from her arousal and Rafael's orgasm.

"See you on the floor." I hold the curtain to the side for her to sneak back into the club. When she's through, I let the heavy fabric drop, leaving myself alone at the entrance. Robotically, I walk over to the coat room and return the fallen garments to their hangers.

Get through this shift.

Just get through this shift.

When I'm home, alone in my bed tonight, I can figure out my next step.

I can decide if my short stay in Phoenix, in my fantasy of a relationship, has come to an end.

Chapter Forty-Two

CAT

Aspen has been weird all night. Not blatantly, but I'm getting a vibe off him that something isn't quite right.

I force a smile as I set down glasses of whiskey on a VIP table and hurry away before they can try chatting with me the way customers sometimes like to do. Any other night I wouldn't mind because it means bigger tips. But right now, my mind is too focused on the security guard heading across the floor to take his shift at the front door.

Normally, we lock eyes and share a grin, or a wink, or a funny face. But he doesn't look around for me.

I chew on my lip and fiddle with my tray. Was he really put off by Rafael and I having sex at work? Maybe it was hypocritical of me to get mad about Rafael belittling my job, then fuck him in the coat room the next day.

Does Aspen think I start fights for no reason?

Do I do that?

Silently, I admit that storming out of the diner wasn't the most mature move. I should've stayed and explained to Rafael why what he said was hurtful.

"What's with the frowny face? Any of the customers giving you trouble?" Mia studies me as she sets the next round of drinks on my tray.

I shake my head. "Just thinking about things. Probably worrying over nothing."

But at the end of the night, as Aspen walks me to my car with my work bag hanging on his shoulder, I find myself hesitant to ask what has been a normal question for the past few weeks.

"You ready to head to Rafael's?" I try for a lighthearted tone, longing to see the Petal Pusher's beard crinkle with a smile. "Should we take bets on if he's still awake?"

Aspen doesn't meet my eyes. "I'm kind of beat." He opens the door to my back seat, carefully placing my bag inside before closing things up and giving the top of my car a good-to-go pat.

He's he going to leave without a goodbye?

My heart stutters and cramps in my chest, begging me to cling to him. But I don't want to force him into anything.

Luckily, familiar warm hands cup my face, tilting me at the right angle for his mouth to meet mine. Aspen kisses me deeply, his tongue stroking into my mouth to dance with mine until I'm gasping, moaning for him to do more.

Touch me. Take me. Prove there's nothing wrong.

But he ends the kiss and holds me in place before I can maul him.

"Bye, Cat." Aspen touches his forehead to mine before releasing me and taking a purposeful step back.

No. My fingers press hard against my lips, and my eyes are suddenly watery as I watch his shoulders slump as he walks away.

That sounded less like "Bye, Cat. I'll see you tomorrow," and more like "Bye, Cat. I'm going to miss you when I'm gone."

Tense with panic, my fingers shake as I turn on my car and drive to a familiar address. I find the key to the back door under a potted cactus and let myself in, then sprint down the hall to the bedroom, coming upon the only person who can help me fix this.

I grasp Rafael's shoulders and shake him awake. His handsome head bobbles back and forth for a moment before he blinks sleepy eyes open.

"Hey, sexy lady," he purrs the greeting as he reaches for me, gaze already melting hot.

"None of that," I slap his hands away then clap mine in his face to get his attention. "I need you to wake up. All the way up. Something is wrong."

That has the Squid sitting upright, rubbing a hand over his face as if sleep is a sticky film he just needs to brush away.

"What did I do?" Rafael asks as I pace beside his bed, his eyes tracking me then flitting around the room. "Where's Aspen?"

"That's the problem." I gesture to all the empty space in the room. "He didn't come. He said he was tired, but he's been off all night. I think something is wrong."

"Wrong, like he's sick?"

"No. Wrong like he's mad. Or, upset, I guess. Does Aspen ever get mad?"

Rafael's mouth opens as if to provide an example, but then he shuts his jaw and tilts his head thoughtfully.

I fill the silence with my insecurity. "Do you think it's because I hooked up with you at my job after getting mad that you said it wasn't real work?"

"Again, I'm sorry. I didn't mean—"

I cut him off with a wave of my hands. "I know. That's not why I'm bringing it up. I'm just...do you think that Aspen is annoyed I lost my temper so easily? That I yelled at you?"

Rafael frowns as he ponders the explanation I came up with. "No. I don't think that's it. After you left, he was more unhappy with me. He said I should give you some space to cool off." He snatches my hand as I pass by. "Maybe that's how you and I work through stuff. We have a little fight, take some time to think and breathe, then we come back together and work to be better moving forward. Just not twelve years this time." He offers a smile I try to return but can't quite, still stuck on the Aspen conundrum now that Rafael disproved my theory.

"And he didn't say anything the rest of the night? Something that might hint at what's wrong?"

Rafael shakes his head. "He headed back to his place after the diner. We didn't spend the rest of the night together."

"You didn't?"

"Nope. Don't worry. You didn't miss out on any wild sex with your boyfriends while we were on the outs. Of course, that means it's been over twenty-four hours since Aspen got some. Maybe he was testy because he was horny," Rafael jokes.

"You and he didn't…" Realization burns through me with the speed of a painfully hot wildfire. "That's it! We slept together without him!"

Rafael frowns. "We're not allowed to have sex unless we're all present?"

"No. Maybe. Ugh, I don't know the rules of throuples." I tug my hand out of his. "Maybe there aren't any. But I do know this…" Digging into my pocket, I pull out my phone and navigate to my email. As I scroll through the messages Aspen and I shared over the years, I settle beside Rafael and tilt the screen his way. He props his chin on my shoulder to read.

"Here it is. This is what he said a few months before he broke up with the last couple he was dating. When I asked how things were going." Together, we silently read Aspen's typed words.

I'm not sure. I thought we were serious, which is why I agreed to move in. But they're going to visit David, their oldest son, for the holidays and didn't invite me. I don't think their kids know we're together.

"Shit," Rafael mutters. "He was living with them, and they didn't tell their family?"

I nod then scroll to a new message. "This too."

Shawna and Ryan are in Vegas for the week. It's a work thing for Ryan, so only Shawna went with him.

"They didn't tell their coworkers about him," I clarify. "I think people just thought he was renting a room in their house."

"That's fucked up."

With a few swipes, I make it to the message Aspen sent telling me about the breakup. He didn't go into a lot of detail, but I point out two sentences in particular.

It felt like they were a couple, and I was an add-on. That I would never be a truly equal partner in the relationship.

"When he walked in on us…" Rafael starts.

"We seemed like a couple. And he probably felt like an add-on," I finish the horrible statement. The pair of us stare at each other, anguished to know that we inadvertently brought up this painful reminder of a past failed relationship. That we might be making the same exact mistakes that could drive away the man we care about.

"He thinks we don't need him," I whisper.

Chapter Forty-Three

ASPEN

I've been staring at my bedroom ceiling for the last few hours, unable to sleep. Instead, I've been twining myself in tight, suffocating knots thinking about staying in a relationship with two people who don't love me the way I love them, versus leaving those two people and never having any part of them.

A loud click at my window distracts me, and I glance over in time to watch the lower frame slide up. I'm too shocked to react at first, and by the time I've regained the ability to move, a familiar face with a head of tousled, honey-brown locks appears over the sill.

"I told you this wasn't hard," he stage-whispers to someone over his shoulder, then proves himself wrong by overbalancing and toppling the rest of the way into my bedroom, landing on the floor in a crumpled heap. "Fuck."

"Rafael?" A sneaker, then a pale leg, then a tight ass in cut-offs appears. Cat straddles my windowsill and tucks her torso through the opening, finding her boyfriend on my floor. "I told you it's best to go feet first on the ground floor."

"Noted." Rafael shoves his body into a seated position then extends a hand, which Cat grasps for balance as she finishes her smooth entry.

Even as my heart aches at the sight of them, I find myself smiling. "You call that stealthy?"

The pair face me, finally acknowledging I'm in the room.

"I told you where the spare key is," I add.

"Yes, but this is symbolic." Cat waves toward the window. "Kind of a tradition."

I push myself up to lean back on my headboard, my brief flare of humor fading away. "Symbolic of what?"

"That you're worth climbing through windows for," Rafael announces as he pops up to stand at the foot of my bed. "Now, let's get those briefs off you and your dick in my mouth."

"Rafael!" Cat gives the Squid a proper glare, but he returns a playful smirk.

"I'm still going with the '*Aspen needs to get laid*' route. What say you, big man?" My boyfriend—at least in the current moment—sets one knee on the bed, dipping the mattress, then proceeds to crawl up my body until his mouth reaches my bare chest. The Squid flicks his tongue in my belly button, before running his teeth along my waistband.

"Take them off," I croak.

Tomorrow, I can take steps to preserve my state of mind. Now, I can't think past the idea of the two of them naked, pressed against me.

Rafael drags the elastic over my half-hard cock, then down my clenching thighs until he pulls my briefs off completely.

"Fine," Cat sighs. "We'll do this your way." The fiery woman strips off her shirt, toes out of her shoes, and shimmies her hips until her shorts pool at her ankles. She's not wearing a bra or panties.

"Shit, Cat. Warn a man." Rafael has his body draped over one of my legs, and I can feel him thickening where his hips press against my calf. Leisurely, the man wraps his hand around my dick, circling his thumb on the head and applying the perfect amount of pressure to have me hard as oak in his palm.

The bed dips again as Cat climbs on. I hold out a hand, ready to guide her to my side or maybe to straddle my torso. But the Pyro scoops up my hand, presses a kiss to the palm, then grips my shoulder and tilts me forward until she can slide in behind me.

I recline on Cat, her thighs splayed wide around my waist, her soft breasts pressing into my shoulder blades, her warm breaths teasing over my ear, and her hot core kissing my lower back. My breath drags into my chest as I attempt to catalogue all the pleasurable ways the three of us touch. Then, Rafael wraps his lips around me, swallowing deep, and I lose all brain function for a moment.

"Gods," I bark, my hips jerking up, my toes curling with sensation. Meanwhile, Cat circles her arms around my torso, smoothing her hands down my chest as though seeking to calm me. Her plush lips press to the pounding pulse in my neck, over and over, an unending display of gentle affection.

The Squid has me in a firm grip, and I'm a second away from spilling on his tongue. As if sensing this, Rafael lets me pop free of his mouth.

And his hand stops moving.

And Cat's kisses pause.

"How are you doing, Aspen?" she asks, low and sweet against my ear.

"I-I'm about to come," I groan out. *Please, don't stop. Give me this just a few more times.*

"We'll get to that in a second." Cat's voice dances over the skin on my neck, and her fingers gently scratch my beard in a subtly pleasant gesture that threatens to roll my eyes up into my head. "I meant, how are you doing since your move back to Phoenix? Have you started studying for the bar?"

"You..." My hips give an involuntary rock, my cock seeking out the warm, wet suction of Rafael's mouth, but the devious Squid just grins up at me and traces an idle thumb over my sensitive head. "You want to talk about that *now*?"

"Mm-hmm." Cat drifts her lips along the shell of my ear. "How do you study for it? Is there any way we can help?"

Confused hope tightens in my chest, and I struggle to breathe. "I don't know," I gasp. "Maybe."

"Good. You let us know how, okay? Because we're here for you." Her teeth pinch my earlobe, and I pant and clench my hands, wishing I could see her. That I could understand what's happening.

Then Rafael starts to idly stroke my length. "How about after you pass? Any law firms you like the look of?"

"Um..." *What the hell kind of dirty talk is this? And why is it working so well?* "There's a-a copyright office. Downtown. An old school friend works there." I reach down to tug on my balls, desperate to achieve the release that's *right there*. But Rafael—the demon—bats my hand away as if my cock is just for him.

Which only makes me hotter.

"They'd be lucky to have you." The Pyro teases my neck with a slow lick. "Did your parents mention the cookout in a few weeks?"

Well, that throws me off even more than this odd interrogation already has.

"Could we not talk about my family? You know, because..." I gesture to where Rafael continues to grip my erection, and I give a subtle press back against Cat's bare pussy. She giggles, burying her face in my neck, and Rafael drags his thick tongue from base to crown, setting off twitching all over my body. My palms are heavy as lead, filled to the brim with earth magic.

Because...damn it. How did they do that?

Because I'm *so* fucking happy right now.

Needing release, I siphon a portion of the power off, sending the paranormal fuel to my shelf full of plants on the far wall of my bedroom. I watch from the corner of my eye as glossy green leaves unfurl and vines drop lower, reaching to the floor.

"Sorry," Cat chuckles through her apology. "I only meant that *all* our families are going to be there. And I thought it'd be a good time to let them all know we're officially an item. But we're not calling ourselves Ratpen. *Or* Assfat." I can hear the glare in her voice on that last sentence.

Rafael smirks, then dips down to press a kiss to my hip bone. All the while, his hand maintains the steady, slow stroking, as if he plans to hypnotize me with the movement.

"What do you say?" the Squid asks against my skin.

Hope rises as fast and thick as my impending orgasm, but I'm worried my mind is too fogged with lust for me to protect myself.

"I can't be some side addition for you two," I manage to force the worry out, taking an axe to my protective bark and revealing my sensitive inner rings "Not a couple plus one—plus me."

Cat's feet sneak around my torso until her ankles hook together. Then, she hugs me with her entire body.

"We're not complete without you," she says, the confession burning against my ear. "You're the glue that holds us together. Everything falls apart without you."

"We never would have found our way back to each other without you," Rafael adds, his hand pausing at my base, but not letting go.

"But now you are together," I manage to point out even as a desperate part of me begs not to push. "You don't need me anymore."

Cat's hug gets tighter. "Don't say that. We do. We *need* you, Aspen." Her hand presses against my cheek, turning my head until I meet her eyes over my shoulder. "I need you. You're mine. I'm yours." Leaning in, she presses her rosebud-scented mouth to mine, and I groan into the kiss. "Say it," she commands softly against my lips.

"I'm yours," I sigh out, loving the sound of the words. "And you're mine."

A sucking pull at my cock demands my attention, and I meet a serious set of eyes. "You're mine. I'm yours," Rafael growls, resting the tip of me on his lower lip. "Say it."

"I'm yours." I hold his eyes. "And you're mine."

"Good man." Then he swallows me, relentlessly bobbing up and down until pleasure chokes me. With one hand I clutch Cat's thigh, with the other I delve into his messy curls. Then I give myself over to the almost unbearable sensation of being surrounded and claimed by the two people I love.

"You're ours," Cat informs me between kisses to my erratic pulse. "We're yours."

Ecstasy collides with joy and envelopes me. I groan an animal sound as I spill down Rafael's throat. Green power smelling of earth seeps from my palms and vines crawl across the floor of my room, but I don't care because, Cat and Rafael are here, and they know me, and want me, and we're in this together.

"Aspen!" Cat gasps out my name on a laugh and scoops up my hands that are glowing green. "Rein it in before you build a rainforest!" She presses kisses to my palms as she scolds me, not really helping calm my libido or dampen my happiness, but I tug back on the power as much as I can.

A fact snags in the back of my mind: how I never truly struggled to control my magic with Shawna and Ryan. I'd felt it in my palms, but they never knew that truth about me, so I always held it back.

And there was always a shadow of sadness in between me and them.

With Cat and Rafael, I'm finally, fully content.

Chapter Forty-Four

RAFAEL

These kinds of gatherings never happened when I was growing up. I stare around the large property in wonder, knowing that all the attendees of this picnic are either elementals, or know about our kind.

"This is massive," I mutter.

Okay, the collection isn't *that* huge, but there are definitely over fifty people here. When my family moved to Phoenix, my mom told me they found others like them through whispers and hints. It's hard to connect with other magical beings living in a world surrounded by humans who might want to do weird experiments on us if they find out what we can do.

Sorry, but the only people allowed to stick probes up my butt are standing next to me.

"I think Yasmin has this grand idea of building an elemental utopia in Phoenix. Or something like that." Cat names the owner of The Jewelry Box, who apparently is a very rich Airhead judging by the size of her sprawling house. I wonder if everyone here knows a strip club is paying for this property. As a group of kids runs by, I would guess *no*.

"Isn't that what Damien's trying to do?" Aspen asks, which has me pondering the regular get-togethers my friend holds for elementals at his backyard pool. I always figured he was looking for a good time, but now that I think about it, those backyard BBQs have given us the chance to relax with each other. To de-stress somewhere other than our own homes.

And I thought *his* backyard was beautiful, but Damien's place is a puddle compared to this true oasis. Yasmin has multiple acres of property landscaped to perfection with a skillful blend of natural plant life, winding paths, and stone patios shaded from the sun with awnings and palm trees. Everything is centered around a pool that has three separate waterfalls and beckons me to peel off my dress clothes and sink below the surface.

But not before I strip down Cat and Aspen too.

I shake my head and refocus on the family-friendly get-together. At least, as family-friendly as a gathering held by Yasmin can be. My guess is, the woman has more business ventures going on than a single—if well-earning—strip club.

"Maybe they should team up. Yasmin is well on her way to convincing my parents to move back here from Tucson." Cat gestures toward a couple I haven't seen since I was a teenager. Mrs. Byrne looks most like Quinn: tall, with centerfold curves and silky red hair down to her waist. And yes, adolescent me was very aware of the term MILF. Long ago, I vowed to never share that brief crush with anyone, for fear of word getting back to Cat and her melting my favorite pair of lucky soccer cleats.

"Hey, friends!" Hands clap on my shoulders from behind, and I recognize the overeager energy of my best friend. Sammy moves to dig an elbow into my side. "Mrs. Byrne is looking spicy as ever. Am I right Rafe, my boy?"

And now, I belatedly recall how, on a white-water rafting trip in West Virginia, I got drunk one night by the campfire and spilled the secret to Sammy.

Damn past me. That guy can't hold his moonshine.

"For everyone's safety," Cat keeps her voice soft and face serene, "I'm going to pretend you didn't say that."

"You're right. I'm sorry." Sammy's apology sounds surprisingly sincere, and I gape at the man, wondering if the humans already got to him and replaced my friend with a less-outrageous android.

"Ready to head in?" Aspen asks, his voice a touch gruffer than usual. Cat and I share a look before focusing on our boyfriend. The guy fiddles with the collar of his button-up shirt as if trying to get the perfectly ironed piece to lay flat. And I know it's perfectly ironed because I'm the one who did it. In the past month, I've made it my mission to help dress the man. Not that I want Aspen to do away with his everyday mountain man chic, but how's he going to win any court cases wearing a wrinkled suit?

He likes to argue that his suits aren't wrinkled and fit him fine, and he doesn't even spend time in the courtroom that often with the kind of law he does.

Conclusion? He's wearing a new shirt Cat and I picked out for him.

"Aspen." Cat glances my way then back up at our man. "Does your family know about us?" She asks the question carefully. This topic—who knows about us three and when—was a big issue in his past relationship.

After our sexy ambush—and a few hours of sleep to recover—Aspen told us more about how things had fallen apart between him and his exes. Turns out, the two of them made him jump through a hell of a lot of hoops, more than he talked about in his emails to Cat, to keep up the illusion they were a two-person couple. One time, they booked him a stay in a local hotel so he would be out of the house when their kids visited. Then, they had the gall to show up one night during the visit for a quicky. Another time, they convinced him to go on a date with Ryan's boss's daughter.

He had more examples, and each one broke my heart. Cat's too, from the devastated look on her face. Also, she accidentally melted the metal spatula she was holding while making pancakes. No one faulted her for the lapse in control.

"Geneva does, obviously," he says. Of course, as she was on the birth control road trip. "The rest know about us in theory. I told them." His beard crinkles with a hopeful smile, though his eyes still hold worry. "But they never met my exes. This is new to them. I just...hope it goes okay." He returns to fiddling with his collar.

I face him, batting his hands away and making sure the fabric lies straight, then I drag him in for a PDA-inappropriate kiss. When I let up, the Petal Pusher's eyes are dilated, he's panting, and I smell earth in the air.

"I'm worried my mom is going to think I'm the same as my dad," I confess. "A playboy who can't commit." I tilt my head Cat's way. "She's the baby of a family that could set us on fire if they want, and they're about to meet the two guys fucking her. We've got a lot of hurdles to get through today." I snake my arm around Aspen's waist and guide him forward at my side. "But we're gonna crush them together."

"You don't crush hurdles. Or family members," Cat corrects as she slides her hand into Aspen's, so we flank our boyfriend. "But yeah, we'll get over them together."

"Me too?" Sammy asks from behind us.

"Only if you don't make things worse," I warn, fully aware that my friend could cause a drama storm if he gets bored.

"Cool. I'll be the trailer on the back of your tricycle." Takes the guy two seconds to change his mind. "Scratch that, I'm the plow hooked to the front. You all walk too slow." Sammy dodges around us and strolls into the party.

"Okay. Together." Aspen's arm settles as a warm, reassuring weight over my shoulders, and I see his fingers lace with Cat's. "Which family first?"

That's the question, isn't it?

"Looks like Ms. Aguado found my mom," Cat points out. "Let's start there."

My Mom and Cat's parents.

I coax my water magic to the surface in case I need to put out any fires.

Chapter Forty-Five

CAT

As the three of us make our way through the gathering of elementals, I debate about the possible outcomes of this interaction. When I spy Harley joining my parents when we're almost to them, I try not to cringe.

As far as I know, she's still not a Rafael fan.

"Hey Mom! Dad!" *Is that too cheery?* From the way their eyes widen, my guess is yes. Far more upbeat than normal. Harley smirks, seeing straight through my bubbly facade.

After another squeeze of Aspen's hand, I let go so I can give my parents hugs. Ever since they moved to Tucson, I don't see them as often. This time, it's been close to a month.

"Missed you, little ember," my dad says, engulfing me in his meaty arms for a hearty hug. He smells like burning cedar and home. When he sets me down, I catch a curious twinkle in his eyes as he glances toward my boyfriends.

Just you wait, Dad.

My mom is almost as tall as Aspen, standing a good few inches above my average-height father, and she has to bend over to give me her own hug. "How are you doing?"

Her question has a not-so-hidden one.

Who are these men you brought with you?

I didn't consider the fact that she wouldn't recognize either of them.

"Felicity," Ms. Aguado—noting my parents' confused stares—says my mom's name with a jokingly scolding tone. "You don't remember my darling boy?"

Rafael greets his mom with a quick kiss on her cheek, and my mother's brows practically disappear into her hairline. "Rafael? Rafael Aguado? I haven't seen you since..." She trails off, face contorted with thought.

Since before our fight, probably.

"It's been a while, Mrs. Byrne. Mr. Byrne. Good to see you both." He's wearing his charming, I-can-melt-any-heart-I-want smile.

The grin works on my mom as she clasps him in a quick hug. My dad seems unaffected as he shakes Rafael's hand. Harley wrinkles her nose like she smells dog poop.

That's something I'm going to need to work on.

I recapture my Petal Pusher's hand, tugging him forward into the group. "And you remember Aspen? I know he has a beard, but he's the same softy underneath." I give his stomach a poke, earning a gruff chuckle.

"Aspen Baumann?" My mother says his name the way she would say *"Free Louboutins?"*

"Hi, Mrs. Byrne. Ms. Aguado. Mr. Byrne." Aspen leans forward to hold out his hand for a shake but my mother is too busy engulfing him in a chokehold hug.

"Are you and Cat back together?" she asks, but doesn't wait for an answer. "When did this happen? Do you live in Phoenix now?"

"Mom!" I consider prying her iron grip from his neck but have no idea if I can break her hold. "Calm down. You're strangling him."

The threat of murder has her loosening her grip, but she keeps her hands on his shoulders and looks him over. "You're even taller! I'm sure Cat doesn't mind. Short ladies love a tall man. Short men love a tall lady."

"That's the truth," my father agrees with a jovial smile, while I silently beg Harley with my eyes to make our mother stop.

My sister gives me a too innocent eye bat as she shrugs and mouths, *What?*

Traitor.

Glancing over to Rafael, I find him staring at the exchange between my mother and Aspen with a wistful expression. No doubt he wishes his greeting had been as enthusiastic.

"We're all dating!" This comes out far too loud, but I'm too far gone to turn back. Apparently, awkward yelling is how I update my family members on my romantic life. "Aspen, and me, and Rafael. All together." Then in a panic, I start pointing. "Him, him, me. One, two, three." I rhyme and count us off like our parents are a class of preschoolers.

"A-B-C," Quinn adds, appearing at my side with August in tow. "You're finally telling them about Assfat?"

"Oh my gods," I groan at the unfairness of unhelpful sisters. "That is *not* our throuple name!"

"Yeah, sorry Quinn." Rafael, cheerier than a moment ago, hooks his arm around my waist. "We're sticking with Ratpen."

"Rafael, Cat, Aspen," Harley explains to the confused parents.

"This was a mistake," I announce. "I'm calling it off!"

Rafael clasps my chin, holding me in place to plant a loud, smacking kiss on my mouth in front of the whole group. "Too late. We're not letting you get away."

Aspen steps away from my mom with a nod and a grateful smile, then raises my hand to his lips for a more family-friendly kiss that somehow feels just as intimate. "I second that."

"Motion passed," Rafael declares with a nod.

I roll my eyes, even as a grin plumps my cheeks. Then, my eyes find their way back to my parents, and I steel my spine to take whatever probing or judgmental comments come next.

Which is why I'm left confused when my mom slaps a hearty high five against Ms. Aguado's hand, and my dad mumbles, "They seem like two nice young men. There's beer at this party, right?"

"Yeah, Dad. I'll find you one." Harley blows me a kiss then hooks her arm around our dad's shoulders and leads him away.

That went better than I expected.

"Mom," Rafael has lost a touch of his bravado from before. "You're cool with everything?"

Quinn and August meander away, giving the five of us some privacy.

"Little guppy." Ms. Aguado sighs with a happy smile, and I use all my willpower not to snicker at the nickname. "It's Cat and Aspen. Of course, I'm okay. I love this for you."

In one stride Rafael returns to his mother, scooping her up in a hard hug. The sight is so touching, I find my arms sneaking around Aspen's waist too. His solid, comforting hand rests on my back, stroking gentle circles. And that's when I notice the flowers blooming on a nearby cactus. I decide not to mention to Aspen his magic might be overflowing.

Meanwhile, Mom's wide, happy eyes flick between the two men before meeting mine.

Nice, she mouths, offering a double thumbs up.

Gods, my family is embarrassing. But damn if I don't love the hell out of them.

Same as I love my Squid and Petal Pusher.

This is going to work.

Chapter Forty-Six

ASPEN

After the loving acceptance from the Byrne and Aguado families, I held high hopes for mine...

which crashed and burned within seconds of finding the Baumann clan.

"The three of you? You were serious?" My brother Birch looks between Cat, Rafael, and me as his wife herds their two kids away with a furtive glance, like we're about to start detailing our sex life. But it turns out, us three aren't the ones to bring intercourse into the discussion.

"But do you plan to have kids with both?"

If I thought Cat was naturally pale before, my mother's question proves me wrong. All the blood drains from my girlfriend's face at the probing inquiry, and I pull my Pyro back against my chest and drape a protective arm over her front.

"Mom. Come on. We just started dating," I reply, even though my mind is already set on forever with them. "When we have that conversation, you're not going to be a part of it."

My mother presses a palm to her chest and her face crumples, as if I wounded her. My guts clench at the sight, but Cat's hot, trusting hand around my forearm roots me, and Rafael's presence at my side supports me.

"All I meant to say is, you love kids," Mom presses. "I hope Cat knows that. I mean, two dads in the household. That's lovely." She offers an encouraging smile that doesn't make me feel better. "And no offense to you, Rafael. It's just that Aspen is such a great uncle. And I think it would mean the world if—"

"Gods, Mom!" Geneva shoves in between us, a whirling ball of righteous fury. "You already have *thirteen* grandchildren. You're really that hard up for more? Are you going to start sneaking Cat prenatal vitamins? Maybe poke a few holes in their condoms?"

My mother gasps, but my sister is on a roll.

"Not everyone wants kids! And they definitely don't want their parents pressuring them about it! Welcome to the twenty-first century" —Geneva extends her hand for a shake—"my name is '*Smashing the Patriarchy*,' have we met?"

"Oh, the Earth Mother tested my patience the day she gifted me you," my mom huffs at my baby sister. "I cannot speak to you when you're like this." As the elder earth elemental stalks away, Geneva strides after her, sending me a thumbs up over her shoulder.

"But I thought you *love* kids," she shouts at my mother's retreating form. "Well, here I am, Mom! Bask in the glory of your progeny!"

Though the party continues around us, voices floating through the space, silence lingers in our little throuple. Of course, Rafael is the first to break it.

"I want your sister to be *my* sister," Rafael declares. "And I guess she kind of is, now. Never had siblings before."

No, Rafael is an only child with a mom who wants his happiness without conditions. Cat's sisters have both accepted me, and despite a little awkwardness on her dad's part, the Byrne parents are supportive.

Fuck. My family is the problem. Are Cat and Rafael going to want to deal with this for the long term?

"Rafe," Cat tugs on Rafael's shirt. "He's panicking."

Belatedly, I realize she's talking about me. And next I know, a set of entrancing gray eyes captures mine. "Hey there, big oak. We got you. We're not going anywhere."

At the sound of my nickname, a seed of relief sprouts in my chest. Then, Rafael is kissing me hard, and he's so fucking good at it that actual tears clog up the back of my throat. When he finishes with a gentle nip to the corner of my mouth, I'm centered again. Still, shame at the way my family acted has me searching for words to make it better.

"I'm sorry, Cat. I never expected that. I mean, I know my mom likes kids, but still..."

My Pyro meets my gaze, hers full of loving understanding as she holds my hand, fiddling with my fingers. "It's okay. Your family needs some time to cope. That doesn't change things between us."

"What she said." Rafael kneads my shoulders, working to loosen the knots tightening my neck. "It'll be fine. We've got time. And magical birth control."

Cat grins, and the beautiful sight paired with Rafael's hands on me finally eases away the tension.

"Yeah. Okay. We've got time," I agree.

"Hey."

The three of us turn at the sound of the greeting to find Harley snuck up on us, three glass beer bottles expertly clutched in one hand, while the other holds an open one she sips from.

"Here. Looks like you three need these." As she passes them around, I notice her sultry sense of humor is missing. When the Pyro extends the last bottle to Rafael, she keeps a hold of the neck, locking them together momentarily. "I'm sorry." At the admission, Cat gives a little gasp, and I realize I'm witnessing history. The oldest Byrne sister's lips twist then straighten, her face relaxing into acceptance. "People change. You obviously have, in a good way. And I don't want you—any of you—thinking I'm against your relationship." Harley lets go of the bottle and stares into her little sister's eyes. "I'm for you being happy. Always."

My boyfriend's face turns blotchy, and he blinks faster than usual. "Thanks, Harley. That means a lot."

She smirks, the serious note gone and replaced with her customary *I own this room* aura. The dominatrix steps forward and wraps her arms around Rafael and me, pulling the two of us in for a hug. "Welcome to the family."

"Oh no," Cat whispers with a gleeful smile. "Say hello to your new outrageous, overprotective big sister."

Chapter Forty-Seven

CAT

A few months later

"And what is...*novus*...gods, what is this? I don't even know if I can pronounce it." Failing at my flash card duties, I extend the card to Aspen so he can read the legal jargon.

"It's Latin. *Novus actus interveniens*," he says. "That refers to an intervening act that breaks the chain of causation."

"Ah yes, of course." I flip to the next one and stifle a groan. "I swear you're making these up."

Aspen's laugh booms through the relatively empty club. Tuesdays aren't normally this slow, but there's a big music festival, which is both drawing customers away for the night and clogging up the roads with traffic. Still, Yasmin insisted on opening, claiming we'll probably get a huge influx when the shows are over, but people want to keep partying. For now, I'm trying not to bother my single customer as he gazes at Jade's expert pole work.

Instead, Aspen and I are using the slow night to study. Well, he studies, and I'm doing my best to help. I thought I could at least handle quizzing him on vocabulary, but apparently lawyers like to speak in a dead language.

I'll get my revenge in the fall when I start back at school. Already, I've received two acceptance letters from universities with marine biology programs. Now, I just need to choose. And we'll see how well Aspen does sounding out all the scientific names of the sea creatures I'll be studying.

Luckily, before I have to try pronouncing another nonsensical word, a familiar face pushes through the curtained entry. Rafael scans the room and spies us at the bar. He makes a short detour by the stage to toss Jade a bill and a wave, then comes toward us.

"Hey you." He cups the back of Aspen's head and brushes a kiss over his mouth. "And hey you too." Rafael smiles down at me, giving the same delicious greeting before settling on the stool at my side. "It's dead in here, huh?"

"Festival," Aspen and I say at the same time, and he smirks at me.

"What'll it be, pretty boy?" Mia asks, looking as bored as the rest of us.

"Something fruity. Surprise me."

A spark lights in her eyes. "Dangerous words. Let me see what I can whip up."

"Here." I hand Rafael the flashcards as I spy the curtain parting again. "Gotta work for five minutes."

After swinging by my already seated customer and checking that he's good with his Jack and Coke, I search the club until I spy the new arrival in the VIP section—another familiar face.

"Hey, Sammy. What's your poison?" I greet the Squid with zero of the menace I used to. Since we talked it out—or, I guess, wrote it out—I find his brand of humor much less annoying. Also, he's dialed his cocky bullshit down a few notches, which helps.

"Red. You look gorgeously bored this evening." He reclines back on the plush leather sofa that would look at home in an old castle library. Something a handsome duke might sit on.

"Why thank you," I affect a curtsy. "What do you want from the bar? Mia is whipping up a secret cocktail for Rafael. Did you see he's here? Aspen is working tonight too."

"Ah, okay. They're here. Cool. Cool, cool, cool." The handsome Squid suddenly seems a few notches less confident, and I immediately realize why. With all my willpower, I suppress an evil grin, wearing my sweetly innocent mask instead.

"Drink?" I press once more.

"Uh, yes. Sure. Whatever Mia's specialty is." His eyes stray to the main stage, where Jade is making her way off and toward my Jack and Coke. I silently wish her luck and a big tip and try not to look like I'm running when I hurry back to the bar.

"Sammy wants whatever you're making Rafael," I tell the Airhead as she shakes the mystery drink, and she gives me a pleased nod. Job done, I skip up to my boyfriends, trying not to cackle in glee.

"Did you say Sammy is here?" Rafael glances around the club.

"I did! And you're going to want to see this. You came on a good night." I clasp Rafael's shoulders and turn him to face the VIP section. From this angle, we can only spy the top of Sammy's blonde head, but that's going to change soon.

Aspen gives me a confused look, which only has me grinning wider.

"You've always been working the door when this happens!" I'm basically squealing now, no longer bored in the slightest. "Ugh, this night just got *so* good. Watch."

Both men follow my direction, observing the general area where their friend is. The music changes, along with the lighting, which is how it always goes when a new dancer takes the stage. The lights are a shimmery white, and the song has a slow sensual beat.

Then, Pearl takes the stage.

The woman always reminds me of Marilyn Monroe, only with longer blonde hair and no adorable mole on her lip. But the sensual curves and natural sex appeal are there in spades. She has on silky shorts that show the bottom curves of her ass cheeks, a filmy sheer top showing the shadow of her nipples, and her bare feet sparkle with the same pearlescent glitter that coats the rest of her skin.

And, as always, a lacy mask covers the top half of her face.

Dancers approach their sets in different ways. Some stick to the edges of the stage, flirting with the crowd. Others utilize the pole to put themselves on creative display and to inspire the imagination.

But Pearl, I've always felt like she enters a meditative state when she gets on the stage. Like the dancing is all for her.

And that disinterest in everyone but herself—plus the mystery of her disguise—draws the customers like moths to a glittering flame.

One customer in particular.

"Watch this," I urge again.

Pearl smoothly enters her set by climbing the pole, then effortlessly descending in ways that would freak the hell out of me. But she's controlled and provocative the whole time.

Sammy levitates from his seat, caught by her movements. The Squid tries to play it cool, straightening the sleeves of what I now see is a *very* expensive suit, and meandering closer to the stage.

He's not fooling anyone.

There's a portion of the main stage that butts up against the VIP section. Sammy pauses there and pulls out a bill from his inner pocket, holding the cash up in two fingers. Pearl is on her knees now, practically making love to the pole, oblivious to Sammy's existence, even though he's the only one offering her money. Jack and Coke is thoroughly engrossed in Jade at the moment.

For half a song Sammy stands there, money out, eyes on Pearl. When she makes no move toward him, he reaches in his pocket to pull out another bill.

Mia sets two red cocktails on the bar beside me, then covers them with a large glass globe. "Give it a little smoke?" Her eyes hold a mischievous sparkle, and I can't help an eager smile in return.

Carefully, I press my fingertips to the glass and pull on the slow pulse of my magic. This is a trick I can't pull on busy nights with too many eyes. But with so few customers, my powers can play. Not a bit of me is angry, so I have to use more effort, but with a delicate task like this, a slow draw is better. Soon the orb is filled with smoke, and my skin is a touch tender. Mia nods in thanks, lifting the covering and letting the gray tendrils drift toward the shadowy ceiling. She sets one drink on my tray and slides the other to Rafael.

"Also, just FYI, those are hundreds." Mia's nods toward Sammy.

"Seriously?" Rafael glances back at his friend, who's now holding up three crisp bills and giving them a wave as Pearl spins in a slow loop around the pole. My boyfriend sips from his drink, then takes a longer pull. "That's delicious."

"I call it Smoking Hot Goddess," she winks at me, then braces her elbows on the bar to join us watching the Sammy show.

After the first song ends and the next starts, we all spy the moment when Pearl finally makes eye contact with Sammy. We let out a collective breath as she deliberately turns her back on him. Our friend deflates, all his arrogant bravado gone. He leans as far over the platform as he can, tossing the money her way. Then he settles in his seat, crossing his arms on the edge of the stage, and rests his chin on the pillow, gazing up at Pearl like a pathetic, devoted puppy.

"He does this a lot?" Aspen turns to me with a raised brow.

I shrug. "Every couple of weeks. She never gives him the time of day." Maybe I should feel bad for him, but I don't. Sammy needs to be knocked down a few cocky pegs now and then.

"It's not just him. Pearl doesn't interact with any of the customers," Mia points out.

"True. And I don't think she keeps the tips," I add. "She donates it, or something. Yasmin lets Pearl come here and do her thing on the stage, then she heads out."

"If not for the money, then why come?" Rafael asks, both he and Aspen stare at me.

I open my mouth, then snap it shut and give a definitive head shake. "Sorry. Nope. You're both his friends." I wave at the pathetic Squid moping in the VIP section. "I can't have you accidentally spilling her secret to him."

"So there *is* a secret?" Rafael leans closer, a smolder in his eyes, but I dodge away, grabbing my tray on the retreat.

"My lips are sealed!" I call back.

Sammy murmurs a distracted thanks when I drop off his drink. When Pearl makes her way off the stage after three songs, she scoops up Sammy's money without another glance his way, and our bar group gives her a whooping round of applause because the woman truly is a talent.

Around ten, things pick up in a big way, just like Yasmin predicted they would. Suddenly, Tuesday turns into the busiest night of the week. Luckily, Yasmin had arranged for two more waitresses to come for the later shift and had more dancers on call. By the time three a.m. rolls around, I'm ready to chop off my feet, then count the massive wads of cash in my pockets.

Having lost track of my boyfriends in the mayhem, I'm sure Rafael wandered off home at some point. But I look forward to meeting Aspen at our customary place just outside the back entrance. He normally waits there to escort the dancers to their cars. Hopefully, he'll carry me to mine tonight.

But I get a shock when I exit the back door and find Aspen with his hands full and mouth busy.

Turns out the Squid didn't call it an early night.

Rafael has Aspen pinned against the brick wall of the building, his hand gripping Aspen's neck while the other is shoved down the back of the Petal Pusher's pants. Aspen, meanwhile, has a firm grip on Rafael's ass, pressing their hips together as they make out.

Despite the ache in my feet, I stay where I am, leaning a shoulder against the wall and taking a rare moment to admire the two of them. We had an honest talk about how two of us being intimate without the third partner did not mean we cared for the missing member any less. All it meant was we wanted intimacy in the moment with the person we were currently with. Framed that way, Aspen was able to work through his discomfort. Rafael and I still make a point about being open about the times we spend together when he's not around, and both of us eagerly ply Aspen with affection when we have him to ourselves. Which is why I'm happy to simply observe this moment, knowing I'll soon be in the middle of that sexy sandwich.

As if hearing my thoughts, Rafael breaks the kiss, and both men glance over to discover my voyeurism.

"Don't stop on my account," I tease, grinning wide.

They move toward me as a team, Rafael claiming my bag, and Aspen grasping me around the waist, easing a large portion of my weight off my feet. I moan in relief.

"Not such a boring night after all," Rafael comments as we approach our cars.

"I cannot wait to lie down," I admit.

"I was thinking the same thing." Aspen's voice drops an octave, and my nerves thrum with anticipation. We pause by my car, and Rafael tilts my chin up to meet his eyes.

"What do you think, Red? Have enough energy for us to climb in your window?"

I smirk. "How about one of you use the back door?"

Two sets of eyes go wide.

But I figure when you're in love, nothing should be off-limits.

Thank you for reading! Did you enjoy? Please add your review because nothing helps an author more and encourages readers to take a chance on a book than a review.

And don't miss book three of the *Casual Magic* series, HEALING MAGIC & PLAYBOYS, available now. Turn the page for a sneak peek!

You can also sign up for the City Owl Press newsletter to receive notice of all book releases!

Sneak Peek of Healing Magic &
Playboys

AVA

The evenings after I teach, I refuse to wear the proper stripper uniform. I'll still put on the lacy, bedazzled bra that adds enough push-up to make it appear as though my D-cups are about to spill out. And I'll tug on my matching panties that seem sheer but have crystals clustered over all the important parts. I'll even coat my skin in the glitter-infused lotion that makes my normally beige complexion look like I'm covered in glittering gems.

But I will not wear the heels.

The soles of my feet ache from hours standing in front of college students, trying to explain how Wikipedia may be a good starting point when learning about a new topic, but it is not a viable source to cite in a research paper. When I first applied to library school, I didn't expect there to be an instructional component. I imagined I would be tucked away in some archive, examining old books, or I'd be cataloging collections in a public library. But I settled into higher education, and academic librarians wear many hats.

Though, I'm not sure how many of my colleagues across the country have a stripper hat in their skillset closet.

I technically don't have a hat either. But I do have a mask. I tie the lacy disguise over the top half of my face and secure the material to my hair with a few strategically placed bobby pins.

But—due to my five-class-in-a-row-day—I do *not* put on the six-inch-tall pleaser heels.

Barefoot, trying not to wince at how even flatfooted my soles are still tender, I push through the door that leads from the dressing room to the area behind the main stage.

Without the soundproofing, I can hear the last bit of "Champagne

Shit" by Janelle Monae. As the final cords trail off there's the sound of cheering, the crowd showing their appreciation for the performance.

"Club is busy for a Tuesday," Blue says. They pause beside me with a janitor broom. The cleaning implement looks badass with its chrome handle and pitch-black brush head. The Air Elemental is in charge of cash collection tonight, sweeping up all the loose bills after each dance. They make a big show of moving the broom around, but us magic types know Blue is actually manipulating the air currents to direct the money off stage. Making sure they don't miss any. On slow nights we collect the bills ourselves, since it's only a handful.

Not that I keep the cash.

"Oh," I say. "Good."

Blue snorts, hearing the lack of conviction in my voice. Most dancers would love a building full of eager customers. A part of me is glad to hear there's a decent showing.

The problem is, I only need a few audience members to earn the payment I'm looking for. The more people there are, the more likely there's someone in the crowd who voices dissatisfaction over my not-so-classic stripping style.

Also increases the chances someone might recognize me.

Stop it, I silently scold myself. *No one from your job would come here. And even if they did, they wouldn't recognize you on stage.*

The curtains part, and Jade saunters in, her light green G-string stuffed full of bills. Normally we're the same height, roughly five foot six, but since she didn't forgo her pleasers, the woman towers over me. Jade swings a curtain of braids over her onyx shoulder to show her top is equally adorned with cash.

"A birthday party," she announces by way of explanation, gesturing at her haul. Blue sneaks around the dancer, ducking through the velvet curtains and heading out to sweep up any earnings Jade received that didn't end up in her panties. "Though, this one"—Jade tugs out a bill that sat snug under the bikini strap running across her collarbone—"was from your man."

She waves the hundred dollars in front of my face and my heart rate trips. But not because of the amount.

He's here. Of course, he's here.

"I don't know what you did to that man." Jade grabs my face in a gentle but firm hold and plants a loud kiss somewhere in the mass of my white-blonde waves. "But gods, I love you for it. He tips me like he thinks I'll put in a good word for him." She tilts my chin up to grin directly into my face. "So here's my word. Keep making him into a needy puddle of goo for at least a few more weeks. I'm almost done saving for my trip to Brazil."

Jade—who's working under a nom de plume like we all are—shared with me that she started stripping to pay off the student loans from her computer science degree. But she decided to keep going because The Jewelry Box is a decent place to work, and the combined salaries means she can fill her condo with luxuries and jet off to locations all around the world whenever she wants. Also, sitting at a computer all day is a demon on the body. Pole dancing is her workout.

I roll my eyes. "I didn't do anything to him. I do the opposite of *do*. I ignore him just like I ignore everyone else."

Jade lets out a husky chuckle. "I know! It's delicious. I'm going to see if I can find a lap near him to dance on so I can watch his face when you give him nothing." She kisses my cheek then lets me go. "You make Tuesday nights my favorite of the week."

The beginning strains of "In Too Deep" by WDW drift to us just as Blue reappears, pushing a stack of crumbled bills in front of them.

"You're up, Pearl." All of us dancers choose what songs we perform to —after running them by our boss Yasmin for approval—and we can change them up as often as we like. But this is one of my favorites and everyone knows it. I'm a sucker for a good boy band.

Jade smoothly squats so she can scoop up handfuls of the cash and deposit her earnings into a nearby bin with her name embossed on it. There's a container for each dancer. Ruby's is also partially full from her earlier performance.

It might seem odd to leave cash basically lying around back here. But the workers at The Jewelry Box respect one another. Plus, a protection witch spelled the boxes to only allow the dancer whose box it is to reach inside.

The pros of working at a strip club run by and staffed with magical beings.

Speaking of magic, time for me to go get some.

I breathe through the tingle of nerves that always sends goosebumps racing across my skin the moment before I step in front of a crowd. I had the same reaction this morning before I walked into the intro level history course where I was set to teach a group of thirty about research databases. Now I'm preparing to tease a crowd of half-drunk club-goers with my body.

An interesting life I live. But I'm used to it.

Mostly.

As my fingers clutch the heavy velvet, I pull on my emotionless mask, wearing it underneath my masquerade one, then I step onto the stage.

Eyes turn toward me. Another jewel on display.

I saunter down the thin stretch of elevated walkway that leads to the round main stage, my bare feet making no sound on the cool wood. The bulbs along the edge of the platform fade from green to a soft white glow. Jade to Pearl, the shift silently announces. Though the lights highlight me, there's no spotlight. No strobe lights or disco balls. Yasmin, the owner of The Jewelry Box, wanted her club to stand out and stand apart from the seedier joints in Phoenix.

The moment a patron makes it past the bouncer, they know this isn't an average strip joint. The floors and walls are different shades of dark wood, the surfaces polished to the point they reflect a muted glow of the candles flickering on high shelves around the perimeter of the spacious room. All the club's lighting is warm and low, providing a sensual ambiance. All the seating is simple and comfortable, and the couches in the VIP section are soft supple leather. Strips of silk dangle from the ceiling, appearing gauzy and delicate as the material shifts in subtle air currents, but each one is plenty strong enough to support the acrobatic dancers that dangle from them as part of their routine. Elegant chandeliers hang from the ceiling where the silks don't, the only items that sparkle in this room other than me.

The first time I toured the place, the word that came to mind was *speakeasy*.

The Jewelry Box provides a sense of elegance along with erotic tantalization.

There is still a pole, and that's where I head, knowing once I reach it my tender feet can leave the ground. Still, this short walk already has my body relaxing. Partly because I'm comfortable up here, completely in charge of this space.

But more than that, my tranquility arrives on a cloud of lust.

The men, and some women and thems, stare at me with hungry expressions, dragging their eyes over every bare inch of my body. In their gazes, I can see them imagining what it would be like to touch me. To fuck me.

Go ahead and wonder, I silently encourage them. *Get creative.*

I want them to fantasize about me. To play out personal pornos with me as the star.

Because every ounce of lust directed my way fills my internal magic cauldron. The often empty well in my chest that holds mystical fuel so I can cast spells.

The problems of a half-witch, half-succubus.

Well, more like a quarter, since it was my grandmother who decided to summon an incubus demon and sleep with him without using birth control. Two generations later, and I'm a healing witch who needs other peoples' arousal to power my spell work. My mystical fuel is all external. Without these dancing shifts, I wouldn't be able to access my magic.

And without my magic, I'm fucked.

A few more steps to the pole, and I'm already juiced up. So much that I'm tempted to direct some of the power toward my feet to ease the ache.

Don't do it. You need that power. You'll regret using it.

Since I've got my stoic stage mask on, I don't sigh in annoyance. But the aggravated noise wants to get out. After working with Elementals like Jade and Blue, and most of the other Jewelry Box employees for the past two years, I've grown envious of how they seem to have an endless supply of magic. Jade, a Fire Elemental, can bring flames to her fingertips with only a touch of concentration. The heat lives in her always. And if she wants to supercharge it, she merely needs to strongly feel a particular emotion. For her, it's annoyance, but each Elemental is different. Fire, water, earth, air, and metal. More often we use the silly nicknames, Pyro, Squid, Petal Pusher, Airhead, and Stoner.

Descendants of the Elemental gods, they carry magic in themselves and don't have to syphon power from the surrounding world like I and many other witches have to.

To distract myself from my pity thoughts, I turn the last few steps into light skips then grab the pole and swing myself around, adjusting my grip and eventually bringing my legs to the smooth surface. With a burning flex of my biceps and a strategic squeeze of my legs, I climb, knowing by the end of the night I'll have light bruises on my inner thighs from the moves I plan to do, all to keep my feet off the floor. As I let the set of songs I picked out guide my body, the pain eases to the back of my mind, and I enjoy the strength and sensuality of my movements.

And I keep my focus away from the VIP section.

Away from him.

I know he's here. I would've realized even if Jade hadn't said anything, though I don't like how she labeled him as my man.

But I guess it's better than calling me *his*.

That's what he wants. I can tell from the way he continues to show up. Continues trying to get me to the edge of the stage by holding up larger and larger bills. Bills that I ignore, just like I ignore him.

But I ignore everyone, so he's not special.

Only, he is. Slightly special.

Not that I'd ever tell him.

His lust tastes different. When the power converges on me, I breathe the force in, the magic passing over my tongue on the way to my chest where the force settles and heats my skin from the inside out. Lust magic tends to taste like cocoa, and it's like everyone hands me a generic milk chocolate bar. But he slips a decadent peanut butter cup between my lips.

A little different.

A little more delicious.

And not something I plan to thoroughly examine. I'm here for magic. Not for some rich playboy interested in a stripper only because she's the first person to ever ignore him.

Still, I should get a medal for effort because the guy is hard to disregard.

Even now, as I hang upside-down on the pole, my attention tries to latch on to him. I spy a perfectly tailored suit covering a tall, lithe body.

A flicker of golden-brown hair, the color richer in the club's warm lighting.

But I force my gaze away before I'm caught in his dark eyes.

I right myself and slide the rest of the way down the pole in a sensual glide that belies how strong my grip is. My toes touch the ground, and I let my body drop lower into a crouch, then arch my back and try not to shiver at the onslaught of lust that tastes largely of chocolate but leaves a lingering aftertaste of peanut butter.

My last song in this set is almost done, and I stand, considering if I want to climb once more. I like being high above everyone.

Then a movement at the edge of the stage teases the corner of my eye.

It's him. My body knows it's him.

My tastebuds tell me how much he craves my attention.

How high will his offer go this time? He went up to a thousand two weeks ago. But even if I want the money—which I don't—he still eventually lets it fall. Those ten hundred-dollar bills scattered at my feet when I wouldn't look his way.

I didn't keep it. I don't keep any of the money. One more wall of safety, like my mask.

Still, I find myself curious.

Instead of climbing, I hook my leg waist-height on the pole and take some lazy spins that match the beat. Meanwhile, I allow my peripheral vision to focus on his hands.

No bills appear in them. Not this time.

His fingers cradle a velvet box.

Different. Intriguing.

I expect him to open it. To show me whatever treasure he brought to draw me in. Instead, he sets the box down on the edge of the stage and waits. The hand that didn't deposit the mystery gift in my territory clutches a glass with amber liquid. He brings the drink to his mouth, but I don't watch him sip the rich alcohol. Don't risk a glimpse of his lips.

Leave it. Walk off the stage at the end of the song like normal.

The problem is...it's a box.

Money is money. I know what that is. But a box...

It's a mystery.

Damn the gods, I love a good mystery. My favorite part of my day job is when a student brings me a fun research puzzle to solve. When we search through databases to discover an answer together.

The box is a puzzle.

Don't do it, I tell myself even as I slow my spinning. *This dancing is for you. Not for him. He doesn't get anything from you.*

But...looking inside the box isn't giving him anything, I reason as I step toward the gift.

A gift I swear I won't keep. Still, I need to see what it is.

What does he think will win me? What price has he placed on my attention?

In a graceful move, I glide across the stage and drop to my knees, thighs spread so the velvet box sits between them.

A wave of lust rushes down my throat, and if I didn't have my mask of disinterest in place, I'd let out a dry chuckle. Or a groan of relief. My internal magical caldron is filling to the brim, and I'm set for at least another week if not more.

He likes seeing me on my knees.

But who cares what he likes? I'm not here for him. I'm here for the box. Impatient for the mystery to be solved, I open the lid with a snap, the velvet soft and teasing against my fingertips.

Inside, nestled on a silk cushion, is a string of pearls.

Pearls almost the exact same shade as my milk-pale skin and the white outfits I wear and the mask I don. Pearls like my stage name.

Pearls like the person I pretend to be.

And nothing like the woman I truly am.

Disappointment creeps up my spine and through the nerves in my body, shoving out the brief respite of dancing and leaving behind all the new and old aches of the day. I extend a single finger, hooking the necklace and lifting it from the box until the jewelry dangles in the low light of the club. There's a gasp from nearby that sounds like Jade. She must've found a lap with a good view to occupy.

I lift my eyes to the unbuttoned collar of his dress shirt, up the strong, tan column of his neck, past his defined chin, and stop at the easy grin on his face. No need to meet his eyes when I can spy plenty of self-satisfaction in the pleased curve of his mouth.

He thinks he found my price. A string of gems in exchange for one.

Pompous playboy.

When will he learn that I can't be bought?

Before he realizes my intention, I extend my arm, the pearls swinging in my grasp. But they settle with a satisfying thunk when I drop the entire necklace into his glass of whiskey.

The song ends, and I rise to my feet in a smooth move I perfected by the age of eight. There's money strewn across the stage, tossed there while I spent my entire set on the pole.

But I'm not here for the cash. Blue will sweep it up, and Yasmin will donate it to the local animal shelter.

I leave every bill behind as I stride off the stage.

And I leave Sammy Reyes behind, too, not feeling even a pinch of guilt over the shocked expression on his handsome face.

The Squid can keep his meaningless gifts.

All I need is the decadence of his peanut butter lust.

Don't stop now. Keep reading with your copy of HEALING MAGIC & PLAYBOYS available now.

And visit www.laurenconnollyromance.com to keep up with the latest news where you can subscribe to the newsletter for contests, giveaways, new releases, and more.

Don't miss book three of the *Casual Magic* series, HEALING MAGIC & PLAYBOYS, available now, and find more from Lauren Connolly at www.laurenconnollyromance.com

Ava Bellerose may use men to charge up her healing magic, but that doesn't mean she wants to date one.

She's fine living life as a single witch working a day job as a college librarian and spending nights as the masked performer Pearl at The Jewelry Box. Every routine on the stage means more magic power in the bank, courtesy of the customers craving her body. One man in particular can't seem to get enough. Ava finds perverse pleasure in ignoring his money and denying him anything more than a distant dance with zero eye contact. His admiration is intoxicating and the magical boost is all she needs from him. But the guy becomes impossible to ignore when he shows up outside of her apartment.

Their meeting must be fate...

Sammy Reyes can't believe his luck. While visiting a new build site for work, he spots a heart-shaped behind and a pouty set of lips he'd recognize anywhere. Unfortunately, Pearl—or Ava—seems less than enthused to have her secret identity revealed, even if he promises to take her secret to a watery grave. From her hostile greeting, the gorgeous witch might be the one to bury him at the bottom of the Mariana Trench. But Sammy has spent his whole life charming people, and he's determined to prove himself as more than a faceless fuel tank of lust. Especially when Ava makes it abundantly clear his money has no sway on her affections.

To woo the librarian, the water elemental will have to dive deeper than his normal surface-level charisma. But just as Sammy starts to show the vulnerable heart behind his confident mask, Ava's two lives collide in the worst way. Can she risk stepping out from behind her own protective walls, or will she leave him wanting?

Please sign up for the City Owl Press newsletter for chances to win special subscriber-only contests and giveaways as well as receiving information on upcoming releases and special excerpts.

All reviews are **welcome** and **appreciated**. Please consider leaving one on your favorite social media and book buying sites.

For books in the world of romance and speculative fiction that embody Innovation, Creativity, and Affordability, check out City Owl Press at www.cityowlpress.com.

Acknowledgments

Thank you to everyone who helped this book come to life! My beta readers, my book friends, my fabulous agent Lesley, and of course Yelena and the whole City Owl Press team!

About the Author

LAUREN CONNOLLY is an award-winning author of contemporary and paranormal romance stories. She's lived among mountains, next to lakes, and in imaginary worlds. Lauren can never seem to stay in one place for too long, but trust that wherever she's residing there is a dog who thinks he's a troll, twin cats hiding in the couch, and bookshelves bursting with stories written by the authors she loves.

www.laurenconnollyromance.com

facebook.com/LaurenConnollyRomance

x.com/laurenaliciaCon

instagram.com/laurenconnollyromance

About the Publisher

City Owl Press is a cutting edge indie publishing company, bringing the world of romance and speculative fiction to discerning readers.

Escape Your World. Get Lost in Ours!

www.cityowlpress.com

facebook.com/CityOwlPress

x.com/cityowlpress

instagram.com/cityowlbooks

pinterest.com/cityowlpress

tiktok.com/@cityowlpress

www.ingramcontent.com/pod-product-compliance
Lightning Source LLC
Chambersburg PA
CBHW020651030726
47498CB00002B/462